The Wishing Well
A Collection Vol. 1

The works in this collection explore themes of death in many of its facets. As in life, death is indiscriminatory in the following stories.

This is your warning.

Proudly human-crafted.

First Round

THE WISHING WELL

A COLLECTION VOL. 1

BY CHRISTOPHER RUÍZ

ILLUSTRATED BY AMY MYERS

PESADILLA
PRESS

TABLE OF CONTENTS

To whom I dedicate my love and this collection:

Amy, my devoted wife, illustrator, cover designer, and support. Your belief in me far surpassed my own.

Leticia, my loving mother; always there. You read me stories in childhood. Now, you read my stories in adulthood. If I ever come to befriend success, it was you who first introduced us.

Alex, my brother, the indefatigable soldier. Though you have been estranged from rest and leisure since donning the campaign hat, you have unhesitatingly offered your readership and support.

You've Been Lost

THE CAPTIVE

*T*he Wishing Well. Those three glowing words pierced through the darkness like a beckoning lighthouse. They spoke to me. Every other week, they taunted me, those three tantalizing words. I could hear them—even from here—I could hear their buzzing declamations. *Hey there, sailor. You look dry. You've been lost, alone, adrift in the vicious waters of sobriety.* Those three buzzing words. *Come ashore. It's safe here.*

That sign. That awful sign. It was not even mounted correctly, the damn thing was canted. Not one or two but three letters did not light properly. That horrible, haunting sign. It was a flame burning hot in the night and I knew it offered only immolation, for I was nothing more than a moth; too weak and stupid to resist its lethal radiance. That was why I was here, yeah? Despite knowing I was the moth, I chose this gas station, the one directly across the street from The Wishing Well, every other week because I was a weak and stupid piece of—

Moth.

I had been urged by the group not to degrade myself, not to "reinforce negative core beliefs," as they put it. But what did they know? Hell, what did I know? I know I hated that sign. I hated that sign almost as much as I hated myself. Yet, here I stood. Not seconds but minutes after the gas pump clunked shut, I remained standing, staring, perseverating.

The attendant is probably watching me, I thought. *He knows. He*

1

knows I'm a piece of shit. He's probably thinking to himself, "Look at this piece of shit. He wants to go to that bar but he has no self-control, so he can't." And then he'd laugh. I'm being watched and I'm being laughed at.

I was getting worked up. With hands behind my head, I leaned back and pretended to stretch while inhaling deeply, slowly. It was a "trick-nique" learned in the group. I know I'm calming myself with deep breathing, but to the rest of the world, I'm relaxing, stretching.

I set the gas pump back in place, slid onto the cracked leather of the driver's seat, and was mindful not to slam the door shut. I ached— body, mind, and soul. I was as dry as the hay I had been baling all week. I was in pain, always in pain, and always the remedy was just out of reach. I curled raw fingers around the chipped gearshift, moved toward the street entrance, and began turning the wheel right, in the direction of home. I paused. Straight ahead, just to the left of my rear-view mirror, glowed those three terrible words. *The Wishing Well.* To the right of those words shined the interior lighting of the gas station; and if I focused my eyes just right, I was sure I would see the at-tendant—that judgemental prick—watching me instead of mopping floors or whatever the hell else he should have been doing.

I straightened the wheel and drove forward.

I let the idling engine move me through the mostly empty lot at a leisurely pace, like a sailboat carried on a soft breeze, until I found a spot that was not too close, but not too far from the bar's entrance. With controlled adrenaline, I set the gearshift to park. There I re-mained, my hand on the stalk, body motionless, while my mind sank swiftly into a perpetual pool of self-pity and temptation.

The windshield was aglow with the sign's hot incandescence. That sign. That judgment. That mocking testament to my grievances. It was a neon spotlight trained upon me, alerting all the world of my shameful flaws. Three fiery words, like a branding iron ready to mark me for eternity.

"The Wishing Well," I finally muttered. The words trembled from my mouth in a thin fog. I trembled, though I was not particularly cold. I moved my gaze from the glowing sign to the front entrance. It was merely a door. It was more, though. It was forbidden.

Yet, who forbade my frequenting this place, this goading establishment? Me? Society? My family? No, not my family. I wanted to believe my sobriety was yet another restraining shackle of marriage and parenthood, but every moment I spent gazing upon this building I could see everything I had done. I knew, with certainty, I had only myself to blame. Each passing minute spent in longing in front of this bar, I relived every drunken mistake, every fit of rage, that led to my abandonment of booze over five years ago.

Five years.

Five years was a long drought. Five years was more than enough time to heal old wounds, wasn't it? Sure it was. But not for *her*. Not even five years was enough for *her*. Five years and her face still remained tainted with disgust. And not just *her* but also *him*. Even after five years, *five*—half the damn kid's age—there were still moments when he would flinch in my presence. What was worse was that five years of sober thinking and self-reflection brought forth the realization that, while I definitely hated myself, I hated my situation more; I hated my whole damn life. Though I earned forgiveness from the courts, I would never be forgiven by *them*. I was forever imprisoned the night I struck the little bastard. It was enraging. I was a captive of grief and regret with no freedom in sight, forever damned. Nothing could be done to earn their forgiveness—to earn my freedom. The sobriety, the withdrawal, the suppressed anger ... no penance would garner their approval. So, what harm could possibly accompany the consumption of a single beer? What difference would it make to *them*? Would they hate me any less?

They could hate me more ...

Now, that I could see. That I knew. I wrung the cracked, grimy steering wheel with callused hands as I envisioned my family's disapproval—no, their *hatred* of me upon their forthcoming discovery of alcohol on my breath.

But, again, would a clean breath attract no less hatred of me? Five years of sobriety, five years of damnation, told me that I was damned either way.

I scanned the parking lot, sure to see some spectators observing my torment. The few cars about the lot were vacant ... probably. Probably not. I could feel it. They were watching. I needed to act, enter or leave, or be observed like some pitiful spectacle.

I unbuckled my seatbelt but held the clip in place for a moment. Last chance to turn away.

The belt retracted.

I pushed open the truck door. Its hinges creaked in protest; a warning of sorts. No, they were mocking me; audibly thirsting for lubricant as I thirsted for intoxicant. Knees popped as I stood to behold the bar's sign. *The Wishing Well.* Its dull glow blinded my judgment. Its electric hum deafened my conscience. It was entrancing. That beautiful sign. It was alluring. It beckoned. I was beckoned to it; I, the moth.

I slammed the door shut and stepped toward the bar. My heart quickened with fear and excitement. I felt something stir within me as I approached the entrance (*I should have parked closer*); a well-known, dreadful feeling: control. Control not in the sense of agency, as that was a notion absent from my life beyond recollection. At that moment, nearing the door, I was overwhelmed with a sense of powerlessness. I was being controlled. It was fate's hand that reached for the door's handle, not my own.

No, I thought. *Don't do that. Be accountable. I'm doing this. This is my decision.*

But it wasn't. Not entirely. Over the years, I assured myself each time I passed The Wishing Well, each time I fueled up across the street, that my restraint was of my own volition and not *their* bidding. But that wasn't true. I knew then as I knew now it was ultimately *their* commands I obeyed, not my own. Commands unspoken but no less commanding.

Or …

Or, perhaps it was *her* will that I did enter the bar; that I did approach the bartender; that I did order a drink. After all, she hated me. She wanted a divorce. She would never admit to it—might not even consciously know it—but that's what she wanted: separation. All she needed was an excuse. I knew this. Unspoken but no less perpetually hanging in the air like some foul odor.

Perhaps.

Or, perhaps I really was an addict. Perhaps the hand that trembled toward the door was being coerced by my own addiction, and not by her manipulation.

"But I'm not an addict," I whispered. *I'm doing this. By my own will, I'm doing this. I earned this. It is my right. I am a free man.*

I'm free …

An effortless grin cracked my face as I reached again for the door's worn handle. And when my fingers met the cold metal, I paused again. Like the ringing of some distant church bells, I could hear *his* faint sobs echoing in the back of my mind.

Not this time, I thought, shaking the thoughts from my head. *It's been five years. It'll be different this time. I've changed. I've earned this. I've earned it, damn it. Fuck! I'm not a piece of shit anymore, I've changed and I've earned this.*

I withdrew my hand and placed both behind my head, interlocking fingers, and holding a deep breath as I feigned a stretch. My heart rate slowed a touch; enough. I drew in one more reassuring breath, pulled open the door, and stepped inside.

· ℘ ·

The Wishing Well was … rather underwhelming. It certainly had the physical appearance of a bar but lacked the atmosphere of one; at least, how I remembered bars to be when I was last in good spirits. Like the exterior, the interior was exceedingly quiet, although it was only a Thursday night. A classic rock song leaked out of speakers so softly that the song's identity was indiscernible. I saw maybe a handful of people scattered about in pairs and a few more drinking stag.

My first step brought an unexpected crunch under my scuffed boot. I looked down to see a dreadfully scarred, wood floor carpeted with peanut shells. A loud *crack* shattered the hushed atmosphere, thrusting my attention toward a lone, tired-looking man shooting pool at the bar's only billiards table.

Tired-looking, I thought. It was a fitting descriptor for both the bar and all its occupants; all save for the bartender, whose gaze and beaming smile had remained fixed on me since I first entered. The bartender's stupid grin widened as I approached the bar top. He had all the persona of a starving car salesman. And I hated salesmen of any type.

"Welcome to the Wishing Well, sir. What's your wish tonight?" the bartender asked. He even spoke and gesticulated with a salesman's panache. He was young, good-looking, and flamboyant. Worst of all, he seemed hyper-social and, by effect, hyper-verbal. He possessed every quality I detested in a bartender. And then there was the manner in which he stared at me; as though I were out of place, strange and broken; as though I didn't belong; as though I had a problem. I didn't like him. I didn't like him at all.

6

I took my place atop the torn, pleather seat of the nearest stool and studied the bar's selection of beers and liquor. I then spotted a small, stone pool, which had been built into the floor between two of the liquor cabinets behind the bar (or had the bar been built around the well?). A small pile of glittering coins coated the pool's floor. I supposed it was a clever gimmick to get that much more from the customer.

I gestured toward the well. "You ever fall in that thing?"

"Not yet, but the night's still young, sir," he answered in a possibly genuine chuckle. "What's your wish tonight, sir?"

Pushy, happy-go-lucky little shit. Repeating himself like an assertive salesman, like he's hurrying me along. Like the serpent in the Garden of Eden, this asshole was here to tempt—to force—my decision. I could order when—*if*—I wanted to.

"I don't know yet, kid," I retorted. "Shit, I just sat down."

"Hey, no prob, sir. I'll check back in a minute and you can give me the deets." At that, he stepped back, maintaining his stupid salesman's smirk ... and the stare. Oh, how I hated that unbreaking gaze of his, particularly how it accompanied that crooked smile. It was too genuine. It was voyeuristic.

"You gonna keep staring at me like I got some dick growing out of my forehead or are you gonna bugger off for a minute while I get settled in?" I briefly considered the dangers of biting the hand that feeds and added, "Please."

"Sorry, sir. Just eager to please. I'll give you some time, but I'll be back for that wish!" The bartender departed, but, for a brief moment, he held his gaze, his smile widened, and his head seemed to cock, a subtle but no less noticeable gesture.

As he tended to another customer, I gave the bar a further look-see. It was then that I noticed all the signs in the bar advertised only a single drink: a wheat beer called "Whet." One sign asked, "How do you spell desire?" And another spelled the answer with flashing letters: "W-H-E-T." A chalkboard sign read, "Thursday night is Splash Night. Get Whet." There were ads everywhere, some decades old even, for a beer of which I'd never been aware. Above a liquor cabinet glowed the word "WHEAT" in a bold red while the letter A flickered on and off. There was even apparel: a t-shirt hung by two nails against a wooden plaque with "I got Whet at The Wishing Well" printed across the chest.

As I returned my gaze to the well, the bartender returned to me. "Before we get to your wish, sir, I just need to sneak a peek at that ID."

"Wh—really?"

"A formality." He gestured toward a sign sitting a few feet down the bar top, which read "No card, you're barred" in larger print with "from drinking" in smaller print.

For less than a moment, I considered this opportunity to leave. I could tell him I had left my ID in the truck and then simply go home. Go home and feel like the piece of shit I was, the kind that chickened out over a single beer because I had no self-control.

I removed my wallet and handed my license to the bartender.

His eyes were fixed on my own. Even as he took the ID, his eyes did not break their hold. Stranger still was how unmoving those eyes seemed to be. Any typical pair of eyes would dance about as the pupils took in the entirety of their subject, but his just held, like the fixed eyes of a wax figure.

"Carson McDonnell!" he announced like a gameshow host. I jumped in my seat.

"What the hell is your problem? Keep it down." I turned about, my back cracking, scanning, sure to find *her* watching, having been summoned by the shouting of my name. If not *her* then someone we knew was surely in earshot, eager to report me to *her*. I untwisted myself. The bartender continued to hold his unblinking gaze. Had he actually checked my ID? Had he even moved? He must have, for he had placed a half-poured plastic cup of headless beer in front of me; a child's cup. "What the hell is this?" I asked.

"It's what you need, sir," the bartender stated as a matter of fact. His salesman's smile had been replaced with an expression of veritable concern, as though he were setting a bowl of water before a dying dog. But his eyes ... "A taste of desire," he spoke at just more than a whisper. His eyes would not shift.

I looked again at the cup. Ridiculous. The absurdity of serving me anything in a child's cup. I reached for it, either to push it away or throw it back at him. My hand was trembling, not unlike the shaking to which it had grown accustomed so many years ago. I looked at the cup's contents. It's what I needed?

How dare you, I nearly spoke aloud. I didn't *need* anything. I certainly didn't need some punk bartender making that determination, as though I looked like someone in need of some kind of—

Fix.

Just one more ...

I'm almost ...

I was being watched. I could feel them: someone's eyes crawling up and down me like shivers along my spine. I threw glances left and right but only caught the attention of another patron who then raised his own glass toward me, as though prompting me to drink. Shit, even the patrons were in on it. I stared back at the cup with a sense of dread. *I shouldn't be here*, I thought.

"Is something wrong, sir?"

I hesitated. I wanted to tell him that if I was to be treated like a child, I would leave. This was it. This was my chance to escape, my last chance. I'd still be a piece of shit but I could leave here a sober piece of shit; a five years *and counting* sober piece of shit.

"N-no." I cleared my throat and imagined walking away without another word, without a single sip. I nearly willed it to be. But everyone was watching. They would know, the moment I stood from this stool, they would know how fucked up I was. I was a joke—a literal joke. A guy walks into a bar and … leaves. How unorthodox. How embarrassing. How could I ever return?

Five years.

I owed it to myself. I was no failure. I refrained for five years and I could do it again. This drink did not represent failure, it was a prize five years in the making. It was a reward. I was merely scratching an itch. No one was getting hammered. Well, someone was likely getting hammered tonight, I was in a bar after all, but it would not be me. Yeah, it was more likely than not that someone in this bar was either drunk or becoming drunk and no one would take that as evidence of some kind of underlying problem. Lots of people get drunk, they wake up hungover, and they carry on with their lives. Some don't, but that wasn't my concern because I wasn't getting drunk. I was just having a drink. I was thirsty for God's sake. Yet, as I began to reach for the cup, it seemed an action more emblematic of betrayal than of quenching thirst.

I pulled my hand back and faked a cough into my fist. I then shot an accusing eye toward the bartender. That creepy gaze of his …

"Look, I want a bartender, not a damn spectator."

"Of course, sir." The bartender raised his hands as a way to demonstrate his harmlessness. "My apologies." He began to walk away and turned another smile my way. "I've got a feeling about you, sir."

I trembled with anger and racing thoughts.

What the fuck is he implying? That I'm a drunk? That I'm some kind of freak?

I placed my hands behind my head and breathed deeply and

slowly.

I looked at the cup. How could a mere six-inch-tall, plastic vessel hold so much power over me? It didn't. It couldn't. It was inanimate, unable to force my hand. *They* were the well from which my unease sprung; *her* and *him*. Or was it foresight? I knew, as did those closest to me, we all knew all too well how reactive I could become with a little inebriation. My hands fidgeted in the lap of my stained, faded jeans.

Reactive … impulsive … angry …

But that was the old me. The new me, the man voluntarily sitting at this bar, had five years of impulse control and self-regulation under his belt. The new me needn't worry about the old days; about them; most certainly not about some surveilling bartender.

Fuck him, I thought, giving the bartender a quick glance. *And fuck them, too. I don't need anybody's permission to drink just like I don't need anyone to tell me not to. I will or will not by my own choosing. I'm my own man; owned by no one but me, myself, and I.*

I reached for the cup and again I stopped short (*fuck!*), resting my quivering hand on the sticky, splintering bar top. *It's one drink,* I told myself. *You're not getting blind drunk. It's one drink. So, pick it up. Something to stop the shakes. Just a quick f—*

I grasped the cup with such force the plastic walls partially caved. I took a deep, shaky breath in a vain attempt to calm my nerves (*there's only one remedy for that*). I swirled the cup with trembling hands, brought it up to my nose, and inhaled. My nostrils flared, almost dilating in response to the pleasant aroma like pupils fixing on a love interest. It was pacifying. There was a hint of orange. I loved oranges. Oh, the memories that scent recalled; memories of my father, of peeling an orange in the backseat of his truck during a failed road trip to the coast. It was the closest I had ever come to leaving the state.

I set the cup's lip to my own and tilted its cool, fizzing contents into my mouth. As the brew rolled over my gums and sloshed onto my tongue, I visualized a calming ocean tide dissipating along a warm, sandy beach. I had never walked along a beach; never set eyes on the ocean. Yet, in that moment, the musty stench of a dive bar had been replaced by the salty air of an ocean-side beach. The memories of soft whimpers and fear emanating from *his* room were drowned out by distant squawks of seagulls and crashing waves. I wanted—*needed* it. I needed that feeling. I needed a cold beer at the end of a rough day. I needed that cool condensation soaking into my hot hands in the setting sun; the cool warmth of a dulling tipple bathing my parched tongue and spilling down my dry throat. I needed a revival. I needed Whet.

I searched for the bartender. He was chatting at the end of the bar top with a man about his age; no doubt a longtime friend of his the way they carried on.

"Ahem." I was loud and guttural. The patron gave me a side glance and then leaned into the ear of the bartender, speaking under his breath. The bartender snorted a laugh. *Here I sit with empty hands while he brays like an ass with his buddy*, I thought. *They're laughing at me*. "Hey," I raised my voice. This immediately stole the bartender's attention. I raised the empty cup to him. "I'm thirsty here, kid. Where you at?"

"I'm here, sir," the bartender reassured me as he walked in my direction. He glanced at the cup and that disgusting salesman's smile spread across his face. He tossed the cup away, poured me a full glass of Whet, and added, "As I've always been." I wasn't sure what he meant by that, but I really didn't care. The bartender was holding the only thing I really cared about at that moment. The bartender set the glass down in front of me. "*Whet* your whistle, sir," he said with a beam of satisfaction. "Ah? See what I did there?" I ignored this.

"How much?"

"Am I correct in saying this is your first time getting Whet, sir?"

"Yeah, I guess," I replied. *You don't have to be weird about it.*

"Then, it's on us, sir." I was about to object to his charity when the bartender added, "The customer's first wish is always on us, sir." He inched the drink closer to me. The cup's cold condensation was already forming alluring beads of sweat for which my fingers thirsted. "But the second will cost you."

"That so?" The bartender nodded. "All right." I wasn't sure if this was an actual bar policy or not but decided not to turn down a free drink.

I steadied my hand with great might, and with greater will I forcefully guided it toward my prize: that sweet, bubbling damnation. I was nearly impelled to thank him. My eyes began to wet themselves. It was over. Five years of beating myself with the fists of remorse, of throwing myself into the depths of guilt, was over.

With the glass in hand, I felt a longing to relive the memory of a paradise I had never physically experienced. I gave the beer a hearty sniff and again drank a visualization of a sun-drenched, sandy seashore. The more I drank, the more I became aware the experience was more than mere visualization. It was an actual memory real and true; a vivid recollection erupting to life in a mere mouthful of beer, each gulp a surge of acuity.

My father was never keen on being photographed. And, in the years following his early death, I had forgotten his face. I had, that was, until now. Until I got Whet, as was apparently the saying. Whet was considerably more than a simple wheat beer. Whet was a prescription for the mind's eye. I was blind no longer. I could see myself—truly see myself—as I was and always should have been. What was more, I could see my father; I could see his once forgotten face. Every crease around his soft, smiling eyes was in perfect depiction. I could make out every stubby whisker in the day-old shadow that coated his jaw. The moment was real, indisputably so. There we walked, side by side along the rolling tides. The warm surf splashed our bare feet. Gritty sand wedged itself between our toes. We were laughing. We were eating oranges. We were free.

And then, we were not.

The tide retreated and the sand grew dry and hot. The orange in my hand rotted. I turned to my father, whose face was contorted in sorrow. I reached for him, for his reassurance and comfort, but he vanished. Crumbling into dust, his remnants were carried away on a gust of wind. And, still, I remained; isolated in a void of burning sand with two shackles about my ankles and a half-buried sledgehammer just out of reach.

I clenched my eyes shut, erasing the vision, and returned to the bar upon my reopening them. My glass was empty.

"No," I whispered.

"Something wrong, sir?" The bartender had again materialized before me. Ever-present, ever-watching, and his smile growing as he fed on my anguish.

"Yeah, I would think so. I'm holding an empty glass, here. C'mon." I jiggled the glass in front of the bartender, who was unmoving, ever-smiling. "Am I drinking tonight or juggling your dirty dishes like an asshole?" I removed a credit card from my wallet, slid it toward him on the bar top, and patted it. "Open me up a tab, kid."

"I'm sorry, sir," the bartender said, shaking his head.

No. "What, are you cutting me off? I look like a drunk to you? Or you just don't like making money?" My head started buzzing.

"Dreams have no monetary value, sir."

The buzz was growing. Holy shit, was I really getting drunk off a single beer? No. This wasn't drunk. What was I feeling?

"Besides, you didn't come here to drink," the bartender said in a factual tone.

"W-whaddya mean?" I was spinning a bit. Not enough to lose balance, but I was spinning.

"It's not the beer you want, sir. You came here in pursuit of a dream. So, let's not drag this out any longer."

"You d-drug me?" I stammered.

"What's your wish tonight, sir?" the bartender repeated. He spoke more like a weary interrogator than a salesman. I wanted to tell the guy to go fuck himself, but some unseen force compelled me to answer. Or was I impelled to do so?

I sifted through racing thoughts, which was no easy task in this state. "To get out of here," I finally answered.

A vicious grin parted the bartender's chapped lips. He looked parched himself, deprived even. In fact, the more I examined his face, the more withered he looked; like a flower at the tail end of a drought. How had I not noticed before? The bartender leaned toward me, the corners of his mouth crawling towards his ears as his grin broadened. The bar top creaked under his weight.

"Do tell."

"I'm a prisoner." I spoke as if in hypnosis. My muted voice was scarcely audible over the whispers and moans (*pain or pleasure?*) now emitting from the speakers. "I've been robbed of free will, robbed of life." The heat of embarrassment and despondency swathed my face. Stinging tears blurred my gaze, which remained relentlessly held by the bartender's. The bartender's eyes seemed dilated to an inordinate degree. Through my unfocused vision, it appeared his pupils flooded the entirety of his eyes, as though they were black yolks spilling across egg whites. Overhead, the speakers grew louder, more clearly exuding the moans of tormented souls alongside a whispering chorus.

"So, what do you wish for?"

"Release," I choked out.

"Oh, yes," the bartender spoke with pleasure. "Release," he repeated. "You are Carson McDonnell?"

"Yes."

"As in the farm up the road?"

"It was my father's."

The bartender gave the bar top a jubilant slap. "Well, sir, I can grant your wish." His voice returned to its salesman's mannerism. "Say, you wouldn't happen to have a coin on you, would ya?"

Without much thought, I reached into my pocket, as I had done every other week, and brushed my fingers against the coin within, as I had done every other week; the coin the group presented me.

I shook my head.

"Worry not, sir. You'll get that wish." He reached into his pocket, removed his hand, and then grabbed mine as if to shake it. There was something in his palm. "But, this one will cost you." He released his grip and I turned my palm to see what had been left behind. "It's a contract, sir."

At first glance, it appeared to be a quarter. Upon further scrutiny, however, I discovered my name was minted where "In God We Trust" should have been.

"How did you—"

"You know what you have to do, sir." The bartender stepped aside, leaving the wishing well in full, unobstructed display before me.

For the first time, I truly observed the well. It was the only thing in the bar that was well-maintained, or well-lit for that matter. Its serene water seemed to hush the bar and the ensuing peace brought forth the realization that this was more than just a well. It was the embodiment of hope.

With the flick of my thumb, I sent the coin ringing through the air. It plopped into the well's placid water. Ripples danced along the water's surface, and as they faded, so did my stupor.

The bartender stepped once more into my field of vision. "The rest will come naturally," he stated. "Like muscle memory." His smile widened. "Like a craving or compulsion. It will happen almost entirely without thought."

And it did. I didn't even remember driving out of the parking lot.

· ∽ ·

The night was exceptionally dark, such that I was having difficulties seeing the road. Further, while I was not drunk, I was not really sober. There was something off in my mind and it made focusing on the road, specifically staying within one lane, quite the challenge. I set both hands atop the wheel and pointed my trigger fingers skyward; a little "trick-nique" from days long past. All I had to do was keep the painted lines in line with my fingers. And if I passed a law enforcement officer? Well, hello, LEO. I'd turn it into a howdy-do. Just a couple of fingers off the wheel. Yup, the ol' Montana howdy, no drunk driving here.

Why, here was one such opportunity approaching on the right-hand side. An SUV was sitting perpendicular to the road, announcing to all in loud letters that it belonged to the Ravalli County Sheriff's Office. As I approached, I cocked a hand in a steering wheel salute and stayed the course, putting the deputy behind me.

Red and blue flashed in my side and rear view mirrors. My heart raced.

I turned onto the next dirt road—my road—McDonnell Road (*I was almost home, tripped up at the finish line*), maneuvered the truck to the road's shoulder, and set the gear shift to park. With hands behind my head, I breathed. I could do this. It would come naturally, just like the bartender said, right? I retrieved my wallet from my back pocket, removed the insurance card, and—

Son of a bitch. He didn't give it back. That son of a bitch did not give me back my license.

A light rap of knuckles at the window gave me a start. I rolled the window down. It was Deputy Little Whirlwind. Of course it was. Even my sober tongue struggled to speak his name without tripping.

"Oh, Mr. MacDonald." The words fell from his mouth, slow and heavy with disappointment. I could feel that old familiar geyser of rage rumble within me. The stupid nursery song with which I had been taunted and bullied year after year in school. That stupid, annoying, infuriating song. I had never been rid of it, not in college, not even in adulthood. No amount of fists dealt or received had ever changed that. I was forever branded Ol' MacDonald.

"I thought you put all this behind you," the deputy continued. "In fact, I had so convinced myself we'd never see each other like this again that I legitimately thought somethin' was wrong with your headlights when I seen you drivin' without 'em. I thought, 'Surely, Ol' MacDonald (*there it was*) wouldn't be drivin' *my* roads drunk again.' Then I seen you swervin', and even then I says to myself, 'Well, maybe he's fiddlin' with the lights or somethin'.' But when you rolled down this window and I caught a whiff of that breath ..." He shook his head. "What would your wife say?"

I squeezed the wheel with all my might. I held my gaze forward, I would not—could not—look at him. I could only watch the dust that sloshed through the moonlight like lazy waves. God, I would kill to be on a beach.

"Hmm? How about when we give her a call at detention, what do you think she's gonna say?"

Oh, a hundred possible things. More. A thousand nags. A million bitches and moans. I knew this song and dance all too well. The lecturing and pontificating. Then, the tears. Those inexorable crocodile tears. Like a leaky bar tap. No matter how bad I made things for myself, no matter how evident it was that *I* was the injured, that *I* had been suffering, *she* would don the mask of the victim.

"I think she'll be pretty worried, don't you?" Little Whirlwind pressed. Of course it was Little Whirlwind. It was always Little Whirlwind. The Honorable, the Righteous, the Law ... the Trap. I knew what he was—what he really was. Deputy Little Whirlwind was a venus fly trap. (*Do plants eat moths or do moths eat plants?*) He planted himself here—right here—right before my turn, there on the side of the road waiting for the one and only me to fuck up so that he could finally uproot and snatch his prey. He did this knowing I'd fuck up at some point and come fluttering right into his trap; I, the moth. He was no different from *them*. He'd hold me, bind me, and I'd rot while the rest of the world thrived in my absence.

"Yeah?" the deputy persisted. He always demanded a response, always needed to know he was being listened to, heard.

"Indeed." My voice croaked like a decades-old door breaking free of rust.

Deputy Little Whirlwind inhaled, as though he were about to spew that old familiar reprimand like years past, but he instead refrained with a sigh, like ... like he had given up on me. Then he asked, "What about your family?" But it didn't seem like a question posed to me, more a wandering thought meant to dissipate into the cooling night air. "Well, then, I suppose we'll just get right to it. Step on out." He pointed toward the shoulder. "Side of the road, license, and insurance and all that. You know the drill. And for goodness sake, MacDonald, give me the keys that idiot bartender failed to take from you."

It wasn't supposed to be like this. It was just one beer. I set my forehead against the wheel and closed my eyes. I could feel the vertigo. This wasn't right.

19

"Carson," I grunted through clenched teeth.

"Nuh-uh. Only friends call each other by their first names. I ain't your friend tonight." He opened the truck's door. "Let's go get you cleaned up. Your wife can have you out by Saturday, and you can pray about it Sunday at mass. You just won't be the one drivin' to church no more, y'know. You listenin'? C'mon, Mr. MacDonald. We don't need to be going hands-on here."

"McDonnell!" I screamed. "McDonnell! McDonnell!"

"All right, get the hell out of the vehicle."

The would-be captor reached across my lap to unbuckle my seatbelt, which he may have been able to do had I ever gotten around to installing those running boards I leaned up in the corner of the garage so many years ago. I wrapped my left arm under his jaw, locking his head against my lap, and shifted the truck into drive with my right. I set pedal to floor. The truck didn't have much get-up-and-go in its current age and state, but it was able to hit fifty-five before the captor managed to free himself. Legs skidded across dirt and gravel. Arms flailed. Hands grasped. He slapped at the brake. I stomped his hand with my left boot and kept the accelerator pinned with my right. We were gaining speed.

"Stop!" he shouted. Wind and engine and rocks and tires and all manner of sound bombarded me through the open door, and so I couldn't quite hear his next words. "(You'll) kill me." Or maybe it was, "(You're) killing me." "(You) will see?" Nah, he was in no position to be threatening me. And it certainly wasn't, "(It's) chilly," as that would be as silly for the situation as it was illogical. The night air was rather pleasant, even at this speed.

The incarcerator attempted to pull himself upright by the steering wheel. The truck's front tires jolted left and the driver side tires, though still spinning, floated from the road, rising higher and higher like uplifted spirits. I closed my eyes.

Vertigo.

· ⁊ ·

When I was able to reopen my eyes, I saw (not easily, as the wind-shield was completely shattered) that I was within walking distance of my home. Not too close but not too far—just the way I liked to park. I removed the keys from the ignition, planted my boots against the center console, and climbed out of the driver's window. The truck had come to a rest on the passenger side after rolling. As a side sleep-er myself, I could relate.

Golly, why would that come to mind? That's a bit out of character.

This was my dad's work truck. We used to eat oranges in this truck together. It would never run again (*much like me after high-school*). Old me would be pretty upset by this. Was new me upset? I couldn't tell. My hands were shaking, yes, possibly from rage. Of course, they could be shaking from the booze, or adrenaline, or some-thing else.

What was wrong with me?

Moans.

No more than twenty feet down the road, mostly in the ditch, the enslaver writhed. He must have been thrown from the vehicle, or crushed by it, or both. I started toward the truck bed and near-ly collapsed when my left hip painfully declined to hold my body weight through a full forward step. Behind me, the enslaver gave a loud grunt. I tried to give him a look over my shoulder and found my neck was unwilling to allow it.

I focused again on the truck bed and limped my way around the tailgate. I drummed my fingers along the truck bed toolbox, forced open its stubborn latch, and limped back away from all the tools that spilled forth. I kicked around the spilled pile of steel, reached down, and retrieved my claw hammer—the nice one, the demolition hammer; twenty ounces of birthday present with a straight claw like an exclamation point. I twirled it in the air and caught it like a baton. Here was my key, the tool to break free of my shackles, just as had been shown to me in the bar. My God, it was happening! I could feel it. I could sing.

I limped toward the trapper, shuffling through the rock-littered dirt that marked my family road. Soon, these heels would know the inviting warmth of soft sands. My elation afflicted me with a nearly uncontrollable compulsion to dance, but the urge could not overcome the pain in my hip.

"Guess you should've been more concerned with putting on your own seat belt than trying to take mine off." Like my breathing, my speech sounded odd. Did the airbag break my nose? Had I not noticed?

The jailer moaned something unintelligible. It was clear his jaw was broken, and not lightly.

"Impossible," I remarked. "The great pontificator, is speechless?"

The great pontificator drooled blood through broken teeth.

"You know what I'm thinking?" I continued advancing toward him. "I know you don't care what I'm thinking, but I'm going to tell you anyway, because that just seems to be how our relationship works." The cager rolled one eye side to side in search of something; the other was closed shut to prevent the entrance of a trickle of blood from a gash in his eyebrow. Like so many discarded peanut shells, gravel crunched and scraped underfoot as I neared his broken body. "'I'm thinkin','" I continued in an imitation, "'Surely this ain't Lirrel … Litter …'" I cleared my throat and pointed at the cager with my hammer. "You, asshole, 'bleedin' all over *my* road; makin' a mess all over *my* road. Yeah? You listenin'?'" I swept gravel at him with my uninjured right foot. The cager was grasping at the handheld fastened to his belt. The radio clicked static. I reached down, removed it, and cast it aside. "Two reasons you don't need that: one, you can't speak, you dumb prick; two, you don't know my fucking name, you dumb prick!" Spittle and blood peppered his already bloodied face. God, I was thirsty. "But don't you worry. You'll learn. You'll go to your grave knowing my name. I'll teach it to you the only way you dumb pricks can learn it." I raised the hammer. He raised a weak arm. "Ol' *McDonnell* had a hammer! You listenin'? Put that fucking hand down and sing it. E-I- Sing it, asshole! E-I-O!"

The captor let loose a guttural moan.

"With a—" I grunted as I brought the hammer down twice, meeting the detainer's skull first with a thud, then with a wet crack. "Here a—" *grunt*. "There a—" *grunt*. "**EVERYWHERE A—**" I swung erratically, cackling in hysteria. I was dripping with sweat, or blood, or both. My arm and shoulder grew tired, but the hammer continued to rise and fall.

· ℰ ·

I gazed upon my home in much the same way I used to gaze upon The Wishing Well. I dreaded this place. It was a voluntary prison to which I submitted myself daily. Well, perhaps not a prison at all, actually. For even prisoners are permitted freedoms. This was a stage, and I was a puppet coerced into handing over my strings by an uncontrolled masochism. So masochistic was I, that I married my own puppeteer.

I stepped onto the oil-stained dirt that comprised my driveway. Soon this pebble-littered dirt would be long behind me, and I'd have only seashell-littered sand ahead. I needed only to break free of my chains.

The bedroom lights flashed on. I glanced up at the pale, yellow luminescence that glowed life into the two curtained windows above me. Windows? No, eyes. Two square, jaundiced eyes bathed me with radiant observation.

With a little hum, I limp-danced my way up the steps to the front door, which I found to be locked. No surprise. Just like the old days. I gave a light tap on the door with the hammer. Years of experience told me *she* was waiting just on the other side. *She* always laid in wait, like some creature ready to lash out with a venomous tongue.

"Baby ..."

"Don't 'baby' me," she exclaimed in a hushed shout through the door. "You've been drinking, haven't you?"

"Aw, baby, don't do me like this."

"I knew it! I *knew* it! Have you no consideration for your family? For your son?" She slowed herself with a quick breath. "I thought you changed." There was a long pause.

I have changed. Oh, how I've changed. "Just—Just let me in and I'll explain myself. I've done some self-reflecting, you know, like the group taught me." I stifled a giggle. "And ... I want to resolve some conflicts."

Another moment of silence, which was at last broken by the sound of a turning lock. The door cracked open a sliver, only as much as its chain would allow, as much as was needed to look at me (*they're always watching*).

"I'm sorry, Carson. But you're not welcome here." Not one note of concern could be heard in her voice. No concern for my health. No anger over a missing truck. No shock at my bloodied face and clothes. No worry, no distress, only indifference; like ... like she had given up on me.

"Let's not do this. Just open the damn door."

"You didn't call. You didn't even text."

"Honey, we don't—"

"No, do not 'honey' me, and do not tell me we don't have service. I walked down the road to check and you know what happened when I got service? Nothing! Because you don't care about us! You don't even look at us anymore!" She steadied her breathing and lowered her voice again. "I walked, with our son, who you said you loved so much you'd quit drinking forever, and obviously that was a lie, and I walked with him, and we were scared, and there was nothing on the phone, nothing, because you don't give a shit." She drew in another breath (*or did she let out a hiss?*) as though to continue speaking but bit her tongue for an instant. Then, "I hope you find peace somewhere, Carson." The door began to creak shut and I threw the hammer's clawed edge into the open frame. "What are you—"

"Finding peace," I snarled. I slammed my body into the hammer's handle and the chain tore loose from the door frame in a splintery crack. I threw the door open, knocking *her* yelping to the floor. "There are no strings on me tonight, baby," I growled through grinding teeth. I stood over her like I stood over the would-be captor. *It would come naturally*, I was assured in the bar, *like muscle memory*. With hammer in one hand and adrenaline in the other, I placed both hands behind my head and breathed. Deliverance was imminent. I looked down at her. She looked up at me. There were those inexorable crocodile tears running down (*scaly*) cheeks. I made an involuntary step back in disbelief, setting weight on my injured leg and falling onto my tailbone. "I-I-" I stammered. "I can see you."

It writhed in pain on the rug for a moment, clutching its elbow (*do they have elbows?*), and let out a quiet sob. "I can't do this anymore," it cried. With all the strength of an enervated marathoner, it stood and hobbled toward the kitchen. "I'm calling the police," it lied. There was almost never service here. "I want you gone."

For a moment, I stood cemented to the floor in shock and bewilderment. It hadn't looked at me with the hate-quivering eyes to which I had become accustomed over the years. What gazed upon me through the darkness were two golden discs with black streaks in their centers. I could finally see. All these years it kept me dry, blind. But I saw it now, its eyes. They were the eyes of a constrictor.

"Did you hear me, Carson?" it called out in deception through the darkness. "I'm calling the cops. You need to leave."

I heard. I understood. The constrictor was working with the incarcerator.

It appeared in the kitchen's entrance. Not a woman. Something. Something only just resembling a woman's physicality, barely playing the role of a wife, but I saw it now. For years, I had seen *her* through eyes both sober and inebriated, but now ... now, I was able to see her true form ... through Whet eyes. It was unmistakable. Two reptilian eyes above a fanged mouth.

It approached me. My heart shivered in trepidation.

"Leave," it cried. My grip on the hammer's handle tightened. It attempted to shove me. "Get the fuck—"

I swung the hammer in a quick, upward motion, somewhat blocked by a shoving arm but still catching its chin (*did they have chins?*) with the hammer's head. It shrieked, fell back, and slithered on all fours toward the stairs that led to the bedrooms. I gave injury-hampered chase and caught it by an ankle (*tail*) halfway into its ascent. It fell forward, striking its face against a step. It rolled onto its back and kicked at me, screaming.

"I hate you!" Venomous spittle sputtered. If nothing else, I had that in common with the thing.

I jerked it a few steps lower, so its reptilian face was in range, and raised the hammer overhead.

"Carson, please!" the constrictor begged. "I'm the mother of your son!"

"I see you!" I bellowed. The hammer fell. It blocked the blow with its forearm and kicked wildly, landing a heel on my stable knee. My leg buckled and I fell from the stairs to the floor. The constrictor twisted up the staircase.

A week of baling hay.

My fingers were locked with lactic acid, my forearms cramped. I clutched at the handrail and pulled myself to my feet.

A rollover wreck.

My neck could not swivel. My hip was failing.

A strike to the knee, a fall on my back.

I limped up the blood-splattered stairs. The constrictor was crawling on hand and knees, dragging a limp arm. The thing was headed for the juvenile. How broken it was already. What a freeing sight, like the crumbling wall of a tomb only a few quick blows from revealing a world of freedom and life. My liberation day. I could sing.

"Old McDonnell had a farm." My voice was deep and slow. "E-I-E-I-O."

"Why, Carson?" the serpent bawled.

"And on his farm, he had a wife." I was on top of it once more, rolling it onto its back. It was quite submissive, hopeless even. The fiery strength that burned within it just moments ago had faded entirely. There was that reptilian brain in action: fight, flight, or, in this case, freeze.

"Please," it squeaked.

"E-I-E-I-O."

"Don't touch him."

And many strokes, though with a little hammer, broke through and dismantled the hardest steel restraint.

I heard a gasp (*hiss?*). Its offspring was peering at me through a crack in the door and I leered back. A puddle of urine was forming around the snakelet's feet. (*Now, certainly, snakes didn't have feet. Toes, perhaps? They had to move somehow ...*) Its python face was melting into a semblance of human shock and terror. I raised the hammer—my key—in its direction. A wet mass of brain matter dangled from the hammer's head. I moved toward the snakelet but faltered on my pained knee and hip. The snakelet slammed the door shut and joggled the lock. I smirked. Tonight belonged to fate. The snakelet was merely delaying inevitability.

"And on his farm, he had a son."

I grasped the handle and rattled the door in its frame. "E-I-E-I-uh-oh. What did we say about locked doors in the house, boy?" There was nothing in response; no cries, no shuffling about, only silence on its side of the door and labored mouth-breathing on mine. My nose still offered no sufficient airway. "Your father asked you a question."

I raised the hammer to destroy the handle and lowered it again. The snakelet was trapped. Last summer, after sneaking out in the middle of the night and burning down half the field with a firework, I screwed its window shut.

Fate. I smiled again.

"I'll wait for you right here, boy. I'm going to knock some respect into you." I paused, listening for any type of disturbance. Nothing. It knew. It knew that I knew. It was no boy.

I tiptoed down the stairs, to the extent my injuries would allow. There was a gas can in the garage next to the ATV. It was always full. It was always full because I never poured it into the ATV. I never poured it into the ATV because the fucking ATV never worked.

Fate.

I vainly dug around the junk drawer in search of matches, which were an uncommon resource in a non-smoking household. The matchbook I did find was the one that little shit used to destroy my property, my months-long work. I remembered I kept it locked up in the toolbox to keep its matches out of the snakelet's grubby little hands. I chuckled.

Tonight truly belonged to
Fate.

With fuel and fire in hand, I returned to the top of the stairs. I hummed that infernal nursery rhyme in sync with the splashing of gasoline on outdated floors and over-decorated, picture-littered walls. Funny, the family looked fairly human in those frames. Deceptive little fuckers.

"With a—" *splash, splash,* "here. And a—" *splash, splash,* "there." I danced from one room to the next, staggering on a protesting knee. A picture of a bathroom in the bathroom? *Splash.* Decorative pillows not to be slept or sat upon? *Splash.* My Bachelor of Agriculture, because kicking shit around a field required an education? *Splash, splash, splash.*

In the master bedroom, I found packed luggage. What of the contents? New me did not care. Old me would be quite upset by this. Old me would have considered this a betrayal of trust. The thing that once posed as my wife had just assumed I fucked up, because I was a piece of shit. I could have rolled my truck in a ditch, but its first thought was, "The piece of shit fucked up. Better pack the bags." Well, new me cared not. I doused the baggage. My belongings, its belongings. It would all burn the same. Everything burned.

The fumes were growing strong enough now that even my broken nose could smell it: salvation. I had to pause to reflect on how genuinely happy I was. What a foreign feeling. Happiness was an elusive thing, and I had once again found it in this moment of triumph. In this *Whet* moment.

"Mommy?" A soft cry through the snakelet's door. The voice cracked in frightful anticipation.

"You'll be with her in a minute, bud."

I trailed the remnants of the gas can downstairs and flung the can back upstairs. I removed a single match and, in my last act of self-liberation, sparked it to life. I set the steps ablaze. A whoosh and crackle ensued as the flames raced onto the upper landing, eager to feed. I stood before the hot glow, hands on hips, joyful tears welling in my blood-speckled eyes. This must have been what a beach sunrise felt like.

I wiped my hands clean on my jeans and stepped out onto the porch, reborn. Triumph! Hellish triumph! I was bursting with it, such that it escaped my smiling mouth in a short explosion of laughter.

The night air was just as pleasant as it had been during the carpool home. The air smelled of campfire. The cattle lowed. From the horizon—that always out of reach horizon—grew the nearing wailing of sirens. Howling captors on the hunt.

Truck Time

THE SUBSTITUTE

I watched my feet as we walked through the parking lot. My shoe lights didn't blink anymore. I wished they did. I wished my feet didn't get so big. My toes were always smushed.

"Straighten up. Walk with pride, boy," Dad said. "You're a Miller. Act like it."

I didn't want to look up; I really didn't. But if I didn't do as Dad told me, he was going to give me more truck time.

"You hear me, CJ?" He grabbed the back of my neck really hard and lifted me to my toes. I whined. I tried not to, but it hurt. "Stop that crying, boy, or I'll give you something to cry about." His voice got low. He always meant it when his voice was low. "Now, walk like a man—like a Miller."

I stood up straight like a stick, sniffed the wet in my nose, and rubbed my eyes with my sleeve. I looked at the door we were walking to. There were cracks in the glass like a spider web.

"You see that?" Dad pointed at the cracks. "Don't you ever let me catch you throwing rocks. Punks throw rocks. And you know what punks get, right?"

"Truck time." I said it quiet.

"Truck time."

He opened the door and we walked in. It smelled stinky and the floor was sticky, too, like the bathroom at the baseball games. There were boxes everywhere and price tags on all the chairs and tables.

"Hello, hello!" There was a funny-looking fat man waving at us from behind the counter. "Welcome to The Wishing Well, gentlemen."

Dad looked around at all the boxes as we walked to the counter. "Business a little slow?" Dad asked.

"Brother, I'm in the business of makin' dreams come true, and let me tell ya," he looked down at me and smiled big and scary, "business is boomin'."

"You here for the pool table?" Another man asked from a door in the back.

"Yeah, that's me," Dad said.

"You're a little early, Mr. Miller," the other man said.

"Yeah, at that price, if it looks as good as it does in the pictures, then consider me the early bird."

"Well, c'mon back." The other man waved at Dad to follow him.

"Stay put, CJ," Dad told me. "And don't touch anything." He went into the back room.

I looked up at the man behind the counter. He was looking back at me and he wasn't blinking. He was probably really good at staring contests. His eyes were big, too. And so were his nose and eyebrows. He didn't have any hair on the top of his head but he had lots of it on the sides, big and puffy. He looked like a clown without any paint on his face.

He gestured at a stool and I climbed up on the seat.

"Why, hello there, little man. I don't suppose you're up for a drink?" The clown-man giggled like a girl. "What'll it be, little man? Tall glass of juice, straight, no chaser? He-he!" Again, he made the girly sound. I wanted to laugh. It was funny to hear a grown-up talk giggly. But I wasn't supposed to laugh at grown-ups. Only punks laughed at grown-ups and I was still sore from the last truck time. "What's your wish today?"

"W-wish?" I wasn't supposed to talk to strangers either. Only punks talked to strangers. But Dad talked to him and he was just in the other room.

"That's what I said. What do you got cotton in those ears?" He reached toward my ear and I flinched. He jumped and dropped a cotton ball on the counter. "Well, I guess you're not here for the jokes, are ya?" He got a serious look on his face. "You know, little man, it's getting harder and harder to please child patrons." He giggled. "But, seriously, what's your wish? What do you hunger for, little man?"

What do I hunger for? I was hungry. I didn't get to have cereal after wake-up because I was acting like a punk. "Um, mac 'n cheese?"

The clown-man stopped smiling. "Mac 'n—" He tilted his head and his eyebrows got wrinkly. "Mac 'n cheese? Hmph." His voice got grumbly and shaky. "You think you're funny, you little shit?" He said it through his teeth like when a dog growls.

I got scared and whined. He put a hand over his mouth and raised his bushy eyebrows like he got scared, too. Then he made a grown-up chuckle. "Ha-ha. Ahem. Huh." He turned to his side like he was talking to an imaginary friend. "The little man wants mac 'n cheese." He turned back to me. "That's a good start, kiddo, but let's think bigger." He made a big motion with his hands. "This is The Wishing Well, little man. We're talking omnipotence, here." I didn't know that word.

We just looked at each other for a minute. I didn't say anything. I didn't know what he wanted me to say. His eyes got shaky and then he breathed big. He reached under the counter, brought out a handled, plastic cup, and set it in front of me. "Let's just whet that appetite of yours."

"I'm not supposed to have soda before school," I said.

"Little man," he shook his head and squeezed his fist really hard on the counter. His knuckles were super white and looked like they were going to poke out of his skin. "You think I'd set you up for failure? This ain't soda pop." He pushed it closer to me. "It's a little taste of desire." He leaned in close to me and his voice got really, really low; lower than Dad's when he was extra serious. "It's what you need."

He wasn't blinking again. And his eyes seemed even bigger. They were black, too, like a snowman's. I was getting scared again. I couldn't stop looking at his eyes. It was like they were gone. There was no more shine. I thought if I reached up and poked at them, my finger would just go into his head like a hole. Yeah, just like holes. They were two holes that went forever and ever. They were so empty and dry. Like me. I was really dry. I was really thirsty.

I took the cup and sipped. It tasted like apples. I liked apples a lot. It reminded me of apple juice. It really reminded me of apple juice. Like, when I used to drink apple juice in the living room with Mom and Dad. I could see Dad smiling as we watched TV. I really liked his smile—his real smile. The one he used to have before Mom went to heaven. I saw it now. He was really smiling. We were all smiling.

And then Dad started crying. No. I didn't like that. I couldn't smell apples anymore. It smelled like the time I burnt my hair with the candle. And there were crackles and pops like when I put milk in my cereal. I looked at Mom and she was burned black now. She looked like a marshmallow that was on fire too long; except, when the black flaked off of her it was pink goo underneath instead of white goo. I tried to splash her with my cup but it was empty. My cup was empty. I looked up at the clown-man. The living room was gone. I felt like crying.

"Can I have more?" I was choking.

"Mm, no." The clown-man crossed his arms.

"Um, please?" I asked. My head was feeling kinda funny.

"You haven't told me your wish yet, little man."

I was feeling a little dizzy and, even though I didn't really want to talk, I really, really wanted to talk.

"Smiles," I whispered.

He put his hand behind his ear. "Speak up so us old guys in the back can hear."

"I want everybody to be happy again."

"Oh, smiles!" he said. His eyes seemed normal now. Still big, but not holes. He reached into his pocket. "I've got just the thing, little man." He removed a really shiny quarter and put it in my hand. "I've got a feeling about you."

He then pulled me up over the counter and stood me in front of a big, brick circle coming out of the floor. It was full of water with a bunch of coins at the bottom.

"Any day, now," he said, tapping his foot.

I looked at my quarter and dropped it into the water with a little plop.

"What are you doing back there?" Dad asked from the door.

"Oh, he was just making a wish," the clown-man said.

Dad walked over to us. "I don't want him behind the bar," he told the clown-man. "C'mon, son." He took my hand and then turned to the other man from the back room. "I've got to take him to school but I'll swing around right after with a check if you guys can get the table into my basement."

"Sure thing, buddy," the other man said.

"Buh-bye," the clown-man called out. He flapped his hand up and down.

· ल ·

Dad walked me to class as the first bell rang. Everyone was sitting in a semicircle around a lady who wasn't our teacher. They looked up at Dad and me. My face got hot. I had never been late before and now everyone was staring. The lady turned her head to look at us.

"Come, come and join the fun." She waved for me to go inside. I went to the floor and sat criss-cross applesauce next to my friend, Paul. Dad walked fast down the hallway, probably to get back to The Wishing Well. The lady went to the door when he was gone and shut and locked it. She then went to the whiteboard and wrote her name on it with a red marker. That was my favorite color.

"My name is Carrie S. Miles but to you I'm Mrs. Smiles." She then sat in front of the group with a big, silly smile on her face. A couple of us giggled. "I've many names in different places, played many games with different faces. Though I'm dynamic in my styles, I never leave without my smiles." She took two fingers and pushed the wrinkly corners of her mouth into an even bigger smile. "So, let us start with simple games, that I may learn all of your names." She pointed to Mary. Mary was nice. I liked Mary. "You, you there with curly hair. What's your name? Go on, now, share."

Mary's face got red like a tomato. "Um ..."

"Speak louder, girl. Do not be shy. Give it a whirl. Give it a try."

Mary hid her face behind her hands. "Um, Mary?"

"You go by 'Mary.' Was that so scary?" The lady asked. "You've found your spine. Now, one more time but I insist you try a rhyme."

"Um, I'm Mary. And, um ..." Mary smiled. "I'm hairy," she giggled. The rest of us giggled, too.

Mrs. Smiles didn't giggle, though. "She went about it somewhat wrong but we'll improve, so, move along."

Mrs. Smiles pointed to Miguel. I liked Miguel. He was kind of fat but he was funny.

"I'm Miguel and I smell!" He said it loud and proud. Then he leaned to one side and farted. Everyone laughed. Everyone except Mrs. Smiles.

Mrs. Smiles wasn't happy anymore. She seemed angry and her jaw was moving from side to side. "Hush! Hush! Quiet down. This isn't funny, little clown." Everybody kept laughing, especially Miguel. "I advise you, child, that you keep things mild. You'd hate to see when I get wild." She seemed extra serious now and while some of us started to hush, Miguel kept laughing. He started fanning his butt and laughing harder.

Mrs. Smiles stood and pulled Miguel from the floor, like plucking a feather. He kept giggling as she walked him to the closet in the back of the room. She opened the closet door and Miguel vanished. It was so fast. He was gone in a blink. Mrs. Smiles slammed the door shut and Miguel screamed. The door shook a couple of times and then it was quiet, both in the closet and in the classroom.

Mrs. Smiles came back to the group. She closed her eyes, breathed deep and shaky, and then mumbled in a sing-song.

"The itsy bitsy spider climbed up the waterspout." She hummed for a minute and then opened her eyes. Her big smile was back. "Do not be sad. Be glad, be glad. Think of the time we could've had, had our friend not been so bad."

"What's in there?" Sam, asked. He wasn't my friend. He cut in front of me at the water fountain line once and stuck out his tongue at me.

"In there, back there?" She pointed at the closet. "Just a pet that's set to get the naughty ones that I have met. Her name is Glee. She's much like me, in that she'll need to feed a while. So, do take heed of this, I plead, you mustn't lose that smile." Something was scratching at the closet door. We all turned to look at it. "If you're feeling naughty, pause it, lest you end up in the closet. For if you're there before day's end, you'll find what's there is not a friend."

Mary started crying and then Lacey cried even louder. Lacey always cried and it was always loud; like, really loud. Mrs. Smiles shivered and her head twitched to the side. She shut her eyes really hard and shushed the girls. But they didn't stop. She walked toward them, still shushing, and the two girls got really low to the floor. Their faces were wet with tears and boogers. I felt like crying, too. But only girls were supposed to cry.

I only ever cried really, really hard once, when Dad told me that I bought Mom a one-way ticket to heaven. I let the carpet catch fire when I didn't wake Dad up. Sometimes he fell asleep when he was smoking and I was supposed to wake him up. But, that night, I was at a sleepover with a friend, like a punk. I had to have a lot of truck time.

"Why-why-why do you cry?" The lady was loud and scary. She sounded like a mean dog behind a fence. "Why am *I* vilified? You gaze upon *me* as though *I'm* the beast but you don't know the least of your worries is me. The creature in there's what to beware. So, smile lest you encounter Glee." Mary tried to stop crying but couldn't. Lacey was scream-crying. "Now, listen here, my little dears, I think you'll find I've been sincere. For when I say I want a smile, I want it now, not in a while. And if a frown should cross my path, then it will meet my hungry wrath."

The lady pulled them both from the floor and dragged them toward the closet. They wiggled like fishing worms when you try to put the hook in. They kicked over desks, and crayons and papers flew all over the floor. Lacey just screamed but Mary begged. The lady didn't care.

I watched real careful this time when she opened the door. The black behind the door was like the clown-man's eyes. Lacey and Mary vanished into the closet just as fast as Miguel. I still couldn't see how it happened. Was the closet like a vacuum?

Lacey screamed longer than Mary but both were quiet in a few seconds. Mrs. Smiles waited at the door. We all waited, quiet. Then, there was a little knock at the closet door. Mrs. Smiles opened it and Mary was there. She had a humongous cartoon smile. And she was holding Lacey's and Miguel's clothes. They were all torn up and covered in red finger paint. She dropped them next to the door.

"Feeling better, little one, now that all is said and done?"

Mary didn't stop smiling. She couldn't stop smiling her cartoon smile. "I feel so great. I feel just fine. I'd like to state, I will not whine. But this of you I do implore, if you could please unlock the door. I'll not be naughty, it's true, I swear. I need the potty to wash my hair."

She brushed her hair back behind her ears. It was all clumped together with finger paint. When it was pulled back, I saw two puffy holes on the side of her head between her ear and eyebrow.

The lady led Mary out of the classroom, locked the door, and came back to the group mats.

"Now, let's set our things back in their places and put some *smiles* upon those faces." She must have wanted us to clean up the desks and crayons but we didn't move. "Smiles are contagious things, but happiness is all they bring. And naughtiness will fade away after the games we play today."

The lady walked to us and stood in front of Paul. He made a big smile. The lady crossed her arms. She looked really mad and shaky. "Give me your name and I won't shame but rather tame the pain you contain if you abstain from feigning a smile. A shame it would be for you to meet Glee when me you attempt to beguile."

Paul whined and got up. He ran to the door and Sam did the same. They tried to open it but the lady caught them. They screamed and kicked and screamed louder the further she dragged them to the closet. And they disappeared like everybody else when she opened the door. Now, I was alone.

She hummed and smiled and walked to me really slow. "A simple request, an effortless test. No teaser, your mind will not strain. There's no one to best, you've survived the rest. Now just tell me what is your name."

I was so scared I didn't think I could talk. But I had to. If the closet was like truck time, I had to tell her my name. Dad always called me "CJ" because we're both "Christopher." But I couldn't think of anything that rhymed with Christopher or CJ—not in a hurry. So, I was going to tell her my middle name. My middle name had the best rhyme.

"My name is ... Kyle ..." I swallowed. "I like to smile."

"Kyle," the lady said. She had a huge smile. Her smile was so big, I could almost see all of her pointy teeth. "Now that's a name that is worthwhile. You're not like them, not infantile." She pointed to the closet and I looked at the wet clothes next to the closet door. There must have been a lot of paint in there. "Never mind the pile, Kyle. You'll survive this little trial. For you have wit, you have guile. You wouldn't quit on our last mile, would you, Kyle?"

Her eyes were turning black. Not like the clown-man's. His weren't shiny. The substitute's eyes were really shiny black and growing like blown up balloons. Two more eyes were growing on the sides of her face, one on each side. They didn't have eyelids or eyelashes. She drooled a little bit. When she tried to wipe it away, it stuck to her hand and pulled out like a string on a toy. It wasn't stringy like regular spit, it was more like melted cheese on a pizza.

She walked closer to me and I whined. She was too scary.

"No, don't fear, that's not the way." Her voice was extra scary now. "You've won, my dear, so you should say, 'I win, I win, hooray, hooray!'" She tried to talk like me but it didn't sound like a kid or a grown-up. She talked like a monster. "'Hooray, hooray, I've won today!'" She leaned over me. "You've won, I said, you've won, you've won! And yet it's tears that have begun. Why not a smile, you little fucker?" She hit the floor mat with her palm and I jumped. "What has your face in such a pucker?"

I tried to be a man. I tried to be strong like a Miller. But I couldn't. I cried. I cried harder when the lady picked me up and took me to the closet. Something scratched at the door. I had to stop crying. I could show her I was strong like a Miller.

"Please," I said. "I'm sorry." I didn't know what to say. I could never change Dad's mind once he got me to the truck. "Please," I whispered.

We stood in front of the closet. She didn't do anything but hold me. Sometimes, Dad would have me open the door for truck time because I always brought it upon myself. I knew that's what she wanted me to do. I looked up at her. Two hairy fingers were growing out of her face.

"Oh, rapture is near. You'll meet Glee in here, where joy appears as happy thoughts within your ears." Her face fingers wiped her stringy drool back into her mouth. She slurped.

I looked at the doorknob. The thing in the closet kept scratching at the door. I reached for the knob. The scratching was getting louder. I always opened the door for truck time when Dad told me to. I never wanted to but I always did. I was too scared not to. But truck time was never forever and ever. There was always an after. Sometimes it wasn't until Dad got tired, but there was always an after.

I opened the closet door.

· ℰↄ ·

The closet wasn't like a vacuum. I wasn't sucked in. I was pulled in by long, prickly legs. I was spinning. Something like fishing string was tying my arms to my sides. I was pushed down to the floor on my back. There were spider webs and skeletons everywhere. But not like the skeletons in cartoons. These ones had parts of clothes and meaty bits, like a mostly-eaten chicken leg with some skin and gristle still left.

A grown-up size spider stood above me. It got really close and started feeling my face with its face fingers. Then it bit the side of my head. Its teeth popped into my noggin like the opening of a soda can. It felt really hot and cold at the same time. Something was tickling across my face. They were a couple of normal-size spiders. They ran to my ears. I tried to pull my arm out of the web but I wasn't strong enough. I whined again. The spiders were trying to squeeze into my ears. They tried and tried. It tickled and itched and sounded like when I scratched my hair. My eyes were getting wet and stinging. My head and ears felt muggy like when you get water stuck in your ears and nose at the swimming pool.

My face began to tighten as the moment dragged on. A fluid—I couldn't tell if it was venom, or even if it was hot or cold—was seeping into my skull. With every trace my brain absorbed, I could feel some sort of surge in cognition. And, when the spiders had at last made their way fully into my ears, the whispering commenced.

Your wish will be granted, you will attain joy. We two have been planted for you to employ. The words rang out in synchronous echoes.

My flesh continued to tighten and my facial muscles spasmed before locking into a terrible cramp, forcing an extensive, lip-stretching smile. The spider retracted its fangs and released my cranium. It then unwound me from its webbing. I stood with a bit of vertigo that passed as I approached the closet door. I rapped my knuckles against the blood-stained, chipped wood and the door was opened. Mrs. Smiles greeted me at the door's opening. I felt the last of the venom dissipate into my gray matter.

"Feeling better, little one, now that all is said and done?"

Happiness is all around. There's no need for you to frown. Anywhere you stare it's there, happiness is everywhere.

"While I at first was feeling wary, I now am feeling very merry."

And just behind her, who did I see? Was it my mother? How could it be? Why, a year ago she was found dead. So, who was this lady in her stead?

That is your mother, yes, it's true that she's the one within your view, the spiders said, nestled now within my head.

To her I trod. "By God," I guffawed.

The class a stage on which my mother starred. Her eyes were embers and her flesh was charred. She held with me a glowing gaze, my happiness she set ablaze. I embraced her in a forlorn hug, and she fell to ash upon the rug.

She's something that you hardly had because you lost her to your dad, the voices spoke. An idea they did provoke.

The sub, she called my old man, as according to my plan. Behavior rough, my temper bad, she had enough and called for Dad. And here I waited, with knife serrated, to finish what I contemplated.

Then he came, with rage refreshed, and the knife I buried in his chest.

And the knife I buried in his chest.

And the knife I buried in his chest.

Again, they called. *Again, again. We are enthralled.*

I was joyous now, without a care, for happiness sprayed everywhere. I was drenched with joy from head to toe—a dripping joy, a crimson glow. And as I watched the bloodstreams spring, I felt inside an urge to sing.

"The itsy bitsy spider was waiting for a frown. Then came a child who was feeling kind of down. The spider pulled him in and tinkered with his brain and the child with the frown was happy once again."

This is your peak, it is your ceiling, indulge now in this foreign feeling.

"My peak? But, no, it cannot end. What's after this, my newfound friend?"

We've brought you joy, but there's a catch. The eggs we've laid are going to hatch. And as we helped you conquer sorrow, you'll help our young to eat tomorrow.

Want

THE LAKE

"Hey, Jake," I greeted with a light wave as I crossed the seating area to the bar. I took a bar stool beside him.

"Glad you found the place all right." Jake took my hand in a hearty handshake. "Been a while."

"Yeah, I got a little turned around trying to find you. Never been to Hell Gate before and I didn't realize I'd lose service going through the pass. I'm still not getting much signal here in the valley." I gave my phone screen a confirming look and set it down on the bar top.

"Ah, you don't need it. It's a boating trip, you won't even miss it." I hoped that was true but for months on end that phone had been the only source of entertainment and human interaction I was able to experience outside of work.

"You're looking good," I remarked. He was. He had always been naturally fit but his shoulders seemed broader, the sleeves on his T-shirt seemed tighter, even his legs had thickened well. The guy was blessed with all the right genes, no doubt, but it was clear he had been putting in the work since last I'd seen him. "Looks like you got a lot of sun."

"I know, man, it was brutal. You should've seen me at the start of summer." He examined his arms. "All done shedding now."

"So, what's this place called?" I asked.

"The Wishing Well."

"No, not the brewery, I mean the lake we're boating."

"Oh, sorry. Hell's Mouth. Nate and I hiked to it last year up in the Beartooths. It's all natural. Looks like a man-made dam or something, but it's totally natural. Like a giant, rock bowl … thing," he described, cupping his hands in an attempt to shape a bowl.

"That sounds awesome. And you can drive up there?"

"Seems like it. If not, we'll always wish we could have."

"Wait, we're towing a boat and you don't know if we can reach the lake?"

"It's all good, man. We for sure can reach Emerald Lake with the boat no problem. That's on the south side of the trails that run up to the bowl. Emerald's got a campground and everything. When we hiked up to Granite Peak, Nate and I saw a trail, like a single lane switchback, that runs all the way up to the Devil's Bowl from the east. Should be big enough for the truck and trailer."

Devil's Bowl. I had heard of it before. I had never been in Hell Gate Valley, but I was sure I knew of the Devil's Bowl. I almost reached for my phone before remembering I did not have service. Maybe the brewery had Wi-Fi but I did not want to look dependent on the device, especially since Jake was keeping his in his pocket.

"Didn't some people go missing or something out in Devil's Bowl?" I asked.

"Drowned, supposedly, but that's just an assumption. Rangers never found any bodies, only clothes by the shore. Could've been bears, wolves, some guy with a machete. Hell, a beaver can kill you. Or, look at what happened to that woman who was floating the Madison: mauled in the face by river otters."

"Huh. And there are people who know we're going to be up there? Like, in case something happens?"

"Yeah, kinda. My parents know we're taking the boat up to Emerald," Jake stated.

"But they don't know we're going to the Bowl?"

"No, dude, because Hell's Mouth is off limits to swimming and boating and kayaking and pretty much everything but shoreline fishing."

"What? Why—"

"Probably because of those people who drowned, Corby."

"No, I was going to ask why, then, are we taking the boat up there?"

"Corbin, relax. I've been up there a hundred times and you know how many rangers I've seen?" He held his fingers up in a circle. "Zero. You wanna know how people drown out there? Same way people lose fingers with fireworks. They don't use their noggins," he said, tapping at his temple. "It's all snowmelt, so it's always cold. Numbs you up, so you don't realize how tired you're getting. They obviously weren't using lifejackets and there definitely aren't lifeguards out there. And you know what we've got? A couple of lifejackets and a former life-guard," he said, emphasizing the last statement with thumbs pointed toward himself. "So, again, it's all good, Corbs."

I considered pushing back, opposing the notion that we should put ourselves at risk of fines or even death. Jake could be so frustrating, but he was also intriguing. Jake was a man with stories to tell; the kind of man so undoubtedly unique that every story was with merit, unquestionable. I wanted that, and I would not have it by shutting every door that was held open for me. I was already unremarkable. So unremarkable was I that I still had not been noticed by the bartender despite sitting at a mostly empty bar top.

"Where's the bartender?" I asked.

"A couple of the taps were only spitting foam so he ran to the back," Jake explained. He then finished his glass.

I looked around for a water pitcher or water fountain or anything self-serve by which I could quench my thirst. I had avoided drinking anything for most of the drive, as there were no rest stops when driving through the mountains. Sure, there were pull-offs for "scenic views" and "tire chain installation," but I knew the moment I pulled my dick out of my pants on the side of the interstate a busload of teen girls would roll by and I would be branded some kind of predator. So, it was simply safer to dehydrate myself.

"Man, I'm thirsty."

"You should try the strawberry blonde when the bartender gets back," Jake advised.

"Nah, if we're leaving as soon as the group gets here, I'm just going to have an iced tea or water."

"Why?"

"I'm not going to drink and drive. The cops around places like this have literally nothing else to do but nail you for the smallest infraction. How do you think a ghost town like this funds such a nice town hall? That thing was built on speeding tickets and DUIs, I guarantee it."

Jake chuckled. "You're always worrying, man. You can just leave your car in the lot, you know. We're planning on carpooling anyway. We can all fit in the truck, all the gear's in the bed."

"I don't know if I really want to leave my car at a brewery overnight, though …"

"Constantly worrying." He placed a hand on my shoulder. The *hey, buddy, relax* rhetoric was imminent. But he was right. My mind was always doing that—always running wild with threats and dangers, scenarios both plausible and implausible; excuses, really. Less an internal dialogue, more another impediment in my stalled journey through life.

"Corbin, my friend," he continued, "nothing's going to happen to your car here. It's Hell Gate, not San Francisco. It's all good. You worry about the littlest things: about getting into trouble; about your car; about work. Just relax. That's what the holiday weekend is all about: barbecues; drinking; going to the lake. That's Labor Day, baby.

Celebrating you, the worker," he stated, pointing toward me. With his other hand, he raised his empty glass. The bartender approached.

"Closing out or you need another?" the bartender asked. He was facing Jake with most of his back turned to me.

"I'll do another. We're still waiting on a few more," Jake answered.

"You got it." The bartender moved swiftly to oblige.

"Can I get an iced tea?" I asked.

"Iced tea ..." the bartender echoed distantly as he poured Jake's glass. Once full, he passed it off and began walking toward the other end of the bar, in the direction of another patron.

"With," I began, hoping to stop the bartender as he paced away, "some sweetener?"

"In a minute, bud," the bartender answered without looking at me.

I turned to Jake. "Dude."

"To be fair, that other guy was here before you. You wanna try the strawberry blonde before I drink out of it?" he asked, offering me his glass.

"No, really, I'm good with just tea." To this, Jake shrugged his shoulders and began drinking.

"So, uh ..." I tried to think of a way to steer the conversation away from drinking. "What have you been up to all summer? Where'd you get all that sun?"

"Oh, right." He glanced at his arms again. "Australia."

"Really? So, what do you have left? Antarctica?"

"Yeah, man, that's it. Give her a look." Jake stood from the stool and pulled up one side of his shorts to reveal a tattoo. His "traveler's tat," as he called it, was a globe that wrapped around his thigh. Outlined within were the seven continents, each of which would be colored in after each return trip from abroad. Australia was freshly filled, leaving Antarctica the sole blank outline. "I scuba dived the

Great Barrier Reef, which was actually kind of cold. Our summer is their winter, which is something I didn't really think about until I got there. Not too bad, though. You ever been scuba diving?"

"Not yet." *But you knew that. I'm not a diver. I'm not really ... anything.*

"Dude, you've got to try it. It was life changing. It was like entering a totally different world. Like being in space. Such a surreal experience, breathing underwater and watching all this life go on around you. We did day and night dives. There were sharks. Oh, I gotta tell you about the sharks." Jake carried on. I mostly listened.

The stories Jake would tell: stories of travel, of women, of great gains and losses of money, of epic fights and once in a lifetime concerts. All while still in his twenties. He had lived entire lifetimes before reaching thirty.

And what would be my story to counter his? What was Corbin's tale? The only thing I could report after ten months—nearly a year of potential experiences—was that I had been working extra hours to cover a rent increase. No novel writing, no vacations. This was it. A five-hour drive on a holiday weekend to boat, fish, and wakeboard at an in-state lake. While people like Jake were traveling the world, I would only travel the state. Worse yet was that I had to leave early on what was supposed to be an extended weekend. I was scheduled to work a double on the holiday. Or, rather, I involuntarily volunteered to work a double on the holiday. With rent due Tuesday, an empty fridge in the apartment, and the expenses of this trip, I needed the extra cash.

Was not that the case every holiday, though? Christmas Eve? I needed the time-and-a-half pay to make up for gift shopping. Christmas Day? Hours of phone calls with the family, video calls while opening gifts received in the mail, and then off to work. Thanksgiving? Fried chicken in the breakroom. I had nothing of interest to contribute. Work was all I had to discuss because work was all I was. While not underprivileged enough to die, I was too underprivileged to live.

"How about you, man? You're still working security at the hospital?" Jake asked me.

"Yeah ..."

"How's that been?"

"Well, to be honest," I bit at chapped lips, "kind of rough."

"Sorry to hear it." Jake asked nothing in follow-up. I didn't blame him. We both knew I had nothing thought-provoking to provide. To ask more of me would be akin to asking a paraplegic to jump. Sure, I was not all work, no play. I did have time off. But I did nothing with it. I had no girlfriend. I had neither the time nor money for a girlfriend. For much of the same, I had no hobbies. So, is that what Jake and I would discuss? My lack of life in the face of his grandiosity?

How shameful. Every minute of my existence had been wasted, forever lost to a job that would replace me in less than a moment without the remotest feeling of loss. I had barely contributed to this world and, worst of all, I had contributed nothing to my own life. I was just another meaningless pebble at the bottom of life's river, unmoving, and further buried by other meaningless pebbles and sediments, fated to be forgotten over time. Meanwhile, the Jakes of the world would be like the stones and boulders that broke the river's surface. No, more like the fish that swam its currents. Look at him. He was Jake: handsome, fit, well-traveled, and well-experienced. Who was I? Nobody. I was a security guard at a hospital, escorting vagrants from the temperature-controlled atrium to the hot summer sun or frigid winter night. That actually made me worse than a nobody. I was the villain in the stories of others.

"Just working," I said to fill the silence. I then added, "I'm actually saving up for a big trip myself." *Why did I tell him that?*

"That's awesome, man. Where are you headed?"

"Honestly, I don't really know." I forced my dry throat to swallow. "Yet."

"Well, when you figure it out, let me know. Maybe we can go together. Or at least I can give you some insight if I've been there." He stood from the stool again. "Hold that thought. I need to hit up the pisser and then we can totally brainstorm some travel ideas."

As Jake left for the restroom, I turned my gaze to the mountains beyond the windows. Bodies never found …

I considered all the possibilities surrounding those deaths. It was something I did to pass the time during slow shifts at the hospital. Patients would enter, clutching at pain while moaning, limping, coughing, or whatever, and I would run through every possibility to reason what was going on. There was the obvious, of course. Your broken bones and head injuries, detox, and so on. But I liked imagining the obvious was wrong, that some symptoms were red herrings. In the case of swimmers missing at a remote lake in the mountains, was drowning the obvious conclusion? Sure. Cold water, inexperience, alcohol … It was more than reasonable to assume they drowned. But there were so many other possibilities: a bear attack, like Jake suggested, in which the bear dragged the bodies away or even stalked the shoreline, keeping the swimmers from returning to land; some type of gas—maybe natural for the lake or a product of running their vehicle or something—which caused them to lose consciousness; maybe something in the lake—Hell's Mouth's own Loch Ness monster.

I turned my attention back to the bar top. A glass of what must have been beer had been set before me. The bartender, with his back to me as always, was at the till, seemingly cashing out the other patron.

"Hey, no, sorry but I—"

"It's what you need, bud," the bartender cut me off with a matter of fact tone, like a weary father explaining something obvious to his child once again. He then rushed to the other end of the bar with a freshly printed receipt in hand.

I eyed the glass. *It's what I need?* What was that supposed to mean? Had Jake been talking about me with him prior to my arrival, telling the bartender, as he was so frequently telling me, that I needed to "loosen up and wind down?" This seemed weird. It seemed rude.

I gave the bartender's back another glance (he was chatting with the departing patron) and then turned my attention back to the beer. As much as I did not want to be forced to leave my car in an unfamiliar parking lot overnight, the drink was quite alluring. Steady streams of bubbles raced up from the glass's bottom to feed the foamy head that sat at the surface like an inviting pillow ready to cushion my parched lips. Everything felt so … dry. I parted my lips with my tongue to afford them some relief but there was none; they only lightly clung to the withered flesh. For a moment—a fleeting thought—I considered going to the restroom to drink from the sink's faucet, or just to wet my mouth. But Jake would see this, and what then would he think of me, the lowly Corbin so unremarkable in life he could not secure a drink even when sat at the bar?

Then, an unheard, unspoken whisper. An urging to reach out and grasp the sweating glass; a prompt, rather, to resolve an unmet need. Yes, a need. I did need it, and it was only inches away—barely a moment from meeting my lips. So, why, then, the hesitation? Did I not moments ago have reservations about meeting this need?

Again, I felt impelled to reach forward. I did. My impetuous hand, that autonomous thing, wrapped about the glass like a lifejacket. The glass floated to my mouth. I drank.

I was overcome with the sensation of movement. My body was anchored to the barstool but I was moving somehow, as though my spirit had been jerked from its hull. I was swimming.

I could see everything: people coming and going, venturing, living; events; activities; achievements. The world pulsed with doing, with recreation and exploits and, well, life. They were wonderful, these wondrous sights, utterly wonderful.

Then there was me. There I sat. I merely sat. While all the world lived, I was only sitting. Though out of body, I felt an urge to cry, to vomit. There I sat without restraint, without restriction or impediment. There was no cage, no shackles, no adhesive to be seen. Seemingly the only thing that held me in place in such a dynamic, thriving world was me—sedentary, stationary me. It was an affront. It was sinful. I, a lifelong atheist, understood this inaction, this ... absence of living was indeed a cardinal sin.

Do something. Do anything. Move, damn you. Live, I commanded my inert vessel. It did nothing. I had to move it. I had to act before it died, before it was too late for it to truly live. But I could not simply will it to happen. I had to move. I—

I was moving. No, I was sinking; receding from the etheric to the physical like the drying of the bottom of an empty glass; like the empty glass tilted against my mouth.

I looked about. The brewery appeared unoccupied, devoid of activity, save for me ... sitting.

"Hello?" I called out, either to the bartender or any other listening ear. I sounded like a lost child.

I was again registering sounds, which I had not until now realized were reverberating around me. Clinking. The bartender was just on the other side of the bar top, my ears assured me. He was shuffling many glass things (bottles and glasses no doubt) in some type of organization beneath the counter. My eyes, which could now fully focus, finally discovered him—part of him, anyway. The man was peering at me; an unwavering, unblinking gaze from just over the edge of the bar top, as though his eyes were setting suns resting on the horizon.

Although, the more I studied that gaze, the more apparent it became to me that those eyes were less like suns and more like moons; two dull moons floating in swollen, ink-black orbs; lidless discs bulging forth with the faintest glow at their cores.

"You ache with want," he stated.

"... Yes," I confirmed.

"Speak," he breathed.

"I want—" I started.

"You want," he echoed.

"I was given life ..."

"Say it."

"But I do not live."

"Tell me. What do you wish for?"

"I wish to live. I wish for a once-in-a-lifetime experience—the big fish story. I wish to be exceptional, vivacious. I wish, I wish I was a fish ... the fish that swims instead of the sediment that sits."

A great pause, not just in conversation but in time itself.

"No problem, angler, you'll have your fish!" I was startled by the bartender's now animated voice. He stood, though not much, as he was fairly small in stature. "Here's what I need you to do," he explained through a warm smile. His eyes also smiled, with lids re-laxed, and welcoming wrinkles spreading outward. He brought out from beneath the bar top a small pouch, loosened its opening, and held it out toward me. "Go ahead and reach on in there, bud."

I felt my arm lift toward it, though I could not discern by whom or what it was controlled. It simply moved, and that felt good. I was, at last, doing something.

"Yup, just get a coin—only one, mind you—from the ol' take-a-penny, leave-a-penny. But get to it, bud, this is a limited-time offer," the bartender urged.

I reached into the pouch, which, despite having the appearance of being full, contained only a single coin. I removed it. It was like a quarter. It shone like a quarter, anyway. And, also like a quarter, its face depicted a bust; humanoid, or perhaps …

"C'mon, bud, I've got other fish to fry." The bartender had an air of annoyance. "You wanna be somebody? Toss the coin." He jerked a thumb over his shoulder in the direction of a round, stone well, strikingly old in appearance, particularly amidst the brewery's modern aesthetic.

Flicked metal rang. A *plop* sprung from the water's broken surface. Furniture scraped across the concrete floor. Jake was pulling his bar stool to sit beside me.

"Hey, party boy," Jake exclaimed. "I'm gone for two minutes and you're already pounding brewskis?" He chuckled, then added, "Without me?"

"Uh …" My brain struggled to process … everything: the vision, the bartender, Jake having only been gone for, "… two minutes?"

Jake chuckled again. "You good, dude? When's the last time you slammed one back like that? You gotta ease back in. No rush, it's a long weekend."

"Yeah …" I muttered in a daze.

"So, Nate and the girls just texted me. They should be pulling into the lot any minute." He directed his attention to the bartender. "Hey, man, can we close out?"

"Yeah, whatever you wish, buddy," the bartender replied.

Jake removed his wallet from his back pocket and fished out a credit card, which the bartender accepted. I started to follow suit, removing cash from my wallet, but the bartender, once more, was avoidant of me.

"Oh, sorry, are you card only?" I asked, setting my bills back in place.

"What's the name?" the bartender asked with his back to me as he processed Jake's payment. How perplexing. Was this some kind of game or joke?

"Uh, Corbin." I answered.

"Not seeing an Uh-Corbin," the bartender stated absentmindedly. He was returning Jake's card, his eyes never regarding me.

"I asked for an iced tea but you gave me a beer." Again, he turned his back to me as he reached for a small towel with embroidery reading, "WHET WIPE."

"Well, your face isn't striking any keys in the old memory piano," he said, tapping at his temple.

"Dude," Jake murmured. He leaned toward me. "Don't Judas yourself out of a free beer."

"All right," I spoke to the bartender. "Thanks, I guess."

Jake and I made toward the exit and I stumbled into his side.

"Whoa, there, Corbs. You got your sea legs about a half-hour early," Jake said.

"Shit, man, I'm sorry. I don't know what's wrong with me."

"Don't worry, Corby. I'm actually glad to see you loosen up a bit." He held the door open for me and the bright radiance of a mid-day sun rushed inside on a wave of warm air.

"Catch you later, bud!" the bartender called out from behind the bar top.

· ∽ ·

The world seemed to pass by around me. I was floating through the parking lot like a jellyfish adrift in an ocean current. I drifted along-side Jake as we met up with the other three.

Nate and the girls, who were introduced as Jenny and Bri (Jake introduced me to his sister, Jenny, every time we met up as a running joke), had been cross-loading their belongings into the speedboat attached to the back of Jake's truck. The plan was for everyone to ride in the truck, while the other two vehicles (mine and Nate's) would sit in the brewery's lot for the weekend. Jake would run me back down the mountain when it was time for my early departure and then re-join the group at the campsite. While I was still uncomfortable with leaving my vehicle in an open parking lot, I was in no state to drive. Moreover, I was in no state to continue standing on hot asphalt under a hot sun.

"You all right, Corbin?" Jenny asked.

"The little party animal downed a pint in under a minute," her brother answered.

"Oh, boy," she sighed.

"Square Corb is shotgunning brews?" Nate asked with a laugh.

Sound was becoming disorienting. I think my body swayed, because Jake made to stabilize me. Nate then suggested, with a subtle wink in my direction, that the girls and I sit in the air-conditioned cab of the truck while he and Jake finished loading up the boat, which we did.

I found it difficult to focus on much of anything, particularly with so much stimuli: a country song praising cold beers on hot days; a farm dog riding the back of its owner's ATV; the frequent shifting of the truck as Jake and Nate moved about the truck bed, trailer, and boat; Jenny and Bri chattering away about the lake.

According to the girls, both sitting beside me, Hell's Mouth was so named due to its unknown depth and because everything in the Hell Gate Valley had Hell in its name. Jenny further elaborated that some claimed it was the very opening to the depths of hell. While there was no evidence to validate that assertion, Jenny was sure she had heard of scientific attempts to determine the true depth of the lake, which had been unsuccessful because anything sent to the bottom of the lake vanished. Bri found this absurd. Surely someone could lower a camera on, like, a really long string or something and figure it out. Jenny explained that it was too dark for cameras, that the lake was so deep that light wouldn't reach the bottom. Bri then offered a night vision camera as a solution. Jenny wasn't sure if that would work but, regardless of its depth, she found the lake creepy. She had been there once before, last year when hiking with Nate and her brother, Jake. According to Jenny, the water was unnaturally placid, the lake too serene, and the water too clear. By this time, Jake and Nate had entered the front of the cab and we departed for a gas station.

I sat in the backseat and watched the world move behind us. The parking lot moved past the window. There I sat. The street moved past the window. There I sat. A gas pump filled the window. The truck no longer moved. The world no longer moved. Then, doors opened and passengers departed, but there I sat.

There was a brief discussion about each of us contributing to the boating trip, beginning with some advised purchases from the gas station. Nate and the girls left, the three lured inside by the prospect of recreational provisions, while Jake instructed me to fill the gas cans but not the boat. He wanted to burn the old fuel that had been sitting in the tank. This would be my contribution to the weekend: pay for the fuel, fill the cans nice and full, and load them up securely so they wouldn't spill on the bumpy switchbacks. Further, I was to get some fresh air so as not to vomit in the cab.

I watched as my body completed these tasks, reentered the backseat, and closed my eyes.

· ‿ ·

"Corbin." I was being rocked by the shoulder.

"How much beer did he drink?" One of the girls.

"I'm pretty sure it was just the one." That was Jake.

"Did he get roofied? I heard college kids were doing that shit for fun, not even to rape anyone." That was Jake's sister—had to be Jenny.

"No way. There was, like, one other guy in there." Jake again.

"Then he's gotta be on meds or something and it mixed with the alcohol. Square Corb isn't a partier, so ..." Nate trailed off.

I filled my chest with cool mountain air and blinked heavily at the late-afternoon sunlight. The rest of the group was gathered around the wide-open passenger door. "Hey, everybody," I said, regaining my faculties.

"Hey, dude, you feeling all right?" Jake asked.

"Yeah, I'm feeling much better. Sorry, I don't know what all that was about."

"Had us all a little worried, Corbs," Nate stated. "Only way you're getting to the hospital from here is life flight, and the price tag on those puppies is no bueno, friendo."

"Oh, shit, we're here." I stood out from the truck and squinted at the brightness of a cloudless day while my pupils adjusted.

"Yeah, you missed all the excitement," Jenny said with a smile—that gorgeous smile. "Asshole almost drove us off the mountain three times."

"Oh, fuck off, Jenny. It wasn't even close," Jake said. "There's no other way to make those turns with the trailer."

"We almost died," Bri assured me with a few quick nods.

"Are we boating or pissing away daylight?" Jake asked.

There was no proper ramp from which to launch the boat, though Jake assured the group this would not be an issue. A voice deep within me wanted to challenge Jake on this; that the lack of a ramp was further evidence we should not be boating on this lake—a lake with a history of death. But that voice was unusually subdued.

Jake was the first to undress, an unsurprising act, although unnecessary for launching the boat. He had a body that warranted display, much like his sister, who followed his example. Through genetics, familial wealth, or a combination of both, the siblings had each cashed winning lottery tickets at conception. I, on the other hand, knew only envy. I caught my reflection in Jenny's sunglasses—staring at her—and quickly averted my gaze, which then set upon Bri. Bri's eyes were set on Jake, which, again, was unsurprising. What I would give to be looked at so exceptionally … to be so exceptional … to be seen.

Bri must have felt my gaze and turned to look toward me. I again quickly made to look elsewhere and decided to study the scenery I missed while asleep. We were enveloped by granite. In all directions, there stood an encompassing wall of steep rock peppered with bunches of pines, firs, and spruces. Nestled within this gargantuan geological basin was the most tranquil, silent water I had ever observed at such a size. The stillness, serenity, and purity made it less a lake and more an indigo mirror, with all the towering world that embraced it reflecting from its unruffled surface in perfect clarity.

Bri stepped into that stillness, shrieked, and jumped back. Jenny laughed.

"Holy shit, that's cold."

"Yeah, I told you. It's all snowmelt," Jenny reminded her. She then pointed toward the ridges surrounding the lake. "Look, you can see where all the water runs down when everything's melting in Spring." She then tested the water with her own feet and gasped.

"It's all snowmelt," Bri mocked. She splashed Jenny's legs with a kick. Jenny gasped louder, kicked at Bri, and the two immediately agreed to a ceasefire. They huddled together farther up the shore and bounced in the sun to warm up. Nate, much like me, was evidently watching this from the boat, as Jake had to honk to regain his attention. Nate was supposed to be triple-checking the path into the water from that high vantage point to ensure the trailer could safely navigate the rocky shore.

I removed my shirt, used it to wrap my phone and wallet (Jake had warned me not to bring anything onto the boat I was afraid to lose), and set the wad under my seat in the truck. I then gave the truck space as Jake backed the boat into the lake from the rocky shore by Nate's guidance. The girls stood shoulder-to-shoulder watching the boys work while I watched the girls. They both wore two-piece swimwear, with Jenny in the type of top that tied only at the back and Bri in the type that tied both at the neck and back. I was not given much time to appreciate the two, as Jake and Nate worked quickly to ready the boat, which we promptly loaded at Jake's urgency, again reminded that we were losing daylight.

The boat was barely large enough for its five occupants. Jenny and Bri sat side-by-side in the bow lounge, Jake manned the wheel from the helm seat with me beside him, and Nate sat behind me toward the stern. Beside Nate were the wakeboards, which remained stowed while Jake made a test run to ensure the boat, which had been in storage for a year, was running properly. Additionally, Jake wanted to scope out the unfamiliar lake to mark any potential hazards.

As we gained distance from the shore, Jake picked up speed. Mists of clean, cold water coated me, giving my skin a cool relief from the unobstructed sun. I studied the scenery but always my eyes returned to the girls before me. Their hair flowed toward me in the wind, their scent carried upon those gusts, bathing my face. Jenny stood, embracing the air and Bri did likewise, their partially wedgied bottoms now on full display. Nate tapped at my shoulder and I turned to see his smiling nod. He offered me his fist, which I struck with my own and chuckled. Beside me, Jake shifted his body and gave the instrument panel his full attention, as though in great effort to refrain from glimpsing his sister's buttocks. Nate again got my attention and gestured with a nod toward Jenny. I looked at her—the soft curve of her neck, smooth skin fingertips could traverse tirelessly for hours. Nate tapped at my shoulder more forcefully to again pull my attention from her. This time, still ensuring Jake was no witness, he pointed to Jenny's back, then motioned with his hand as though to tug something free. I returned my gaze to Jenny's back, trying to make sense of it. Her shining hair streamed behind her like a war banner and just beneath those flowing locks fluttered a loosened string from the sole knot securing her top.

I glanced at Jake and then back at Nate and shook my head. Nate responded by throwing his hands up in disbelief. He then waved his hands in a "c'mon" gesture and nudged me forward. I looked back at Jenny. She still stood there, arms out, embracing the wind. I looked at Jake. He still watched the instrument panel. All around us the granite amphitheater circled while we skated across a wet stage. I had been given a role, one I would never typically consider playing, but an opportunity to act nonetheless. I gave Jake another quick glance, leaned forward, and swiftly pulled at the string like a hungry thief plucking a forbidden grape from its vine. The knot unraveled and Jenny's top rode the gusting wind overboard.

"Oh, fuck!" Jenny exclaimed, covering her breasts with one arm while fruitlessly clutching at the wind with the other. She promptly dove port side in pursuit of her lost swimwear.

In a panic, Jake killed the engine. "What the fuck is she doing?" he yelled.

"I think she lost her top," Bri explained.

"Well, she's going to lose her fucking scalp if she does that shit." He turned to me. "Get your eyes on the water, man."

I scanned the water's surface from the boat outward but saw nothing save for the dying ripples from the now nearly motionless vessel. I then focused on looking past the surface. The water's transparency gave sight to endless depths of increasingly black volumes, but no visual of Jenny. "I don't see her," I stated. My heart picked up its pace.

"Why hasn't she resurfaced?" Bri asked with heavy concern.

"Check the prop," Jake directed Nate, ignoring Bri.

"Oh, my God," I breathed. I was overwhelmed with a cascade of thoughts: words and images of fear in random flashes. *Gas.* That long, beautiful hair wrapped around the prop. *Methane—no, carbon dioxide. Wait, methane, right?* Scalp clinging to loose bunches of hair like clods of dirt on freshly extracted weed roots. *This is all my fault.* Blood dissipating, staining that perfect, pure water. *What have I done?* Exhaust from the motor.

Nate leaned over the stern. "No dice," he called out.

"Fuck," Jake moaned, echoing my thoughts. He moved to the stern and readied himself to dive in.

"Wait!" I grabbed at Jake, who pulled away from me in anger.

"What, dude? What?"

"Don't jump in. What if it's methane or something?" My voice rose in panic.

"What?" Jake asked.

"That's why we're not supposed to be out here. We need to get off the water. It's methane." I wanted to pace but the boat afforded no such room. I instead attempted to shake the anxiety from my hands.

"Nah." Nate spoke too calmly for the situation. "If it was methane, we'd smell it."

"No, no. N-not out in the wild," I stammered. "Methane only smells when they add the smell."

"You're thinking of propane, dummy," Nate assured me. "Now, just calm down, Corbs. You're scaring Bri."

"No he's not," she corrected him.

"Then carbon monoxide," I continued. "From the engine. Jake, you said it, man, you said that you wanted to see if the engine was running okay and what if it wasn't and what if it's carbon monoxide—"

"Slow down, Autismo." Nate raised his hands, gesturing for me to stop.

"Or she got her hair caught in the propeller and you stupid assholes are letting her drown," Jake said. Allowing no further impedance, he dove into the water with an olympian's grace.

"We're outside, Corbs," Nate informed me.

"What?"

"It couldn't be carbon monoxide poisoning because we're outside," he explained further.

"Nate," I took a breath. "Indoor, outdoor, it doesn't matter. You can be poisoned either way."

"I'm just saying, like, no, you can't, dude."

"How long can he hold his breath?" Bri asked.

"Uh," Nate gave this some thought. "I dunno. He used to be a lifeguard. So, probably a while."

"Shouldn't he have come back up by now, though?" She sounded on the verge of tears.

Fuck, what have I done. I've killed them. "Yeah, Nate, I think we need to do something." My pulse was thick with growing fear. I peered over the side again. Blue faded to black. I wanted to cry.

"Well ..." Nate trailed off.

"Like, now, Nate. Right now!" I could hardly control my dread.

"Calm down, Corbin!" Nate shouted. "What the fuck do you want me to do? Should we just keep throwing ourselves in one at a time like prairie dogs? Jake's the lifeguard. Just give him a minute."

"Nate ..." I steadied myself with a deep breath. "Lifeguard or not, no one is holding their breath that long underwater. I think it's really obvious something is wrong with the water. We need to get off the lake and get help before what happened to them," I pointed overboard, "happens to us."

A realization began to change Nate's expression, and for the first time since Jenny went under, true concern began to show; though, perhaps not for the apparently doomed siblings.

"You," he jabbed an accusatory finger into my chest. "You're what happened to Jake and Jenny."

"Are you shitting me? You are the one—"

"You pulled off her top," Nate interjected. "If you hadn't been such a fucking pervert, she wouldn't have dived in in the first place."

"Corbin!" Bri cried out like a mother in shock.

I turned to Bri, who quickly wrapped her arms around her chest as though cold. "No, Bri, Nate—"

I was shoved forward, nearly falling into the bow lounge. I reached out to stop my fall and Bri jolted back away from me, nearly spilling herself overboard.

"Get the fuck out of my way," Nate demanded. He sat at the helm and attempted to start the motor.

"No, don't!" Bri shrieked. "What about their hair?"

"Shut the fuck up, Bri!" Nate shouted back. "And use your brain. You think Jake's short-ass hair is caught in the prop?"

Bri sat down and started crying. "Well, what are you trying to do? We can't just leave them. They'll drown!"

"They already drowned!" Nate again tried the ignition.

"No!" Bri screamed in opposition. "If you two won't do anything, give me the lifejackets. I'll bring them the lifejackets."

"You can't dive with lifejackets, you dumb bitch. Why the fuck …" Nate again tried the engine. "... won't you start?"

"Well, I still want a lifejacket," Bri said, sounding defeated. She then looked at me. "I want to cover myself up. And I can't swim." She turned to Nate. "And you're being mean."

"Actually," I said, "I think it would be best if we all put one on.

Where are they?"

"In the bow storage with Bri," Nate answered.

Bri searched the storage compartment and removed two lifejackets, tossing one to Nate and donning the other.

"Come on, Bri. Get me a lifejacket, please," I said.

"There's only two," Bri informed me.

"Where are the others?" I asked.

"There are no others," Nate answered. "We only ever needed two for wakeboarding."

I fell to my seat. "I don't believe it. I can't believe I let you guys bring me out here. And then Jenny's top." I groaned. "This isn't me. I don't do these things ..."

Nate slammed the bench seat storage shut. "Where'd you put 'em, Corbin?"

"Where did I put what?"

"The gas, Corbin! The gas! Where the fuck are the gas cans?"

My heart sank. "In ..."

"Yeah?" Nate raised his voice. "Jake told you to load up the cans and you said you did, you fucking told us you did."

"I did!" I shouted.

"Then where the fuck are they, Corbin? 'Cause they're sure as shit not on the boat!"

"In the back of the truck," I said, flatly.

"You motherfucker!" Nate postured toward me, fist raised. "You motherfucker! How could you be that stupid?"

"Stop! That's enough," Bri cried.

Nate's shaking eyes challenged mine. He cocked back his arm, I flinched, and he began striking the seatback. "Fuck!" he screamed with each blow. "Fuck-fuck-fuck!"

"He told me to load them up, that's all he said. How was I supposed to know?"

"Yeah, 'load 'em up ...' on the fucking boat! What good do they do us in the truck?"

"Hey, you guys were the ones launching the boat. Don't blame me."

"Shut it, Corbin. I do blame you. Nobody's that stupid."

I wanted to counter that statement but stifled a response both out of fear of being assaulted (I had made it this far in life having never been in a physical altercation, even at work, and I intended to keep that streak alive) and because I did not actually have a valid argument. I had not been in the right state of mind. Had I been sober, I likely would have inquired as to where I should have stored the gas cans once full.

For a long time, no one spoke. For a long time, the siblings did not resurface. For a long time, nothing happened. There was no motion; not even the boat stirred with what should have been a natural sway in such a large body of water. There was only silence, both in motion and sound. Animals, if they were present at all, did not move in the woods that lined the shore. The very air dared not shift. The whole world was muted. Only one thing seemed unaffected by our situation: the sun, which had been steadily retreating behind the jagged mountain tops that surrounded us. Shade was now being cast upon the boat.

Nate quickly stood, giving both Bri and me a start. "Gimme your vest," he commanded Bri.

"But ... I can't swim." Bri sniffled, indicating more tears were imminent.

"You're not swimming, Bri. I am. I'm going to shore. I need that lifejacket to help me bring back a gas can."

"Um," she seemed to think this over. "Can't you just use a wakeboard?"

"No, they're made for riding, not floating."

"They float. I've seen them float!"

"Bri, they float like pool noodles float."

She considered this a moment, then relented. "Okay ..."

With great reluctance, and another glance in my direction, Bri unbuckled and unzipped her lifejacket. She gave it to Nate.

Nate turned toward the stern and froze. Bri similarly was locked in place by the sight of something aft. I followed their lines of sight.

At the aft-most part of the boat, just above the seatback of the stern bench seat, rested a pair of eyes—Jake's eyes. They were as motionless as we were, those eyes. They bulged from their sockets as though something had swelled behind them, pushing them outward. They watched us, those unblinking eyes. They glowed; a faint gleam; a bioluminescence; a dim glow like those old buttons on a remote control.

"Jake?" Nate broke the silence. "You all right, bro?"

Jake did not answer. Jake did not move. Jake did not blink. Jake was simply still.

The most unnatural aspect of Jake's stillness (and everything about the situation was unquestionably unnatural) was that he did not appear to be floating. He was out of arm's reach of the ladder, his hands did not grasp the vessel's frame, his body was mostly in the water, and, yet, he was suspended motionless. He neither moved his limbs to remain afloat nor was he wearing a lifejacket, as we had the only two on board. Even if he was wearing a lifejacket, or something with buoyancy, he should have at least bobbed; he did not. His eyes merely glowed in the waning light.

Nate dropped Bri's lifejacket. "J—" he started.

Jake began to rise, his body ever-motionless. His glowing gaze held Nate's, unbreaking. Slowly, his body rose through the water's surface, arms extended, feet together in a crucifixion pose. He floated toward us, water running steady streams onto the stern bench seat.

Nate took a step forward, hand extended in an offering of assistance. Jake, or rather Jake's body, withdrew from him. Nate took another step toward Jake. Jake slowly retreated. Nate slowly advanced. Jake's eyes, two glow-in-the-dark balls fresh from a lightbulb, held Nate's. They gazed at one another, transfixed. Jake floated over the end of the vessel. Nate moved to the end of the vessel. Jake's body began to descend into the water, his face still locked on Nate's, eyes faintly aglow. Nate reached for his childhood friend. Jake receded. Nate leaned closer. He peered over the end of the boat, inching toward the watery plane through which Jake had so serenely passed.

Water erupted. In the brief instant before droplets of diluted blood struck my eyes, I saw teeth—rows of needles. In only a fraction of a moment, quicker than my mind could process, Nate had vanished. The violence was so swift, so instantaneous, that even the lake with its already calmed surface seemed to question if anything had really happened at all.

Bri inhaled as though to scream but did not. Perhaps her brain needed more time to believe her eyes. My breathing became more rapid, chest swelling and shrinking, swelling and shrinking. Fear had so overwhelmed me in that deadly moment that my heart had forgotten a few beats and was now exhausting itself to catch back up.

"Corbin!" Bri finally bellowed. She stumbled out of the bow lounge and wrapped me in a fear-soaked embrace. In a reflex, I started to fight her off of me, then returned her tightening embrace as I came out of shock.

"Don't move." The words rattled from my mouth to the ear beside my lips. "Be quiet. And still," I added.

"What is it?" she whispered.

How the hell would I know, I nearly spoke aloud. I shushed her instead.

We continued embracing one another, her body pressed against mine, her hair brushing my nose, her warmth feeding my own. Though I presently had no sexual energy—particularly in our current predicament—I started to swell. Bri must have felt this, for she backed away from me. Blood rushed to my face. I wanted to assure her that, despite this involuntary reaction and the earlier voluntary act that set this perilous plight in motion, I was no pervert, but I was muted by embarrassment. Instead, we momentarily looked at each other with sheepish expressions before Bri moved back into the bow lounge. We both sat, maintaining silence in the fading light of an increasingly disappearing sun. Though the sky remained aglow, The Devil's Bowl was now wholly untouched by sunlight.

· ༄ ·

In spite of everything that had happened, time continued its onward march, darkness growing stronger with every step. Still, we sat. Still, thoughts remained unspoken. Still, we were, possibly because we were still.

Then, Bri was not.

"What's up?" I asked just loud enough for her to hear. She had stood from her seat and was beginning to examine the bow lounge.

"There has to be a way for us to get to shore," she answered in a similarly hushed tone.

"Maybe a breeze will pick up at some point and drift us to shore." This was something I had been hoping for all those countless, silent moments.

"You can sit around and wait for things to happen, Corbin," she said, opening the bow lounge storage compartment. She did not appear to find anything of value and added, with growing frustration, "I won't. I'm going to do something. Anything. Whatever it takes." With that, she slammed the compartment shut.

The sound amidst such thick silence echoed out like the report of an elephant rifle. I started, as did she, evidently not anticipating the outcome of her reactivity. Fear held us still once more; even my heart seemed to pause. Eyes fixed on one another's, mouths agape, we awaited our consequence. It did not present itself.

"Bri ..." I exhaled.

A shockwave. A great, blunt force smote the underside of the bow, which now soared skyward as the boat stood upright on its stern, bobbing briefly; an involuntarily perpendicular, throbbing—

"Cor—agh—C—" Bri attempted to scream through throatfuls of water. She had been thrown from the boat, which was now falling backward, upside-down. Gravity was changing direction. My body weight shifted, no longer securing my back to the seat but now rushing toward my head. The lifejacket tumbled past me. I grabbed the steering wheel with one hand and missed the lifejacket with the other. Walls of boat and water alike collapsed upon me.

Skin tightened and muscles locked. The water's coldness forced a gasp and my esophagus filled with its icy fire. Neither up nor down were known to me. For the moment, I let my body thrash ungoverned as it fought for survival. I was trapped under the boat. I had to get away from the boat. I had to move.

I fought to regain control of my limbs. I grabbed at anything that offered a grip and propelled myself in that direction until I felt the steel rail that assuredly marked the frame's edge. I pulled myself past. In one direction, endless black; in the other, the faint glow of a twilight sky. I oriented my body and made for the sky. I broke through the lake's surface in a coughing fit, expelling more and more of the lake with each hack. I could hear Bri losing the battle for buoyancy no more than a dozen feet away. I turned toward the sound and immediately spotted her drowning convulsions. I could easily swim to her. I intended to swim to her.

Then, I felt it—the lack of it—the absence beneath me. As I float-ed in the dark water, legs dangling like bait, like worms on a hook, I felt the emptiness … and everything within. The abyss in which I was adrift was unfathomably infinite. I was hovering in a pool of possibly endless depths in which an endless amount of possibilities lurked; suspended in death's maw … Hell's Mouth.

Then, I saw it—one such possibility: a monstrous mass moving meticulously toward Bri; just under the rippling surface. In the last moments of waning twilight, I saw death.

Long, vine-like appendages spread forth from the creature. Some stretched outward from its sides but most reached forward to meet Bri, whose thrashing was growing more violent. At once, the violence ceased and Bri was pushed into the air by one of the crea-ture's vines, which appeared to be sliding under her skin. She started to scream, but only just started, for she was briskly pulled under the water's surface, whereupon she was silenced.

The water stilled.

I fought every increasing urge to panic. The creature seemed to have been drawn to Bri's struggles. My heart pounded and my still burning lungs worked tirelessly to bring it more and more oxygen. I scanned the water. There was neither beast nor refuge, only the boat and me at the lake's center. I decided to mount the boat's belly, which would require my moving to the stern to climb the ladder. The boat's round, smooth underside offered no alternative. I slowly, steadily moved my hands along the frame to guide my body through the water, checking all directions for any sign of the creature. In the depths of my mind, I could still feel it somewhere beneath me, racing from the black depths to snatch my dangling legs, vines spreading toward me like eels on the hunt.

Adrenaline was surging. Fear was overcoming logic and I start-ed to quicken my pace. Water sloshed from my moving arms and I froze. At least, I tried to freeze. My testicles retreated toward my body and my legs did likewise. I waited.

Nothing.

I willed my arms to continue my progress toward the stern (I was within arm's reach of the corner), but they would not unlock. So, I continued to wait, scanning, feeling, listening, floating like the moon above.

Still, nothing.

My body moved once again. I rounded the back of the boat. There was the ladder, its steel tubes reflecting soft moonlight. I could reach it. I extended my arm, uncurling trembling fingers. Shining metal. Wet fingertips.

Water tension broke just before me. First, water-logged hair, followed by a sunscreen-lathered forehead. Then, two dully glowing eyes distending from their sockets as though by some growing cranial pressure; two eyes that floated on the surface like glow-in-the-dark bobbers.

I panted. I wheezed. Dread had so saturated my body that I could no longer feel the cold bite of the lake's snow-fed water, only the panic-inducing surge of the adrenaline my heart was so frantically disbursing to the very tip of each extremity and back again. I moved. Opposing muscle groups fought each other in a battle of utter chaos. I moved. Every limb, every digit. Water sprayed from my explosive panic. I moved. My eyes, already blinded by tunnel vision, were doused with splashes. I moved, but my fear-soaked brain was unable to coordinate my movements and I made almost no progress toward the ladder.

All the while, Bri watched.

Any moment, my kicking feet would be swallowed. I would be pulled under, pierced and torn while drowning. But I was not. I was only watched.

A hand made contact with the ladder and my mind took control to force fingers to latch on. My adrenaline could neither overcome my fatigue nor the wetness of my hand and my fingers slipped free. I thrust my arm forward once more, striking extended fingers against the frame until I once again found a grip. I pulled my body into the ladder and climbed upward like a crazed chimp. I threw myself onto the boat's belly and vomited. I crawled forward on hands and knees, and saw, but did not yet feel, a dislocated finger.

I gave the stern a glance over my shoulder. The ladder jutted skyward and beside it, Bri's body ascended, floating heavenward like an untethered balloon, its hanging string a thick, slimy vine. Two softly illuminated orbs glowed behind wet strands of dripping hair. Those mesmerizing eyes. I could not look away from those eyes. They were captivating. I turned, still balanced on hands and knees. I needed a closer look at those eyes. I crawled forward but she withdrew. How frustrating. I shuffled forward further. She retreated further, now descending behind the stern.

No, don't do that. I need to get a look at those eyes. Please ...

I inched closer to the prop. She continued her descent into the water. I leaned over the boat's end. The moon was losing and regaining its reflection in the soft ripples of the water's surface. Those eyes, they were just being swallowed up by the water. I shifted my body to lean closer, reaching out a hand to steady myself with the ladder. A sharp pain jolted up my arm. My dislocated finger met the unforgiving steel of the ladder. My eyes were briefly pulled to my injury. I looked back at the water.

A gaping maw; just under the surface. A widening hole lined allround with rows of needle-like teeth. A surface-slanted cavern full of stalactites and stalagmites awaiting the spelunker's plunge before collapsing into one another. Above its mouth, as large as beach balls, rested two dead, clouded eyes as though marred by blindness.

I scurried back, palms and heels slipping on the wet underbelly of the boat. When I reached the boat's center, I flipped prone and gave it a wide embrace. I was exhausted. My mind, body, and, especially, heart were too weary to fight, move, or even fear. I clenched my eyes shut and hugged the boat.

· ❧ ·

I remained hugging the boat for some time. I would have remained like this for some time longer but a chill was consuming my feet. With tremendous effort, I raised my head to look back. The lake was swallowing the boat. What little safety there was to be had was slowly vanishing. I considered the depths below. I considered riding the boat into those depths. In an abysmal pit such as this, I could sink forever …

I scooted toward the bow and looked all around, first at the waters around me, then outward toward the shoreline. In all directions, the shore appeared to be equally far from me, and nowhere, from me to there or there to me, could be found the creature. The boat continued to give up its buoyancy. I was being engulfed, now underwater at the waist. I urinated, unsure if by need or from fear. Warmth spread around my thighs, giving momentary relief before slowly dissipating. I looked in the distance at the truck resting so peacefully on the moonlit, rock-littered safety of the shore. It was too far to swim—every direction was too far for me to swim. But even if I could swim the distance, if I had the strength, I couldn't do so silently.

Perhaps the thing, with all its needles and vines, had forgotten me, or given up and returned to its depths. Or, perhaps it satiated its hellish hunger with Bri. Losing its predatory drive with fullness, it was no longer motivated to hunt me down. Was that not how zookeepers walked amongst monsters unscathed?

The boat departed.

I felt small floating in such a vast abyss. The waters beneath were as endless as the sky above. Tranquility was all around: a breezeless air; a cloudless, starry sky; a slumbering woodline. The moon, a mighty spotlight, hung high above my watery stage, illuminating me, awaiting my action. I gave my surroundings one final scan. From what I could tell, I was utterly without company—be that man or beast.

I floated, this appearing to be my sole resort. I would have to float for the shore silently enough so as not to attract the beast but quickly enough so as not to succumb to coldness. I leaned back, filled my lungs, and gently, carefully swept my arms in the lightest possible strokes. I was unsure what kind of progress I would make with such a maneuver, and I would be unable to check, for I was entirely submerged, save for mouth and nose. I made only shallow breaths to ensure my chest remained as inflated and buoyant as possible. With the exception of my arms, my body remained motionless as I (hopefully) drifted toward shore. It was a painfully slow process. However, the longer this went on, the more secure and hopeful I felt. I stopped once briefly to check my progress and found with delight that I was indeed making progress. I returned to my wide, slow strokes with renewed enthusiasm.

Then, I felt it.

My arm encountered one of the vine-like appendages. My body jolted and my nostrils and mouth took in water. My arm was being wrapped up. I would not be dragged down without a fight. Legs kicked. I screamed and clawed at the strings about my arm, tearing them loose from their grasp. I pulled it from the surface, ready to bite and tear and—

Jenny's top. I had drifted into Jenny's top.

Beside me, within arm's reach, water tension broke. The moon's luminescence set aglow thousands of scales, like shining stars. That pale spotlight, casting its glimmer on my concluding scene, glinted on each and every approaching needle-like tooth, those many, many rows; it glowed false life into large, dead eyes like white embers.

I was seen.

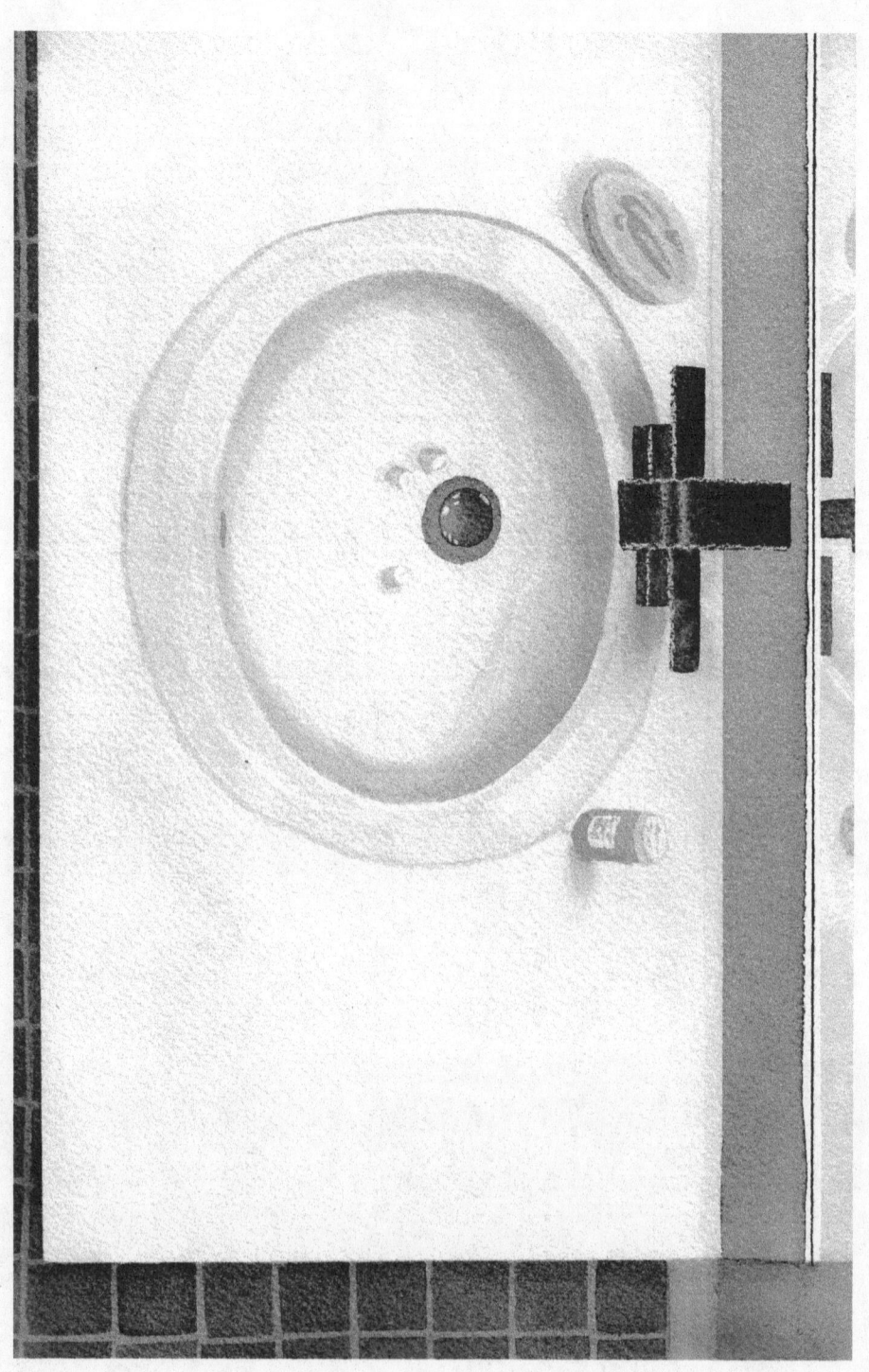

I see him burning

THE SPECTATOR

O ur mission was cut short. The route we were traveling went black due to an improvised explosive device and all movement was restricted. We had to stay the night on Kalsu, a base about four hours north of our destination. Kalsu was supposed to be a blackout base; meaning no white light was to be visible after sunset. However, the presence of women on the base made it mandatory to put up what became known as "rape lights." They were massive spotlights acting as street lights that lit up the living areas. Their purpose was to deter sexual assault. They were far more effective at showing the enemy where we slept.

It was nearing 0300 by the time we were finally assigned our usual living area for the night. Prior to the existence of the rape lights, Kalsu was a labyrinth of concrete barriers and camouflage netting. That night, though, Kalsu had more of a downtown USA look. I watched the sandy air dance around the rape lights like fog, reminding me of how congested my chest was.

I must have had an incredibly skewed perception of distance in darkness as our now visible path to the living area was travelled in half the time it normally took. In a matter of minutes, I was staring at the most inviting thing any base could offer: a sweat and piss stained cot. Perhaps it was not so much the physical object that I valued but the idea behind it. A mere strip of fabric stretched over a metal frame, though oily to the touch and exuding the fragrance of pungent sourness, was my rest, my peace, my escape from the troubling world *in which I lived. That cot was great beauty disguised as something awfully repulsive.*

Dawn had yet to break when the first rocket struck. I had been known to sleep through impacts. So, the first reaction to any indirect fire taken was to ensure my consciousness. It was an unnecessary task this time. Not even the dead could have slept through such a force. In fact, they did not.

The explosion belonged to a 155 millimeter projectile and attached to it was some type of reservoir the likes of a water heater. The receptacle held a mix of gasoline and motor oil, which created a sticky fire upon detonation. The rocket hit a 3rd Army Combat Regiment housing unit and killed the two inhabitants instantly. Eleven others were injured. A twelfth man, the soldier of a neighboring housing unit, lost his leg and caught fire.

The entire base echoed with the sound of the explosion and the sirens that followed every attack. More distant thuds could be heard as rockets and mortars were lifting off from an unknown place outside the base. We rushed for the bunkers. We were a mix of shoeless, shirtless, half-dressed, fully-awake individuals sprinting through shadows cast by overhead lighting. I struck my forehead against the low hanging ceiling of the bunker's entrance and clenched my teeth as pain enveloped my skull. That is when I started hearing the screams.

The soldier who lost his leg—the twelfth man—was crawling halfway out of the doorway of his housing unit. He was ... bright. He was too visible through the smoke and darkness. He was burning. The rockets we had heard lifting off were now striking around us. His screams were barely audible over the thunder the projectiles brought down to Earth but audible nonetheless. They were unlike any screams I had heard before. These were guttural sounds heard only in nightmares—unimaginable to the conscious mind.

I have never heard indirect fire so close. The explosions rattled existence itself, all but time. Time remained untouched, unchanged, and still; an instance so intense, it left all of its participants frozen. Only one thing seemed unaffected, pushing forward through the stillness, out of time's grasp: the man who lay burning in front of us. I had no idea a few seconds could last a lifetime. He burned for an eternity. He still burns. I see him burning.

Then, the thunder stopped. A soldier from an adjacent bunker broke the hold time had placed and ran to the body, thawing everyone else out in the process. Dozens of feet pounded gravel while short, sharp commands were shouted, competing against wailing sirens as stampeding men poured out of the surrounding bunkers. One man doused the corpse with the contents of a fire extinguisher while two others retrieved a litter from the casualty collection point. The stillness of the body made it easy to apply a tourniquet to the leg; however, the hemorrhaging had long since stopped. Between the bleeding and the burns, he had lost too many fluids. No form of care we had to offer would have been life-saving.

Skin and clothing were indistinguishable. Moreover, it was difficult to determine what he may have looked like at all prior to the incident. He was without a leg. He was without most of a leg. Tattered flesh, skin, and ligaments draped liked wet tentacles around the broken bone jutting out of the blistered stump that remained. He was without life. He was without more than life. To me, he was without family, background, or even a name. He was simply the twelfth man. He was a brief moment in time that only became a memory; a fate I am destined to encounter.

· ∾ ·

We sat in silence. I sniffled and wiped at my eyes. She did nothing, said nothing. She hardly moved, if at all. Though her camera was aimed just below her eyes, she appeared to be staring; at me, presumably. I started bouncing my leg and rubbing my hands. I was about to ask if we had lost connection when she spoke up.

"Thank you for sharing with me," she said, unmoving. "Where would you say your anxiety is after reading that? Scale of one to ten."

"Um." I gave this some thought. I could not recall what number I told her before I started reading my homework. "Like, a four or five?" I supposed, hoping it was similar to the initial answer. I did not want to be honest with her. I would not be flat out dishonest, but I could not be truly open. I could not be open because I did not trust her. I could not trust her because this was our first session. She was the third psych provider I had seen through the VA in as many months, and she would likely be the last. If she, too, fled this sinking ship or was another victim of cuts to funding and personnel, I would simply give up. I could not start from ground zero again. Psychiatric care required trust, and trust could not be established without time, without a relationship. "A four, I guess," I said with more caution. I was as of yet unsure how trigger happy this provider was in calling in a wellness check.

I waited for a response. Again, she was silent; a statue visible only from the bridge of her nose to the half of her torso rising from behind her desk. I moved the mouse to check the connection, which was described as both "strong" and "stable."

"Do you know why Dr. Quadri had you write that memoir?" she asked, at last.

"Yeah, it's part of desensitizing me. Exposing me to triggers a bunch so I eventually become less emotional." More silence. More stillness. "Right?" I asked, not so much for validation but to urge her to respond.

She did not—not immediately. My leg bounced more rapidly.

"So to speak," she said, at last. Another pause, then, "Let me ask, and be honest with me, what do you hope to get out of this?"

"Like, therapy in general or this prolonged exposure thing?" She, expectedly, did not answer, and so I continued. "Well, I ..." My face was warming, either with embarrassment or tears, I knew not which. "I just want to sleep." Tears. "Like, actually sleep. Every night it's the same shit. I have these nightmares and I'm up at two or three in the morning and my heart's racing so of course I can't get back to sleep and I'm up pacing around the house trying to calm down and by the time I get back to bed the fucking sun's up ..." I drew in a shaky breath. "Sorry." The apology dissipated into the growing, ever-persistent silence. "I'm tired all the time. I don't have the energy or will or whatever to get out of bed but I can't sleep. Like, I can fall asleep, but I don't stay asleep, you know? I just wish I wouldn't wake up."

At this, she shifted. It was the first time I had seen her move—do anything—on the screen.

Oh, fuck, I thought. *Here come the suicide questions. She's going to call the cops.* "Like, from the nightmares," I clarified. Then, I preemptively stated, "I don't have any active or passive ideations."

She did not speak. She must have known I was being dishonest. She could read me, as all psych providers could, both to the benefit and detriment of their patients.

"Not recently," I further clarified.

Bang-bang-bang.

Three loud strikes at the door bolted me upright, my heart and lungs quickening. I looked across the living room to the apartment's entrance and back to the laptop on the coffee table. Had she somehow contacted law enforcement? Were they here now to subdue me, to punish me for my ideations—for my weakness?

I apologized to the silent laptop and cautiously approached the door. The force of the knocking still permeated the air. Given both its authoritative strength and its timing, I was sure this was a wellness check. It had to be. My breathing now nearly matched my pulse. I had once before been dragged from my apartment by law enforcement in full view of the neighbors. Since that involuntary hospitalization, I maintained a vow to abstain from honesty in therapy, which, until now, had seemingly been effective.

I inched toward the door on silent feet. I would bring them no awareness of my presence. With great care, I leaned into the door, chest pressed against wood, heart knocking against veneer like a woodpecker. I looked through the door. There was nothing visible through the peephole but the closed door of the apartment opposite mine. The hallway was empty, devoid of uniforms or anything else. Had they left, whoever *they* were? Curiosity outgrew my fading trepidation and I opened the door—only slightly—as much as the chain would allow.

There was nothing to be seen but a greasy paper bag and a tall cup, both resting unsupervised on a shoe mat that falsely declared to any of its readers that they were welcome. I shut the door, removed the chain, and cautiously reopened the door to the empty hallway. I looked up and down the hall. Still, nothing. I picked up the meal, warm bag in one hand, cold cup in the other, and shut the door with my foot. I brought the meal to the coffee table in the living room and set it beside the laptop.

The receipt stapled to the bag showed "Moreno," my last name, and then went on to list the contents:

> As U Wsh Combo
> 1xPub Brgr
> 1xSwtPt Fry
> 1xWhetCement
> Note: Knock hard!!!

"That was quick," the laptop said.

"Did you get this for me?" I asked. I had given her my address at the start of the call. The psych providers always started the sessions by verifying my name, date of birth, last four of my social, and the address where I would be situated for the next couple of hours.

"I know it can be hard to open up to a new provider, and with your next homework, I wanted to be sure you were well-fed and well ..." Again, she appeared to be frozen, but the connection showed no issue. "Actuated ..." she finally spoke.

"Actuated?"

"Did Dr. Quadri explain 'in vivo exposure' to you before he left?"

"Um, no. I don't think so," I answered.

"Go ahead and eat. It's from the pub just around the corner from you."

"The Wishing Well?" I asked, opening the bag. A fatty fragrance floated forth onto my face, a warm perfume I had not worn in several weeks. My stomach rumbled with want. "Thank you. I've been meaning to try them."

"It's what you need," she stated, as though indisputable.

"What? Food?"

"These are the things you're missing out on, right within walking distance," she said. "You should give that shake a try before it melts. It's ... seasonal. You might not get another chance."

"Oh, uh, thanks." I picked up the cup, its sides dripping with condensation. "By the way, I think your video is frozen."

"I can see you," she assured me.

"No, I mean you've been frozen on my screen since we started."

"Frozen on your screen," she echoed.

"It's just you looking at the camera." *Staring at me,* I thought.

"What you have been doing now for weeks—please, drink up— is revisiting memories. What you'll be doing next is physically confronting your triggers—all the things you've been avoiding."

"So, like, going to the pub?"

"No. Today, the pub came to you. That is the beauty of omnipotence. Or food delivery apps," she said in what was a poor attempt at an apparent joke.

"Yeah, that's how I get my groceries. It's actually pretty convenient."

"What do you think of that shake?" she asked. "You'll have to let me know, everyone's been dying to try it."

"Oh, are you guys here in Hell Gate?" Most of my appointments were handled via video conferencing, given how rural this part of the state was.

"No, but not a soul in these parts doesn't know The Wishing Well."

"Huh, I thought it was just some local dive. So, what's my next homework, then?"

"The Vet Center is running a ballgame at the softball complex over by Hell Gate High. You know where I'm talking about?"

"Yeah, I used to go there all the time. My sister played for the Lady Owls."

"Well, you'll be playing for the Warriors."

"Will I? When?"

"This evening."

"This evening? That seems a little soon. I ... I don't know." My heart began its warmup jog.

"I asked you earlier to be honest with me."

She knows. She knows about the ideations. Of course, she knows. They're always there. Fuck, I'm going to the hospital. Fuck! All this I thought. I spoke nothing aloud.

"What do you wish for?" she asked.

"I told you. I want to be able to sleep." I swallowed, then added, "Through the whole night."

"With all these dreams and thoughts of death, do you ever ... wish you were dead?" She seemed to ask this with some undertone of pleasure.

Yes, I answered in thought. "No, of course not," I answered aloud. My armpits were dampening. Had I left the thermostat off?

"You feel regret." This was not a question. "About what happened in Iraq. About surviving what the twelfth man did not. About letting it happen. About watching."

Adrenaline surged from chest to fingertips. I tried to shake it out of my hands. The room was growing warmer and I was becoming increasingly aware of a growing need to cool my drying throat. I took the shake, removing it from the moat it was building on the coffee table. The wet, cold cup was a relief to my hand, fueling urgency to similarly relieve my throat.

I licked my chapped lips (how long since last I drank anything?) and wrapped them around the straw, pulling the cup's cool contents onto my tongue.

Oh, I marveled inwardly. I had not the desire to think anything else, for any other thought would only distract me from the wonder melting throughout my mouth.

The texture. Oh, the texture. It was as gritty as the name implied. Rich and thick in its creamy base. A whisper of something earthy or flowery or ... green, definitely green. A cooling celebration on the tongue. A bit of a bite, though, no? Surely not alcohol ... Mint! That was it. A flavor reminiscent of that wonderful trip along the Mediterranean with my sister. I could see her now, shoving a handful of mint leaves at me to chew to freshen my breath.

"Slow down," the laptop commanded me.

I shifted to the edge of my seat and pushed the laptop screen to angle it back. Illogically, this adjusted the view of the psych provider, providing now a full look at her face; an *almost* full look, that was.

The video was glitching and across her eyes was a jumbled mess of pixels like a digital blindfold. The glitch was motionless, though. It was as motionless as the person whose eyes it obscured.

"You should take a PRN," her voice advised. Her mouth did nothing.

I moved to comply. I did not exactly understand why I was complying or why an as needed medication was presently needed. The only understanding was my need to kiss that straw once more, for what it conveyed consumed me as much as I consumed it, and I would need something with which to swallow the medication. Something Whet …

On unsteady legs, I went to the bathroom sink, where I had set my medication after retrieving it from the mail yesterday. I lifted the bottle. It felt heavy in its fullness. My arm felt similarly heavy. I tried and failed to open the bottle with weak fingers. (*Why are my fingers weak?*) I examined the troublesome top. The cap advertised the Veterans Crisis Line, directing me to dial **988** and then press **1**. I did not. Instead I turned to the bottle's body. The label directed me to, "Take one-half to one tab as needed for anxiety," and warned me not to exceed 4 mg in a single day. I tried again to twist the top, this time using a sweaty palm. (*Why are my hands sweaty?*) I opened the bottle, peeled its foil, and shook out a single tablet, which stuck instantly to my moistened palm. Today's mission, should I choose to accept it, called for a full tablet. I raced back to the living room and snatched the shake from the coffee table. I swiped away the new, large, watery ring that had been left behind and gave the shake another pull through its straw.

Despite its delivery by car or bike, in addition to having been sitting at room temperature, it was still creamy, thick, and cool on my tongue. Again that whisper of mint adding to the coolness. I took in more, every pull from the straw an unfurling of a cold, emerald leaf

across my palate. It was more than a mere milkshake. It was a promise—an assurance of renewal, like springtime. It was life. The cup
had grown light and I realized it was nearly empty. I needed to take
the medication. (*Why do I need the medication?*) I opened my palm
but no tablet was visible. Had I already taken it? There were many
nights when I could not recall having taken my medication but those
were usually lapses of multiple hours.

"Did you see me—" I started.

"Always," she interjected. "Sit," she commanded.

I moved to comply. My body sat before the laptop. My eyes, or
perhaps the room itself, seemed to wobble and sway.

"Tell me your desires." She commanded. "What do you wish
for?"

*Whet Cement. I wish for more Whet Cement. Tell her. Tell her
you need it!* I could not relay these thoughts and instead, in a steady
drone, I answered, "To sleep. For the nightmare to end. To stop feeling so guilty. To be able to look at myself in the mirror. To—"

"Well!" Her voice was cheerful and piercing, startling me almost
into sobriety.

Am I drunk?

"You got it!" she proclaimed, as though this was a simple fix.
"I'm going to prescribe you one evening of softball."

"One evening of softball," I echoed.

"Someone from the Vet Center is on their way to give you a ride.
You should get ready," she advised.

I moved to comply.

· ∾ ·

I changed into gym shorts and tennis shoes. I was not sure if a baseball glove would work for softball but decided to bring it regardless.

My phone notified me that a Mira would be arriving in about five minutes in a brown KIA. My heart accelerated. Was I really doing this? *Could* I do this? What would it look like if I could not? I envisioned myself spiraling at the game, panicking, crumbling into anxious debris in front of—

Oh, God. In front of how many others? There must be at least seventeen, if we were playing with full teams. Add to that the friends and families in the bleachers. And the other fields, they were likely packed with players, and their bleachers would be full of people and this town with nothing else going on and only a few thousand people-and-dear-Lord-there-could-be-thousands—

A sharp pain in my chest. I clutched at it. I was having a heart attack, I was sure of it. I was going to collapse, out of reach of my phone, crawling around an empty apartment because who would want to live with someone so broken? And then I would just die on the floor and there I would be, rotting, until someone finds me, not because I was missed, but because I was stinking up the apartment complex, and then they would clean me up—the trash I am—and find another tenant in a snap without a single day of mourning because that is how replaceable I am—

My heart pumped pain throughout my chest. My lungs pumped air in and out and in and out, but I could not catch my ever-elusive breath. I needed an ambulance. I needed my phone to call for help. I needed … a Whet Cement—that creamy elixir—that brief, sweet savor of a secret garden, fleeting but utterly indelible. I could probably order one through my phone. Oh, right, I needed my phone. Where? Where was my phone? The bathroom! Yes, by the medication. Wait, did I take my medication? I had the tab in hand. I had no recollection of taking it. Was this a panic attack? No, I was having a heart attack, right? I had almost forgotten about my heart attack.

I was overcome with the feeling of déjà vu.

I raced to the sink and secured another tablet. The bottle was much lighter, evidencing either a surge of adrenaline or further distance from intoxication, or a combination of both. Either way, my left arm was feeling strong—a good sign. Evidently, this was not a heart attack. Or was a limp left arm stroke-related?

Four milligrams, I thought, observing the tablet. Possibly four. I just could not for the life of me recall if I had taken that initial tablet earlier. *Certainly not, or I wouldn't be having a panic attack right now,* I reasoned.

I drank from the sink's faucet. The water was warm—warmer than the apartment. I double-checked that I had opened the cold line. I ran the water over my hands, feeling for it to cool down, that I could then splash my face with cool water.

My phone chimed; a message from Mira. *Multiple* messages. She had been waiting for me for several minutes outside and would be leaving if I did not get downstairs soon. How long had I been in panic? The water was still running and still warm as it spilled through my empty fingers; disturbingly empty, were my fingers. I had taken the tab, had I not?

I was overcome with the feeling of déjà vu.

A half-tab. I would take a half-tab and dry swallow it. *Then,* I assured myself, *then I'll know for sure. Just a half-tab. Even if I had taken two, surely a half wouldn't be that dangerous. Not compared to a whole tab. And this was an especially distressing situation. I'm owed at least a half-tab.*

I palmed a whole tablet, placed it on my splitter with quavering fingers, and cut it in half. Hyper-focused and hyper-concentrated, I set the half-tab on my tongue and forced it down my throat with several swallows. I then made to exit my apartment with glove in hand.

I stepped into the hallway like a Martian astronaut in initial exploration. I looked down each end of the hall. It seemed much longer than usual, and much warmer than my apartment. I reasoned there must be some issue with the building's air conditioning. I checked my pocket to ensure I had my key, then shut the door behind me, softly, quietly, for some reason fearful of alerting anyone of my presence outside of my apartment. I then jogged toward the stairwell like a child attempting to reach their bed from the light switch before the light vanished entirely. I made my way down both flights of stairs in a near tumble and out the door to the parking lot, whereupon I found Mira. Her waning patience was showing on her face, prompting me to enter the backseat rather than the front.

· ༀ ·

The ride to the softball complex was short, but no less uncomfortable. Mira appeared to be watching me from her rear view mirror, not just occasionally, but for the entirety of the trip. I gave the mirror only a few quick glances but could see it—her unwavering gaze—in my peripheral vision. It was unnerving. It was impossible. I was unable to reason how she could drive with her eyes so focused on me; unless this was a symptom of the drink, or of my medication. Had I over-medicated? I oriented my vision to the outside world, which did not pass by so much as it appeared to spin by. Like a spinning ballerina, I had to fix my eyes on a single point as the rest of the world twirled around it, or I would be driven to vomit.

Inside the car, there was stillness. Even the air held still, despite my failed attempts to move it with my tiring lungs. I felt trapped in a hot, plastic bag.

"Excuse me, uh, Mira? Would it be okay to turn on the air?" I asked.

The car moved, continuing to roll toward the softball fields. I moved about in my seat, seeking unattainable comfort. Mira's arm finally moved, guiding an unwatched hand toward the instrument panel in the dashboard. Mira's eyes did not move. It had to be a trick of reflection—the angle at which the mirror was oriented and my position in the backseat.

Air began moving, though just as hot, if not hotter. With such heat outside, it would likely take the car a moment to cool down. Though we were nearing our destination, I decided to try to engage her in conversation, both to ease the tension and distract me from the heat and nausea.

"So, I don't see many vets driving KIAs." She offered neither response nor reaction. "Or their spouses," I said, considering that she may not be the veteran. Now that I gave it thought, I was not sure how she was affiliated with the Vet Center at all. "You know," I continued, "'cause of the acronym."

· ❧ ·

We reached the parking lot in silence. The air had not cooled down and I was desperate to escape the car before the milkshake escaped my stomach. I pulled at the handle but the door did not open. Mira stepped out and was closing her door behind her.

"Wait, the child lock—"

She shut the door. I was trapped in a mobile oven. She was going to leave me here like a forgotten dog in the hot parking lot of a grocery store. Like a dog, I panted, dry mouth agape, but the air offered no relief. I would have to kick out the window. I—

A metallic *click* and the door opened to fresh air. Mira stood on the other side.

Calm yourself, Casey. You're going to crash and burn like at the cattle branding thing. That was something I could almost be assured would be absent at a softball game: the triggering scent of burning hair and flesh.

Trying to ensure a calm outward appearance in the midst of so much internal chaos, I set forth to slowly maneuver my legs out of the car. This looked more like an awkward dawdle than calm control. When I finally stood to depart the vehicle, I nearly fell out of the backseat in a bout of lightheadedness.

I haven't even made it on the field and everyone's going to think I'm fucked up on drugs and alcohol. Just some junky vet who can't keep their shit together; dependent on booze and pills and everything but positive coping skills ...

"Hey, Moreno, right?" A calm, deep voice from an approaching older man.

"Uh, me?" I asked before I could stop myself.

The older man chuckled. "Yeah, you're Moreno? Here to play softball with us?" He gestured toward my glove.

"Yeah, sorry. Just having a, uh ... bit of an off day."

"That sounds tough. You wanna join us in the dugout and we can talk about it? We've got some ice in the cooler. Looks like you could use some," he offered.

"Y—ahem," I cleared my throat to stifle a cry. "Yeah, that would be really nice."

He led me through hot daylight toward a nearby dugout. The sun was suspended low in the evening sky but still floated above the horizon. The world was bright. I shielded my eyes and realized I had left my sunglasses at home.

We entered the dugout and exchanged introductions. I was offered ice and water, and took both without hesitation. The older man, revealed to be the co-ed team's coach, gave the group a warm-up speech and sent us to the outfield to play warm-up catch with one another. I was assigned to right field and would begin the evening there, as the Warriors had home advantage. Despite the heat, my mind had cooled down significantly. The more I interacted with the Warriors and threw and caught balls and moved around in the open space of the field, the more comfortable I grew, the more confident I was that doom was not impending.

I took my place in the serenity of right field.

The spaciousness of the field, the warm breeze against my damp skin, the soft grass padding every footstep … It was therapeutic. It was liberating; an escape from the confinement of anxiety. Despite being surrounded by bleachers full of spectators, I did not feel trapped. I had all of right field to myself. I had all the sky above me, its clouds set ablaze in pinks and oranges as the sun collapsed onto the horizon.

My gaze descended from the heavens and onto the bleachers, whereupon I became aware of a troubling oddity: all eyes were on me. My heart jumped from its relaxed state and back into the familiarity of distressed rapidity. My face flushed with embarrassment. I had obviously missed a play while staring into the clouds like an inattentive child. I checked all around, from my feet to the fence and back again. There was no sign of a softball. I looked up. My team—every player on and off the field—was looking, not just in my direction, but at me specifically. My face grew hotter. I shuffled on my feet, looked left and right, forward and back. I even checked my glove. There was no ball. There was no hint of a ball. There was only me and my audience.

I jogged toward the center fielder and called out, "Hey, did I miss the play?"

No response.

"Um, what's going on?" I asked, slowing to a cautious stroll.

Silence and stillness were my only answers.

I rubbed anxiously at my neck, which was burning in the rays of the setting sun. I should have worn sunscreen. I looked around at my audience, seemingly the entire world. They tracked me as I moved across the field. Each and every person on and around the field followed my movement, though not simply with their eyes, as their eyes were as unmoving as their bodies. The several dozen spectators moved only their heads to keep me in focus, as though their eyes now entirely lacked mobility. Several dozen heads synchronously swiveled as I swam through sweltering air, halting, all in unison, as I halted.

"Please don't." The words leaked weakly from my mouth. I rubbed again at my neck. If the evening sun was this hot, I was glad to have been inside during its midday arc. "Please …"

My whispered plea went unheeded. I forced a chuckle. Surely this was some sort of prank on the newbie. Mischievous setups like this were my most hated aspect of military culture. I was always the punchline to the joke and my poor reactions only ensured the jokes kept coming. But those jokes did not typically endure like this one. Those jokes usually had a cracked smile by at least one of the perpetrators. This joke employed more than sixty people, all of whom played it unnervingly straight-faced.

"Okay, guys, that's good," I called out to anyone—everyone. Statues they remained, and I, their unwilling Medusa, could do nothing but stand before them, equally statuesque. I wiped sweat from my forehead and brow. How could it be so much hotter now than earlier? How could so many strangers act in such a simultaneous performance?

Because they're acting. They're actors, I reasoned inwardly. Of course, they were. There could be no other rational explanation. I was unwittingly in the hot spotlight of one of those insufferable prank television shows; the kind that required a laugh track to tell their brainless audience when to laugh. I could see it now: me, standing stupidly in the middle of a softball field, broadcast worldwide for all eternity in reruns while all the world laughed at the punchlines: me, myself, and I.

I once again scanned the field, this time searching for cameras instead of a softball. I could see no equipment in the stands. Nothing in the dugouts. I turned to run my eyes along the fence. There was not a lens to be found. There was, however, an exit. A gate situated in the corner of left field presented an opportunity for me to excuse myself without the risk of falling over the fence, or tearing up my clothing on the fence, or taking the long walk of shame in defeat past all those spectators and their unblinking eyes. So much unbroken silence. So many unspoken words. So much conveyed, but not lost on me. They all had the same message: I did not belong.

I picked my pace back up and set course for the gate. This had played on long enough. My escape from the comfort and safety of my apartment was no small feat, and now I found myself a lone sheep having ventured into this den of wolves. No friends were these. Not a kind soul among the crowd; only wolves. Well, I would be damned if I stuck around for the feast. I would retreat back to nowhere and be no one.

They can't torment what doesn't exist, I thought.

As I hurriedly walked past and behind the center fielder, the Warrior's head swiveled to maintain his gaze on me.

"Yeah, I get it. I'm leaving." My voice was rising and straining with anger or sorrow or a mix of both. "You can give it a rest. I'm the joke. Ha-ha."

I continued my stride. He continued to watch, turning his head, rotating only his head in an owl-like pivot, frozen below the neck. The motion was becoming so unnatural—painfully unnatural—that I could not help but fix my own gaze upon him in curiosity. I stepped. He screamed, muffled by his unopened lips, but a scream nonetheless. It startled me and I took another couple of quick steps to distance myself from him. He was stoic, expressionless. His face portrayed no sense of distress. The only indication I had that he was experiencing pain or anything else was those muffled screams, which may have just been echoes of memories and nightmares unforgettable—figments of my haunted imagination. I furthered myself. Still, his head turned as it tracked me, lips suppressing screams until my next step brought the screaming to a stop and the body to the ground.

"Holy fucking shit. Holy fucking shit!" I panted. I squeezed my eyes shut, hoping to reset the world upon their reopening. It failed. The body lay in the grass, supine from neck to toes and prone everywhere else. I looked out at the crowds, who were all on their feet now, still looking in my direction, every one of them. "Help! Call EMS!" I shouted to the unmoving spectators. "Do something!" I pleaded vainly.

My eyes were stinging with sweat and tears. I rubbed fiercely at them with sweaty hands, then dabbed at them with the sleeves of my t-shirt. When my vision was once more clear, I saw them—the spectators, my teammates, my opponents, everyone—every pair of eyes in the vicinity had moved closer to me. They were frozen in place now, but they were all undoubtedly closer, by several feet at least.

"W-what are you doing?" I asked aloud to no one in particular—to everyone. I pulled at my sweat-soaked shirt over and over to fan my body. "Don't do that. Help him." My voice was weak, powerless. It sounded as scared and confused as the rest of me was rapidly becoming. I looked at the left fielder, who had moved almost within reach of me while my eyes were shut. She was giving no attention to the body or anything else apart from me.

My head was aching, worsened by the severe brightness of the world. I squinted and raised a hand against the sunlight as I looked again at the gate—my exit. The sun was a distant explosion on the horizon, its destruction growing nearer, hotter, brighter. A sharp pain behind my eye forced both shut and, nearly instantly, my arm was taken in a powerful grip. I reopened my eyes, flooding my throbbing skull once more with a tsunami of scintillating sunlight. The left fielder had her ungloved hand clamped onto my arm, nails anchored into my skin.

"Let go!" I shouted at her blank face. "Get the fuck off me, bitch!" I pulled my arm free, all but the skin her nails would not unfetter. The act took a surprising amount of force. I looked first at my wound, then up at my assailant in disbelief. I then looked past her to see if anyone else had witnessed the assault.

Pain erupted from my heart and I grabbed my breast with nearly the same force the left fielder had placed into her grip. The spectators were on the field, several encroaching crowds, a tidal wave of watchers as silent in their approach as the owls they embodied. I gasped for air, my lungs reminded of their duty by my panic-stricken body starved of oxygen.

The situation required no further analysis. I took flight.

· ❧ ·

The world was collapsing in on itself. Space was diminishing. Buildings seemed to wilt closer together; I ran through their narrowing gaps. Far, far, and even farther ahead, it seemed, was my apartment complex. Behind, closer and ever-nearer, a flood of racing footsteps in mad pursuit. They were growing in number. Within my burning chest, my understaffed and overworked heart threatened a strike. I pressed on.

A klaxon echoed throughout the fiery sky, reverberating through the melting town. I recognized those mechanical screams. Any moment that synthetic voice, flat and unfeeling, would start chanting, "Incoming, incoming, incoming." Only, there was no such voice. Not the one I recalled, anyway. Something did ring through the air. Perhaps a live voice. It was similar to the recorded warning in its echoing, though much fainter, and difficult to distinguish. For a fleeting moment, I thought I heard, "Clear."

As in, 'All clear?' I wondered. Was the nightmare coming to an end? It was possible. If the end was not in sight, at least my apartment building was.

In disregard of my protesting heart, I sprinted through the apartment building's parking lot. My arm brushed a car door as hot as a branding iron. I jolted and nearly stumbled into another car. I could not falter here, not a mere handful of lunges from the building's entrance. The footsteps behind me, hundreds of them in a stampede, did not relent. I dashed harder.

I grabbed the doorknob of the entrance and screamed. White hot pain was all I gripped, as though I had reached into a fire and took hold of a burning lump of coal. There was no time to reflect on the pain, the stampede was upon me. I forced open the door and spilled through, peeling my hand free from the doorknob by a combination of body weight and impetus.

I sprinted up the stairs two at a time. My legs, lungs, and heart burned, shouting over one another in vain attempts to be heard and heeded as they begged for cessation. I demanded more. My legs pistoned, muscles tore. My lungs pumped ever-hotter air. My heart pumped more and more adrenaline in rapid response, keeping the impossible barely possible. I reached my floor. Every door in the corridor was open, save for mine. Every open doorway was filled with staring occupants. The stampede behind me echoed nearer, louder.

I dashed to my door, key in hand. As I passed the spectating occupants—my neighbors—I could feel them reaching out to snatch me. Fingers clawed at the empty, hot air at my back. Even the toddler from three doors down was in her doorway, eyes as bulbous as her father's nose, trained on me as I approached and passed by. Hot air wafted by my ankle, as though the toddler in all its undeveloped musculature had attempted to subdue me.

I reached my apartment.

I would not have the time to unlock the door before the crowd reached me. I glanced back. The horde froze; an unthinkable multitude frozen shoulder to silent shoulder. More footsteps from the other end of the hall. I turned my head in that direction. Those flanking spectators were now frozen in place by my observance. The others, now unfrozen, shifted. I turned my head back and forth, back and forth, restricting the gains of the sandwiching crowds to mere inches while I jabbed my key blindly at the lock. Metal struck metal. Shuffling neared from one direction. My head spun. Now shuffling from the other direction. I was being surrounded, soon to be engulfed.

The key slid in place.

I forced open the door, turned to slam it shut, and saw a now frozen wave of spectators crashing into my doorway. I kept my eyes on theirs. Dozens and dozens of widened discs, from floor to ceiling and side to side like an unblinking wall of bubble wrap. I slammed shut the door, set the locks, and looked through the peephole. Eyes. I ran to the living room window. There was a crowd gathered below, all gazing upward, all with staring, fixed eyes and swiveling heads like owls.

I could barely see out the window. The sun was in meltdown on the horizon and all the world was alight. I drew the curtains. *Ouch.* They, too, were hot, as though pulled mid-cycle from the dryer. The building shook with the stomping of the ever-growing crowds.

My god, the whole town must be trying to get in, I thought in horror.

I patted my pockets in search of my phone. Nothing. I must have left it in the dugout. I scanned the room. There had to be something with which I could call for help. Everything was smart, everything was connected to the internet. Something should be able to act as a phone.

On the coffee table rested my laptop, undisturbed since my video call with the psych provider. I woke the device and swiped the cursor back and forth on the screen in thoughtless panic. How could I place a call through my laptop? Who would I call?

Alexis, my sister, of course. We had not really spoken since my last freakout but she was the only person I could trust to save me. I placed an audio call. *Allow video? I don't have time for that,* I thought, declining the offer with a click. The digital ringtone chimed. The apartment door, or perhaps the walls themselves, was creaking and cracking with the weight of hundreds of spectators.

"Alexis, please. Please, Alexis," I implored.

"Hello?" My savior's voice.

"Alexis, help. Please! Oh, God, please help me."

"Casey? Are you all right?"

"No!" I shouted.

"What's going on?" True, human concern. I could cry.

"Everyone's after me. And everything's burning." I panted. Something snapped within one of the walls. "I can't breathe, Alexis. I can't breathe!"

"Casey, slow, deep breaths," she instructed. "You gave me all your firearms, yeah?"

"What? Yeah, I don't want to shoot them. I just want them to go away. I want everything to go away. Please help me!"

"I'm going to get you help, Casey. Are you in your apartment?"

"Yes!" I sobbed.

"You're absolutely sure you gave me all your firearms?"

"Fuck the guns! I don't need the guns. I need you!"

"I'm out of town, Casey. Turn on your video and we can do your combat breathing. Together. Okay?"

I took a deep breath. Every thread of my shirt was swollen with sweat and sticking to my body. I glanced at my bulging walls and door. I did not have time for breathing exercises, but I needed relief of any sort before my heart utterly collapsed.

"Okay," I spoke in a quiver.

I navigated the settings in the call and turned it over to video. Alexis filled the screen, all but her eyes which were jumbled messes of pixelation. Actually, not pixels. On closer inspection …

The pixels were hundreds of tiny eyes—thousands of them, rolling and quivering and focusing, all like static on the screen.

"No!" I screamed at the laptop.

"Yes!" the laptop shouted back. "Dear sister, yes. Fulfillment is near."

Bang-bang-bang. Some great, blunt object was hammering against the door. From outside the window, the parking lot was filled with guttural screams—the kind heard only in nightmares. I parted a small gap in the glowing curtains and peeked through the blinding light. The sun had grown so much brighter. Below, dozens of bodies burned and writhed and crawled and twisted and did all manner of things distinctly, save for one collective act: they were all staring up at me. Despite the burning and jerking of their bodies, despite the death throes, they looked on. They spectated. Their burning eyes, those glowing hot embers, still held on me.

"You aren't real!" I screamed at the window. "None of this is real! You're just my imagination trying to hurt me. You're just self-harm."

The apartment was at a boil. The door burst open in a splintery explosion. A pair of owl-like humanoids in police garb stood frozen at the front of a floor-to-ceiling crowd in my doorway. My back was burning.

I ran from the living room window to my bedroom. Countless footsteps followed. I hid behind my bed, crouched on the floor. I watched as eyes slowly populated around the doorframe. I was sweating, I was crying, I was urinating. Seemingly every bit of liquid within me was being expelled. I was withering.

"I'm sorry!" I cried. "Please! I'm sorry!"

I blinked tears away.

They were closer now. Eyes just on the other side of the bed.

My eyes stung with salty sweat and tears.

"No!" I sobbed, rubbing the sting from my eyes.

Closer still. Eyes were now watching from under the skirt of the bed. Eyes were standing over me. The room was sweltering.

"No," I whispered.

The bedroom blinds were sagging with heat. The outside world was unbearably brighter. The inside world was intolerably hotter. The apartment stank of smoke. I backed up into the bathroom, keeping my eyes on the crowd. I coughed as my lungs tried to rid themselves of smoke. I did not break my gaze from the growing crowd in my bedroom, though they neared with every blink. The heat intensified. *Blink*. Closer. *Blink-blink*. Closer still. Hotter still.

My clothes erupted with flames. I shot upright on my feet, pulling myself up by the vanity, and knocking over the medication bottle into the sink. Its hollow bouncing about was barely audible over the flicker of flames. I opened the faucet, which produced only steam. I glanced away from the crowd and caught my bright reflection in a double-take. My eyes. My eyes! Wide and unblinking. Had I still the lids with which to blink? Oh, my melting eyes! They watched the flames consume me. They watched everything be consumed; but that could not be. It was not the end of the world. It was just the end of me.

The Absence

THE CREEPER

I knew all the urban legends. I knew they were mostly false but, as the saying went, where there was smoke, there was fire. I knew all the cryptids. I knew of all the serial killers, cultists, and rapists; all the ones worth knowing, anyhow. I listened to every prominent podcast on malevolence both fictitious and factual. I watched the documentaries and read the news articles. I had researched and listened and watched and read but, still, I was not in the know. How could I be? I was personally without evidence these things truly existed; nothing physical nor anecdotal. So, how could I know I was really safe? That no such evils actually existed?

Well, I reasoned, *how could I know a stove was hot or cool without feeling it?* I tried, though. Many times, I tried to feel the stove. Many times I stood before many mirrors and repeated cursed names twice—always twice—and never more as I could never bring myself to speak that supposedly ill-fated third time.

So, again, how could I know I was safe? Simply put, I could not. I could never know if it was safe to venture out into the night without actually doing it. But, I could never venture out into the night without knowing if it was safe. That was my confining conundrum. I tried to recall the last time, if ever, I had been out alone so many hours after the sun and all its safety faded from the sky. I had been working from home for years. Even before COVID I worked remotely.

COVID, I pondered. There was another threat of which I was aware, by which I was trapped within the safety of my isolation but so unable to know the validation of my fear and response as I had neither become ill nor encountered someone who had. However, my lack of illness did not evidence a lack of the illness's existence, just as my lack of encountering cannibals, murderers, ghosts, and ghouls did not evidence a lack of their existence. I could thus rely only upon popular opinion, which was becoming more and more indiscernible online. The unpopular were just so vocal; fact and fiction were so blurred. I was left without a choice.

I stepped out from my isolation, to set forth for a bar, to set hand to stove. Would I burn? If I did, at least then I would know my avoidance was justified. Set forth I would, into twilight no less, for I could only drum up the courage to walk to the bar while the sun was still half visible above the horizon. That I could do. I would then be forced to brave the night on the walk back. Yup. No talking myself out of that. Not unless …

I found a man, I hoped. Admittedly, that was another unmet need—yearslong unmet, in fact. Over the years, I had become increasingly concerned of being kidnapped, of being tortured and trafficked, of being locked up a sex slave. Or, rather than some newsworthy outlier, I would simply be drugged and raped. *Not tonight,* I thought, opening my purse to check for a fourth time that I had packed the spiked drink test strips. *Not ever.* Would I allow a man to buy me a drink? Sure. Well, maybe. How could I know? I supposed it was one more stove I would need to feel. I just wanted a man so badly; to feel safe in his arms; to feel the weight of his body pinning me to the bed—on my own terms, of course.

I shut the apartment door behind me, attempted to twist the doorknob to ensure it was locked, pushed and pulled to test its inability to be opened, and then tried to look through the peephole. I could see nothing. Was there nothing to see because the cover was closed or because the lights were off? Was there a cover? I did not often think about my peephole, I was unsure if it had one. What if it was bare? What if someone looked in and saw it was empty? They would assuredly break in and then wait for me. I would need to leave a light on, to give the impression the apartment was occupied. I reached for my keys and paused. That was what they would expect, though, right? A single light might as well be an invitation to break in.

I'm doing it again, I thought. *Talking myself out of it. Standing in an empty hall instead of—*

Oh. I had just become aware of that. I, a solitary woman, stood as a lone target in a vast hallway devoid of all but the limitlessness of possibilities and likelihoods: every lethality of which man was capable. I needed to move. The lights would remain off. I took a few steps in the direction of the elevators, then a few steps back to the apartment door. I tried the doorknob once more. I had to be certain it was locked. I was then at last mostly satisfied with the door and made my way once again toward the elevators.

My footsteps echoed throughout the hallway. Every echoing step reminded me of its emptiness—of my solitude. As I approached the elevator doors, I reached into my purse to feel for the pepper spray. The elevator, as small as it was, was similar to the hallway in that it held boundless probabilities within. I could enter an empty space on this floor, but every floor beneath was a possible stop, a possible reopening of the doors, and the subsequent entrance of any possibility. But, what good would pepper spray do me in such confinement? I would be as much a recipient of its blinding burn as my assailant. Then what would happen? He would blindly attack me, I would blindly fight back, and that was only if I did not trigger some sort of asthma attack and die. Did I have asthma? I could.

No, it was safer to take the stairs. Or, was it? Five flights in heels, each step a potential misplaced foot and a fatal tumble. Maybe a group of vagrants was taking shelter from the cooling nights on one of the landings. What then?

Elevator. For sure, the elevator. Unless the power went out. That was a rare occurrence but it had been so long since last there was an outage that we were practically due for one now. The stairs, then? After I checked the door, of course.

· ❧ ·

The Wishing Well was about a fifteen minute walk from the apartment. I made it in just under an hour. Though the shadows were long and plentiful, I was granted more than enough light for safe passage to the bar. The walk was oddly unremarkable, likely because I followed all the rules. I knew all the rules; all the ones worth knowing. I knew never to step on a grave, though my route was thankfully absent of graveyards. I knew better than to whistle at night; so, too, did my body, as it was unable to produce a whistle. And, despite having been estranged from my mother for so much of my life, I knew not to step on cracks. Estranged I was, cruel I was not.

Beyond the obvious precautions over which I had some control, I did not need to act on any unpredictabilities. I passed not a single other pedestrian and hardly any traffic passed me. Hell Gate was small, I knew that, it was one of the reasons I chose to live here; but so uneventful was my walk that I had to consider if it had become a ghost town during my seclusion. What even awaited me inside the bar before which I so hesitatingly stood?

Now fueled as much by curiosity as a desire to conquer fear, I pulled open the door and stepped out of a dead world and into an exuberant one. The music was lively, the colors cheerful, and the crowds … my word the crowds! Why, every resident in the valley must have been here. Expectations of dullness and a handful of tired ranchers as flea-ridden and fur-matted as their cattle dogs had been utterly shattered by this merry mass indulging in unmitigated gaiety. It all set my heart aflutter with excitement and nervousness.

There's privacy in being one of a herd, I told myself. No target of observation would I be with such a multitude present.

I smoothed my dress, held my purse tight, and swam upstream to an opening at the bar. Careful not to make eye contact with anyone, I gave a brief look up and down the bar. There were plenty of men to consider; well-dressed, clean-shaven, a few strong jaws with lovely hints of stubble, and such confident smiles. Things were going me.

"Oh, my gosh!" the bartender called over the music. He was looking me up and down. "You look absolutely adorable!"

"Thank you," I called back through a smile. I adjusted my dress with renewed confidence.

"No, thank you," the bartender said. "This place was in desperate need of some natural femininity, I tell you."

A blush spilled across my face as realization spread throughout my mind. I gave the crowds another scan. Men here. Men there. Male hands meeting male hands. Male lips meeting male lips.

Oh.

My confidence fading, I slouched like a wilting flower.

"Is everything all right?" the bartender asked with genuine concern.

"Yeah, I think I just came to the wrong place."

"Oh, you're in the right place, girl," he assured me. "A safe place. We're all friends here."

"Well, that's both the good and the bad, you know?"

"Hmm." He set his fists to his hips. "How about a drink? I'll bet I can mix you up something that's sure to change your mind."

Thoughts of spiked drinks and lost consciousness flashed in my mind. "Something in a bottle, please. Uh, beer—bottled beer," I stressed.

"You don't want to start with a cocktail? Beer before liquor is no bueno, sweetie."

"Just a beer," I said with a sigh.

The bartender pursed his lips. "I'm going to get you Whet," he said.

"Excuse me?"

"It's a strawberry cider. It's what you need." He reached into an unseen shelf beneath the bar top and set a bottle before me. He turned it to face its label toward me. *WHET*, it read in large letters. Beneath, in smaller print, was listed the flavor, *Whet 'n Wild Strawberry*. "Here," he said, scooting it toward me. "First one's free. You'll love it." He cocked his head in a quick thought. "Like, you'll *love*, love it. And if you don't, then your tongue's as tasteless as that jacket, oh, my God, Anthony, you did not wear that in here," the bartender rambled as he hurried presumably in Anthony's direction.

I looked at the bottle of cider. It was open. Had he opened it beneath the bar top? He definitely set it down open, but was it already open? Did he put something in it? What if it was an unwanted drink that someone else spiked and he put it back? What if—

No, I did not need to go down this rabbit hole. There was a quick solution to this (probably) nonexistent problem. I picked up the cider and made my way to the restroom. Two doors opposed each other in a tight corridor. One was labeled "Handsome in Pink," the other "Pretty in Pink." I presumed I belonged in the latter and entered.

It was quite clean for a bar restroom, though I supposed it did not see much traffic, as further evidenced by its vacancy. I set the bottled cider on the sink and glanced up at the small, decorative mirror above the faucet. Something seemed off, not of the reflection's image, but of its speed. A brief thought occupied my mind, that the mirror was a screen rather than glass and that the reflection was a video playback. I looked again, held my gaze, and moved my face to study the image.

There was nothing abnormal.

"Huh," I muttered, lightly shaking my head.

Still, I continued to look, not so much at my reflection, but into the mirror and beyond. A passing urge—merely a sprouting seed of thought—budded; a mere suggestion; a name ...

I briefly checked my makeup (*even if the men aren't interested, I still want to look cute, to feel cute*) and then pulled my purse to my front. I removed a test strip from my purse, took the bottle from the sink, and splashed the strip over the drain. There was no change to its color. I waited.

Seconds or minutes? I wondered. Surely these types of tests required more expedient results than minutes, right? I aired the strip like an instant photograph and reexamined it. It remained unchanged. Maybe it was a dud strip. I decided to test another, this time pouring even more of the cider onto the strip. Why not? The drink was free after all. I gave this new strip some extra time, but, again, there was no change.

Of course a gay bartender wouldn't drug me. What would be the point? Other than robbing me. Or kidnapping me. Or murdering me. Gays are just as capable of murder as anyone else.

There I went again, spiraling. *I didn't used to be like this. I used to be fun.* I gave the bottle—its contents—my attention. "Liquid courage," it was called. Or, in the bartender's words, "what I needed." Well, I could be both fun and courageous without alcohol, especially with a gay crowd. But, a little loosening up wouldn't hurt. I took the bottle to my lips. *Bottoms up.*

Crisp, crimson carbonation. Each swig a bite of an effervescent strawberry. Sharp on the tongue, like ... like a strawberry bon bon. Like Halloween nights. A chill in the air as crisp as this cider. Sitting cross-legged on the floor, ears overwhelmed by the sound of wrappers, especially the bon bons—each and every crinkly one of them.

My brother would give me all of his. No trades. Bon bons had no trade value in his mind. They were "treats for old ladies," he would tell me. Of course, I would not confess that I enjoyed them, sometimes not even to myself. They were hard candies, not bars or cups or ropes. But, they did what those other candies could not: they lasted. A delayed dissolve, a comforting crunch, and then the creamy, chewy center; all the while my tongue bathed in my favorite flavor. We always rushed with our Halloween haul, but the bon bons made me slow down. The bon bons were a delightful pause. If I could have that again. If I could slow my racing thoughts. Fear did not consume me back then. I did the consuming. There were no worries of poisoned goodies, of spiked drinks, of kidnappings. I just lived.

I opened my eyes. I had not realized they were closed. The bottle was empty. I sniffed the opening. There was nothing left but the whisper of memories long past, a scent as faded as my very life.

I looked again in the mirror, though not at myself, not quite. Again, that budding urge. I could do it. I must. A life in fear was a life unlived.

I inhaled, deeply, slowly. Then, I spoke a cursed name. I spoke it once. I spoke it twice. I paused, glancing at the empty bottle in hand. I took it by the neck, a readied weapon. My gaze flicked from bludgeoning bottle to mirror and back. The danger of an urban legend was surely less probable than the effects of the intoxicant I so eagerly just consumed. So, why the hesitation?

I set my eyes on the mirror. My heart achingly pleaded to take action or stand down. My grip tightened.

The cursed name rode a whispered wave of wavering breath … a third time.

I scanned the mirror. I turned behind to face a closed stall door, bottle raised high. There was nothing at which to swing. I took a step toward the stall and forced my weaponless arm through air so thick and heavy with fluorescence it felt like gelatin. Breathing was becoming laborious. Fingertips met cold metal. Hinges squeaked nearly inaudibly. My forearm burned in a marinade of adrenaline and lactic acid. So, too, did my eyes burn but I dared not a single blink, for that was when it would strike—the unknown within the stall.

A soft *clunk* as the stall door met the partition. There was only a toilet (*hey, that's pretty clean for a bar*). For the first time in what felt like minutes, I exhaled. I blinked. I did both multiple times and then I turned back to the mirror. There was I—I and I alone. There was nothing else to reflect.

I spoke again the cursed name, three times over. Still, there was nothing. The bottle lowered and my mouth spoke a second cursed name, once, twice, and a cool and calm thrice. *Nada, sweetie,* I imagined the bartender would say.

"Huh." More an escape of disbelief than air. "I did it. I mean, I really fucking did it." My heart picked up a beat again, this time in excitement. It was just like that president said: fear was the only thing I had to fear. "Well, I was courageous. Now let's go be fun."

I gently dropped the bottle into the trash so as not to break it, took a confident breath, and left my testing ground.

· ∽ ·

I was invigorated. I felt like an Amish teen let loose into the world of sin unrestrained. I left the restroom a changed woman, and stepped into an equally changed atmosphere. The bright cheer that overwhelmed my senses had been replaced—in only a few minutes, no less—by gloom and despair. No bass thrummed in my chest, no shouts of laughter, no singing. The world had seemingly swallowed itself while I swallowed the cider. Now, there was only absence: of color, of light, of warmth. A chill seemed to seep from the very walls, now only barely visible in the anemic glow of a single, flickering light.

The difference was so incomprehensibly vast and encompassing that I had to re-enter the restroom to verify it was not shared with another bar; perhaps one catering to the goth crowd. I checked and re-checked that I had entered and exited the same door. Inexplicably, there was only a single door. I walked through it once more, and once more I was met, not with the sounds of flamboyant flirtations, but with those of downhearted despondency.

With unadjusted eyes still partially blind to the darkness, I cautiously stepped down the corridor toward the bar, toward groans and grief. The unsettling scent of metal, like old coins, wafted about, steadily replacing any hints of strawberry still lingering in my nostrils. Shadows, dark masses, living lumps or some such things were floundering about the floor like piles of fish in drying mud. Fear was displacing confusion. I backed away, retreating for the safety of the restroom. No fool was I, much less foolhardy.

I worked the handle but the restroom door would not give. Had someone entered and locked themselves in? Surely, I would have heard this. Nonetheless, I rapped my knuckles against the stained, dark wood.

"Hello?" I called out. "Let me in." I continued to work the handle to no avail. "Please. Please let me in." Along the corridor walls reverberated the sounds of stumbling and shuffling. Someone (*something*) was approaching. I threw my shoulder into the door, once … twice … thrice. "Please! I'm scared! Please!"

I turned to face the other door. "Handsome in Red," read the sign. Its handle gave no resistance. With all the impetus my frame could effect, I threw the door and my body into the restroom. The door, having given as little resistance as its unlocked handle, slammed into the wall-mounted stop with a barely subdued *bang!*

"Shit, sor—"

The restroom was bathed in a dim, red hue. On its floor rolled and squirmed more masses, these more clearly visible in the red luminescence. They were the patrons of the bar. Their clothes, once clean, vibrant, flamboyant, were now filthy rags, shredded and bloodied. They writhed and crawled. They clawed, at each other, at the air, at themselves—their throats, as though they could not breathe. Toward me. They noticed and now crawled and clawed toward me. Their panic-stricken eyes—every pair—were focused on me, as though I were the sole occupant of a liferaft amidst a sea of drowning men.

The man closest to the door snatched my ankle in a clawing grip. I attempted to jerk my leg back in response but, unstable already in high heels, I lost my balance and fell back, barely catching my weight with my palms before my head or back met the unforgiving floor. To my side, the stumbling, shuffling figure closed in. Another ragged man, similarly clawing at his throat. He fell forward and collapsed into me, pinning my upper body to the cold floor while the ankle-snatcher, still mostly in the restroom, was pulling himself further up my leg with what remained of his fingernails. Weight— suffocating weight—from chest to legs, immobilizing, restraining. Every exhale was only half-met by its following inhale. Further the ankle-snatcher crawled, pulling my legs, pulling himself up my legs, now wrestling with the man on my upper half. I was both the prize and the rope in a twisted game of tug-of-war.

My lungs were barely inflated, arms trapped, only one leg free with nothing to offer but helpless kicking. The men atop me, starved of air, fought each other, fought at unseen, strangling forces, and fought for, on, and over me in erratic fashion. Then, a shift in weight. I freed my arms, and wriggled and pushed and kicked and flopped like a fish freeing its slippery self from the hands of a novice angler. With both legs free, I braced my heels against the tangle of flailing limbs and pushed myself away. I scrambled for a grip on the open doorframe, that I could pull myself to my feet, as my body was still heavy with the phantom weight of the two men. As I did so, I saw the other occupants of the restroom making their agonizing way toward me. I snatched the door handle and pulled the door and its sign ("DAMNED IF YOU DO") in toward its frame. It stopped against the jerking legs of the ankle-snatcher.

I moved again to try the handle of the opposing door but there was no handle. The door remained. The handle did not. The door was devoid of all but its sign, which read, "DAMNED IF YOU DON'T."

"Help!" I shouted into the darkness. Amidst all the sounds of asphyxiation, of fists and feet flailing against flooring, of crawling and rolling and twisting and thrashing, there was no response—no signal of salvation. Up the corridor behind me was only a wall, which seemed closer with every glance. Down the corridor, toward the bar from which I came, was an orgy of anguish. Something swatted at my leg, scratching my calf. It was one of the two men from whom I had just freed myself. With no alternative, I moved toward the bar.

The floor of the bar was now a quivering quilt of writhing limbs, a minefield of men, a landscape of toppled and tossing bodies amongst all manner of overturned furniture. All was unlit, dark, hardly visible, save for the barricading bar top, which held behind it a single, downward-oriented light hanging at its center like a beckoning lighthouse.

I obliged. I straddled and hurdled, every step in once graceful heels was now a liability—a gamble. The men in the corridor would not allow me the time to strip my feet bare. The men in the bar area would not allow me the space; and even if space allowed, there would be no way I could remove them without drawing the attention of those suffocating.

I strained my eyes against the darkness as I tried to assess my route to the bar top. Chairs, stools, tables, and decor abound jutted out from writhing waves of flesh like jagged rocks ready to sink me. My heart hammered a frenzied drumbeat, that tune I had become so familiar with in recent years.

They'll hear it. They'll hear my heartbeat and they'll grab me. I'm moving too slow. I wanted to run. I wanted to scream. I wanted to curl up on the floor and cry; I visualized this. *Maybe they wouldn't notice me. Just one more body on the floor. No, of course they'd notice.* I straddled a headbanger, momentarily losing and then regaining my balance. *You clumsy idiot. You're always tripping over something. Stubbing your toes. With or without light, it doesn't matter, because you're a clumsy idiot and you're going to fall.*

The thought of falling, of being consumed by clawing fingers, triggered a surge of adrenaline. Just one missed step. But it was more than merely misplacing my feet. The movements of the damned were too unpredictable. My feet and legs were being, more frequently now, inadvertently kicked and slapped, though I seemed to remain unnoticed; for now …

The bar top counter was almost within reach, but a surging tide of bodies at its base seemed to make it unreachable.

You're not going to make it.

"What did I tell you?" The cheerful voice froze me in place. "Did you love it? Or did you *love* it?" The bartender, still as animated and lively in speech and appearance as when I had first met him, stood precisely beneath the hanging light.

"Help," I pleaded in a hushed quaver. Two of the men by my feet jerked their heads, fixing their faces on me.

"What's that?" The bartender cupped a hand behind his ear.

I looked at the men who took notice. They were climbing one another, reaching up toward me as though trying to break the surface of whatever invisible waters drowned them, every muscle fighting in search of even a single lifesaving breath. They were inches from grasping me, from pulling me down to eternally drown alongside them.

I ran toward the bartender. I ran past, through, and on bodies, stumbling but not quite falling. Heels sank into flesh. Balance wavered. A hand caught my shin in an unsecure grip and my heel twisted on a face. I caught the bar top rail and pulled myself up, jerking my legs away from several snatching hands.

"I knew you could do it," the bartender stated as a matter of fact.

"What?" I panted.

"Like Martin Luther said: 'Faith must trample under foot all reason,'" the bartender said.

"Help me," I demanded. He did not. He only stood with his hands on his hips and his head tilted like a parent who just walked in on their child sneaking out of their bedroom window. I slid from the counter and collapsed into a breathless pile onto the floor beside a short stack of stones.

"Whoa, careful there, girlie," the bartender cautioned with that genuine concern of his. He then pointed behind me. "You don't want to get wet." I glanced over my shoulder as I got to my knees. The stones were set in a circle and contained a pool of placid water. "You want to get Whet," he concluded.

I turned back to the bartender, who was now holding another bottle of the strawberry cider. For the briefest moment, I felt an urge—a magnetic pull—to reach for it.

"What's going on?" I asked. "What's wrong with you people?"

The bartender cocked his head in apparent confusion. "What's wrong with us?" He then leaned over the bar top to scan the floor. "Oh, let's just say there's two sides to every ..." He fished for something in his pocket. "... coin," he finished, presenting what was evidently supposed to be a coin in his palm. It did not resemble a coin to me, though. A coin I expected to glint or shine or shimmer under even this one pale light. This did not. If anything, this dark metal seemed to absorb light. On the side made visible to me, there was a face, though not quite a face. No, it was a contradiction—many contradictions. It was shifting; beautiful and gruesome, one moment serene, almost angelic, and, impossibly almost in the same moment, it was grotesque. The only thing that did not shift was its smile, which seemed either warm or wicked when framed by the angelic or grotesque face. The more I stared, the more I thought I could hear something akin to whispers, assurances, wishes …

"Say, you know what would be fun?" the bartender asked. "Making a wish. Yeah," he crooned. "That might just liven the place up a bit, you know? Might be fun. You can be fun, right?"

I pulled my eyes back up to the bartender's face. "What?" I shook my head. "Wha—"

The bartender gasped theatrically. "You didn't drink all of your cider. Oh, you naughty girl!" he exclaimed in a playful tone, wagging a finger at me.

"What? You did try to drug me, didn't you? You tried to drug me! Oh, my God, I'm hallucinating right now, aren't I?"

"Well, aren't you a neurotic little thing?"

I pulled myself up and took a defensive step back. All around, the encroaching crowd gasped, scratched, and clambered. "Did you do this?" I gestured toward the crowd. "Did … did you poison them?"

The bartender peered again over the counter. "Gosh, that is super concerning, huh? Looks like they ran out of all the airs they were putting on. I think that's on you," he said, bobbing a downward pointed finger over the counter.

"What?"

"Well, you know, you took so long getting here, which I totally get. You can't just look at your outfit on the bed. You have to see it on your body before you can really judge it, right? But then you finally get here and you don't even hang out at the bar. You just go hide away in the restroom forever, don't you, you little tease?"

"What do you want?"

"What do I want? You're asking the wrong questions, sweetie. We're in the business of making wishes come true. This is about what you want."

A bottle crashed to the floor beside me. One of the dying patrons was clawing his way over the bar top, knocking over anything in the path leading toward me. I ducked to lower myself out of view of the rest of the crowd.

"No, no. They want me. They want to—"

"Girl," the bartender interjected. "You're the life of a party absent of life. Of course they want you. Isn't that what you wanted?"

"No!"

"Okay. Well, you know what would clear that up?" The bartender lowered himself to a squat to meet my gaze. As he did so, even over the sounds of groaning and gasping and clawing and shuffling, I heard the sounds of creaking leather. I had to check that I was not mistaken, but he was indeed wearing denim. He leaned forward, his face blotted with shadows in the dim light of the bulb hanging just overhead, his eyes unseen in the shade beneath his brow. Lips parted into a shaded smile, his mouth as abyssal as his eyes, the stretching flesh, like a worn mask, bringing more sounds of creaking leather. He again offered me the coin. "Better make it quick. I don't think they're going to wait."

Like waters spilling over a levee, men began falling over the bar top and behind the counter. Every pair of eyes was on me. Every hand was extended in my direction. Every mouth was agape, struggling for air that could not be inhaled.

"Okay! Okay, I wish—" Hands flung wildly from the bar top. A fingernail scraped my cheek. "I-I wish I was safe!"

"Oh, c'mon, girlfriend. You gotta mean it."

"Y-yeah," I stammered, cowering closer to the floor. "Like, all the time. I'm scared all the time and I just want to know I'm safe, even when I'm alone." The truth of the matter was that I was scared of being alone. That would be my wish, if wishes could come true: to not be alone anymore.

Savage fingers took hold of my hair, jerking my head back. I looked to the bartender for aid, and while he lent a hand, it was only to continue offering the coin. I reached out to take it, but another hand grabbed hold of my arm. I fought forward, roots tugging scalp, nails gashing skin, until I inched close enough to take the coin from his hand.

"Honestly, the lack of manners is just atrocious," the bartender said, shaking his head. Hands. Hands and hands were groping and grasping, clutching and clawing. I was being pulled in all directions. Gasps and chokes filled my ears. The bartender, now barely audible, continued speaking as calmly as ever. "You know, honey, you're never really alone. You know that. It's why you keep your curtains drawn, even on the top floor."

The creeper. Even in the midst of despair, the words bubbled in the back of my mind.

With the coin clenched in fist, I punched through a wall of flailing, thrashing limbs and threw the coin at the well's ever-placid water. It tumbled through air and darkness and eternity, falling without end as every surface of my being was jerked and wrenched in every direction. I was going to die. Hundreds of men were literally fighting over me and my death would be the byproduct. My highschool self would have squealed with glee to have been made aware of this fate. All the friends and family and human connection I had in those years. Was my life flashing before my eyes? How easy it was to have become so isolated in this new, ever-evolving world. Would I have been in this position—tearing at the seams—if I had simply kept a friend?

"I wish I wasn't alone!" The unbidden words, born from vocal cords, not mind, erupted from my throat, clear and discernible despite the fingers spreading my lips like so many fish hooks.

As though now permitted contact with the water, the coin struck the pool flat against its face like an expertly executed belly-flop. A wet *slap* resounded like a finger snap, and just as instantaneous, the world was bright.

Let there be light.

"Girl, nothing dims your sparkle," the bartender declared. "I knew you could do it."

I pulled myself up, just enough to peer over the bar top. "What happened?" I asked, looking around the lively bar. Like moments prior, there were men all around. Unlike moments prior, though, not a soul seemed distressed. Men here. Men there. Men holding hands. Men dancing. Men kissing. Men doing all manner of things save for dying.

"You made your wish, silly. What do you think happened?"

"Can I go?" I stood fully and backed away from the bartender. "Just let me go home."

"Yeah, babe." The bartender spoke as though I should have known this. "You want me to call you a cab?"

"No!" Some of the men lining the counter turned to study me. "Uh, no," I spoke more softly, just above the sound of the thrumming music. "I'll walk."

"Well, in those heels, that sidewalk might as well be a runway." I took my purse from the floor, turned from him, and retreated in a controlled but no less swift stride to the door as he called out, "Own that walk, girl!"

· ◌ ·

What the hell (police) happened back there? (Hospital) I'm drugged, I need to (run) go to the hospital or the police. I just want to (look behind you) go home (don't look behind you!). Oh, my God (they're coming), it's so dark out. My chest (calm down) hurts. Please (shut up), let it be over.

Breathe.

It was a fifteen minute walk to the apartment—an eternity. A brain starved of oxygen would die in less time. Hell, it took less than a minute without oxygen to pass out. Was my brain getting enough oxygen? I was panting—hyperventilating—cruising toward uncon-sciousness. Then what? Imagine all the things the nighttime world would do to the unconscious, unguarded, unsheltered body of a wom-an. Imagine—

Breathe, I commanded myself once more.

I kept my pace but slowed my breathing, inhaling deeply, exhal-ing shakily. Damp, cold air in, hot trepidation out. In through the nose … two, three. Out through the mouth. I needed to ground myself—look, listen, and feel.

Footsteps echoed!

My footsteps. Only mine.

An ache bound my chest, a burn tightened my throat, fatigue gnawed my legs. More than anything, my feet hurt, but they did not slow. I walked as hurriedly as my heels would allow. I contemplated removing them, but that would require stopping, and stopping out here, in the dark, in solitude, was an imbecilic notion. So, I was re-signed to careful strides and hypervigilant eyes. A rolled ankle would be a death sentence, an invitation to man and beast alike; for pred-ators both two and four-legged preyed on the weak, the injured, the solitary …

You're never really alone, the bartender's voice reminded me. A chill wrapped its way up my spine like an untamed weed.

I knew all the urban legends; all the ones worth knowing. And no urban legend was worth knowing more than that of "the creeper." No urban legend so dominated my amygdala like "the creeper." "The creeper" was the reason I accepted no apartment lower than the top floor. The bartender somehow knew that. He must have known. Why else would he have mentioned my curtains? Of course I kept them drawn. I was living alone. And, as both the bartender implied and the urban legend explained, no one is ever really alone. You need only look out your window to see that. The creeper always kept watch over the solitary, always ready to provide company. That was why you had to keep your curtains drawn at night. A single glance would suffice as an invitation.

I tried to hurry my pace dangerously further. Every click of my heels rang out into the night like a dinner bell, echoing off sleeping and dead buildings, down alleys, across streets. Every strike of the spindles underfoot was amplified by the utter silence through which I waded. Every awkward, heavy footfall a knock at the door of a haunted house. I could not pry my mind from my shoes. Heel-toes. Heel-toes. Knock-knock. Anyone home? Any*thing* home?

An occasional pebble crunched beneath my heel, threatening to topple me, rolling and grinding, the sound stretching across the soaked cement of the sidewalk like the shadows cast by the pale streetlights that guided me home. Wet leaves spotted the walkway like a leopard's hide, like doormats inviting me to slip upon them. Electricity hummed from each building and streetlight I passed, sounds of the distant applause of a sadistic audience. The night was never as still or as empty as it so deceivingly implied.

I looked up and down the street I was about to cross, but gave no pause. "No monsters here," I spoke aloud, quietly. I spoke in hopes of emboldening myself, but I was now growing more and more fearful that the observation may be interpreted as a challenge of sorts to any of the possibilities lurking in the dark.

I made wide arcs to give alleyway openings extra space. I watched my feet as I traversed curbs and crossed streets. I did not want to offer anyone or anything an invitation by eye contact; especially one thing in particular. Moreover, I did not want to risk a blind step at this speed. Oh, I could only imagine; and I did. I imagined slipping on one of the small piles of decaying autumn foliage. I imagined a great many things in the absence of natural light. It was my well-honed skill; a skill fantastically flexed in solitary situations, and tonight was truly a night of solitude. I fled the bar as alone as I had entered it, and had since encountered not a single stranger with which to avoid eye contact. Not one set of headlights disrupted my night-adjusted vision. There was nothing on which I could focus my thoughts except the limitlessness of possibilities and likelihoods ...

This was why I avoided stepping out after sundown. In contrast to the tranquility of the night, my mind was clamorous, always ablaze with fear-fueled questions. Should I break an elbow—no—should I crack my skull—no, no—should I fall forward and fail to remove my shivering hands from my pockets in time to save my face—my teeth? Who would find me? Who would help? What if evil approached disguised as help?

What a mistake I had made in leaving the apartment; in leaving the safety of routine, of the known, of four walls and a single way in and out five unscalable stories high. What had I gained? A free, drug-spiked drink and a bad trip. Men grabbing at me, holding me down. Was I nearly raped? How much of it was real? Did rohypnol have hallucinatory effects? This was my punishment for leaving home. I had been drugged and now I walked dark streets, vulnerable, assailable.

The stove was hot, and my wounded hand could not yet be pulled from its burning surface.

They're coming for you. They'll suffocate you, tear you apart, finish what you escaped. I did escape, right? No, it would be more reasonable to assume I hallucinated. I could be reasonable, right? Let's be reasonable—rational. Had I been assaulted by a mob of dying gay men?

That seemed improbable.

I was drugged, hallucinated, and fled the bar, right? Was that not a probability? Or, was it more probable that I wasn't drugged? That I would ruin potentially multiple lives through false testimony? That I was a crazy lady who got drunk, freaked out on her first night out in years, made a scene, accused the innocent, and forever shackled herself to solitude because now the whole world would see her as a lying, attention-seeking manipulator? Who would the world believe?

Figure it out when you get home. You're alone in the dark. Ground yourself. Be situationally aware.

I shook the thoughts from my mind and shifted my gaze ahead. Then, for the first time since fleeing the bar, I halted. One final *clop* from my footwear resounded into the night like ripples through crocodile-infested waters.

A shadow at the street corner. There were many shadows along the street. So many shadows. But none had the apparent mass and depth of the shadow at the street corner. It stood the height of a man. That was all it did. It merely stood, as if waiting for me. I remained paused, mind and body, in dreadful observation. It remained unmoving, but remained nonetheless. Standing—a shadow—as though it could; blatantly defying the laws of nature.

They're coming for you.

The bartender. It was the bartender stalking me. Or maybe one of the patrons. Someone followed me from the bar and they were going to kidnap me. I was going to spend the rest of my life in a soundproofed basement.

I reached into my purse, grabbed hold of the pepper spray, and crossed the street to the opposing sidewalk, giving only a slight glance to the curb to ensure my footing. Slight as the glance was, however, I lost sight of the shadow. And despite scanning with night-adjusted eyes, it could not again be spotted. I halted—only my body this time, as my thoughts resumed their race against my heart.

Another drug-induced hallucination? Or an optical illusion? Had I stared into a streetlight and experienced the after effects—a mere spot in my vision?

I pressed on, quickly picking up pace from a slow and cautious start. When I reached the end of the block, I re-fixed my gaze on the opposing street corner. Nothing. Neither sight nor sound. Too cold for insects, too late for people. It was me alone against the night.

You're never really alone ...

I continued the trek, but something was wrong, I could feel it. The hairs on my neck, the skin of my back, my very spine were telling me—screaming—that I was being watched, followed, stalked. I stopped yet again and scanned my surroundings. There was indeed a shadow, a silent observer casting an unseen gaze upon me with unseen eyes. But it was not posted at the street corner. It stood now behind me. Maybe half a block away it stood. But there it stood, clearly stood. Not a man in black. A standing shadow.

My skin tightened. With eyes fixed on the shadow and pepper spray clenched in one hand, I removed my cell phone with the other. Who, though, would I call? The police? And what would I tell them? I'd tell them I was being followed. Just that. And then what? Wait for ten or twenty or thirty minutes until they showed up? I'd already be home if I kept walking. But maybe a car was patrolling nearby. Maybe they'd offer me a ride home.

I turned on the screen and reluctantly pulled my eyes from the shadow to enter my PIN. I then darted my eyes back down the sidewalk and again lost sight of the thing. Again, I checked my surroundings and, again, I was surrounded only by silence and a breezeless, still night. I needed to press on. There was no waiting for an escort. I would be taken long before the police arrived.

I started jogging. My heels struck sidewalk and street like drumsticks beating a piercing, percussive announcement of my presence in the shelterless street. The thin straps of my shoes dug into my ankles, a binding burden with every stride. I jogged. A threatening wobble began in my heels. I jogged. Under streetlights, through deeper darkness and curtains of jaundiced light, I jogged.

The chapel was just ahead. The chapel was halfway to the bridge over the ditch, which was halfway home. I was halfway to being halfway home.

I dared no backward glance as I passed the chapel. I considered pulling at its doors. I considered entering its holy grounds in the hopes that the unholy could not follow suit. But I left this consideration at the back of my mind. What if the holy building offered no such shelter? What if it was locked and I became pinned against its doors? No, I put the chapel to my rear.

Now the bridge was just ahead, the creek beneath it growing louder. Behind me, I could feel the shadow drawing nearer, nipping at the nape of my neck, tasting the fear that trailed me. The rap of my heels became hollow clunks as I reached the wooden bridge. Ice glistened atop the splintering planks. I could feel the thing at my heels and I widened my stride in response, stepping beyond the limitations of my footwear. I lost traction. I slid forward throwing my belongings as I waved my arms in large circles in a failed attempt to swim through the air until I lost balance altogether and fell onto my back. I returned to my feet, scooped up only my phone, purse, and whatever remained of its contents, and resumed a careful stride. Not once did I cast a glance over shoulder. My back was stiff, my breathing ragged, my throat burned with frigid air.

I was nearly home. I thrust my hand into my purse in desperate search of my keys, felt their jagged metal, and, for the first time this evening, relief. I readied the key to the complex's entrance, clutching it like a shank.

I made the entrance.

With my free hand, I grabbed hold of the door handle, turned around, and poised my key-armed hand high, like the cocked tail of a scorpion. I did not sting. There was nothing to sting. I was alone.

You're never really alone ...

I fumbled the key around the lock and paused. Something was waiting for me inside. I could feel it. I knew the moment I opened the door I would find it—whatever it was—on the other side. And if it was not in plain sight, I would find it eventually. In the elevator. In the stairwell. Behind a door—behind *my* door. In the closet. Under the bed—dear Lord, *in* my bed!

No, I thought, *it would find me. Oh, God, it would find me. It's just waiting for the right opportunity. I would open the bathroom door and there it would be. Behind the curtain. In the toilet! I can't go inside!*

But what was the alternative? Brave the night? Walk somewhere until daylight? It was just as likely the shadow or something or someone else was lying in ambush for me somewhere outside—more likely, even! Or-or-or—

Or, it was likely that I was so fatigued, so frightened by my own mind, and still so drugged that I imagined the thing—everything. I likely walked home in a bit of a stupor, like sleepwalking. That had to be it.

I can be rational. I was just daydreaming, I thought. *Day-nightmare-ing,* I corrected myself.

The key tapped and scraped about the lock in my shaking hand. I cringed at the noise.

Why do I have to be quiet? I don't have to be quiet. There's nothing to worry about. If I open the door and something grabs my wrist ... pulls me in ... then I've got something to worry about. If I open the door and—

"Shut up," I whispered aloud. "Shut up, shut up, shut up," I told my mind through clenched teeth.

I opened the door and braced myself. Nothing. I jumped inside, quickly marched to the elevator (my legs and feet allowed not a single thought of climbing five flights of stairs), and ascended heavenward, leaving below me the hell I had survived.

I did. I did survive the night. I actually did it.

· ∽ ·

After having successfully braved the dark of night and the emptiness of the fifth-floor corridor, I readied myself to brave the possibilities within my apartment. I opened the door and flinched. Nothing. I darted inside like a cold plunge and slammed the door behind me. I lit the living room and examined every inch, wall-to-wall, floor-to-ceiling. Still nothing. I slowly approached the bedroom hallway. My neck tingled imagining what awaited me in the corridor: a clawed creature, crouched and crawling across the carpet; some sinister silhouette slithering along the ceiling, stalking my shadow, stretching snatching, serpentine fingers toward me. My heart fluttered, soaking my flesh with chilled blood. It was too much—unbearable. If the monstrous manifestations of my mind did not murder me, then surely my sprinting heart would collapse from fatigue.

Breathe, I instructed myself in thought, as I had so many times before.

I slapped at the hall's light switch and found it empty. With cautious feet, I moved to each room, sliding reluctant hands along dark walls in search of light switches. Nothing here. Nothing there. My furnishings and I cast the only shadows about the apartment, and none had volume. All was still, which only catalyzed my fretting mind.

I had not yet cleared the bathroom, but shut its door, too fearful was I of receiving the punishment of having spoken the cursed names at the bar. Still, I needed to brush my teeth, but that would require a cognitive cooldown; time to bolster my bravery, that I may stand before the bathroom mirror and even look into its reflection. So, I turned on the TV, searched for a cartoon, and gave myself a long, long moment of deep breathing and reflection on the couch.

At long last, I removed my heels and their biting straps. They pulsed with relief. I collapsed backward into the cushions and fixed my unfocused eyes onto the ceiling. I had been drugged. I would go to the hospital and get tested in the morning, in the safety of daylight. I would never again wear heels of any sort. The bar, the shadow, it had all been an effect of the drugs—had to be. I rolled my head from side to side on the cushion, scanning the room once more. There was nothing about but safety and security ... and solitude.

You're never really alone ...

When I felt adequately emboldened, I let my throbbing feet carry me to the bathroom door. Like the shadow on the street corner, I stood. That was all I did. For so many countless, heavy heartbeats, I merely stood at the door, holding the doorknob, but not turning it; bracing it, as though ready to fight against something that may attempt to turn it from the other side. No matter how intently I gazed into the door, I could not see beyond it—into the vast possibilities that awaited just on the other side of the mere inches-thick barrier.

I turned the knob. My sanity required it. My lungs stood by, preparing themselves for dread or relief. I eased the door open, slightly, steadily, slowly. The gap of darkness, of dreadful possibilities, was widening. I froze when the gap had widened enough to fit through my hand. I would have to reach in and feel for the lightswitch. I would have to plunge a hand into that chasm of dangers; my left hand, of course. That was my non-dominant hand.

My fingertips pressed against the smooth, painted wall in much the same way the dense darkness pressed against the back of my hand. Further inward I guided my hand, my wrist now entirely swallowed by the absence of light—the absence of life and of safety and observance. My fingers slid along the wall, feeling for the normal and expected (the plastic switch plate cover) but anticipating the abnormal and unexpected (anything—everything—that lurked in the dark).

Just shut the door. Brush your teeth in the morning. Pee in the kitchen sink. Who would know?

Then I felt it. Jutting from the wall. My fingers felt it. It was the light switch.

I flipped the switch and flooded the bathroom with the safety of artificial luminescence. I pushed the door fully open and took several moments to observe from the hall. At the far end of the bathroom, across the vast distance of the linoleum floor, hung the shower curtain. And behind that? Well, anything …

I stepped toward it, into the sole unexplored expanse of the apartment. One step. The coolness of the linoleum soothed my throbbing sole. A second step. Did the curtain move? A ripple caused by a shift in air from my entrance or by the breathing of something in the tub? No, a trick of the mind. Shadows at play as my eyes observed from new angles. A third step and something appeared at my side. My heart burst, shooting painful shrapnel through my chest. I turned ready to scream and thrash.

It was me. I was looking at myself, at my reflection. I was looking into the mirror. No monsters, no apparitions, only me—crazed me.

I gave an anxious chuckle. "Okay, that's enough."

I took the final steps to the shower, grabbed the curtain and liner, and paused. *You can do this. Just pull it like a bandage. You'll see. There's nothing there. You'll see. You're all alone.*

You're never really alone ...

I pulled the curtain to one side. I pulled the curtain to the other side. Then, I spread the curtain back in place, obscuring the nothingness that inhabited the shower and tub.

After both my heart had caught its breath and a second look-see, I fell back into routine: brushed my teeth, washed my face, looked at myself in the mirror, cleared acne, but, more importantly, cleared my mind. Lastly, I laid myself down to bed, though not before scanning its underside. While no dangers were present beneath the bed, I could not find comfort between the sheets. Something was different, misplaced or forgotten. Too much adrenaline. Too much fear. My mind was clouded.

I scanned the walls of my bedroom from my pillow. The bedside lamp spilled splotches of shadows all about, though none appeared malicious. The closet door was partially ajar (I had wanted to keep an eye on its interior), and I considered for a moment removing myself from the safety and comfort of my sheets to shut it, thereby attenuating the vivid thoughts of the endless, malevolent possibilities within the closet that would assuredly ensue should I leave that gateway open. However, I was sure—so sure—that if I were to place a foot down onto the floor, something would take me by the ankle. Something. Some *creeping* thing ...

No, I told myself. *Calm down.*

I took a slow, deep breath, paused, and exhaled. It was time to sleep, not time to run wild in imagination. I wanted to roll over, to face away from the light and finally rest my eyes, but began to fear the notion that something was lying beside me; that, should I turn, I'd find something gazing upon me mere inches from my face. A face to mirror my own, perhaps; one with twisted teeth in an impossibly wide smile.

No, damn it.

Again, I calmed myself. Again, I breathed deeply. I would need darkness and a serene mind to drift asleep. And so, with much hesitation, I reached out and shut off the lamp. And there it stood; in the corner by the nightstand. It stood. A shadow. It watched. I likewise watched, too crippled by fear to do much else. There I remained watching. There it remained standing. There it remained still. Would it move before I fell asleep? Would it move after?

For a long time, nothing happened. The soft sounds of a muted cartoon played from the living room, but I gave my ears no focus, only my eyes. Nothing, nothing, and nothing. For a longer time after that, nothing continued to happen. It was merely a shadow. An ordinary silhouette. So, why was I still so fixated on it? Why was it so unsettling? I gave this some thought. I had never really observed the shadows in my room before, not at bedtime. There were never any shadows to worry about with the—

I hadn't drawn the curtains. So hyperfocused was I on the minor details within the apartment, on all the shadows on the walls and under the furniture, on the damn bathroom, that I had overlooked the big tasks. The window was bare, an open invitation to the thing I feared most.

I sat upright with my back to the window and turned the light back on. I would need to plant my feet back onto the carpet, just below the skirt of the bed, just before the darkness of the depths beneath the boxspring. My heart rate climbed. I scooted to the edge of the bed and lowered my feet toward the floor in much the same way a novice would dip their legs into a shark cage. Lower and lower, until soles met fibers. I paused, poised, ready to jerk my feet back upward at the first feeling of fingers.

More nothing.

That accomplished, I stood and shuffled toward the closet, never removing my eyes from the gap in the door. They burned, my eyes, but I dared not a single blink. That was when these things struck—the things behind doors. Any moment, it would creak open and an apparition of apparel would amble out. I reached through the darkness, hand outstretched, further and further forward until my fingers met the knob. I gripped and twisted the metal, retracting the latch bolt so as to shut the door as silently as possible. The door returned to its frame without resistance. I slowly returned the knob to its resting position and backed carefully toward the window until my heel bumped the baseboard.

First the blinds, then the curtains. Double protection.

I felt around the wall, the window frame, the window itself in search of the cord to the blinds. Try as I might, my hands could not find it, not blindly.

A quick look. Not out the window, obviously, but at the frame. Just to find the cord. So I can finally get some rest.

My eyes darted to the window frame. There they were. Resting on the windowsill. Two small moons each with a miniscule black crater at their center. Eyes of the creeper.

"No!" I shrieked. I pulled at the curtains to cover the window and the curtain rod was ripped down by my fear-fueled force. I shot to the bed, snatched my phone from the nightstand, and took refuge beneath the covers. The phone emitted a blinding light as I failed twice to unlock its screen with panicked fingers.

The sound of a retracting deadbolt reverberated down the hall.

I tried a third time to unlock the phone, this time succeeding.

The sound of a door softly opening and shutting reverberated down the hall.

I opened the phone app and dialed 9-1-1. Just before the digital trills of the call, I could hear a cartoon child remarking, as though somehow having an awareness of the thing that had entered the apartment. "Uh-oh," the child remarked.

Trill.

The sound of shambling reverberated down the hall.

Trill.

The sound of a door softly opening reverberated throughout the room.

I gripped the phone tighter, clenched my teeth tighter, and lowered the covers from my head. There they were. Resting on the door frame. Hardly pupils to be seen. Merely pinholes in unpainted Easter eggs. Like a fascinated child peering into an exhibit, there was held the unblinking gaze of the creeper; widening eyes above a widening smile.

· ❧ ·

"I didn't look! I swear! I swear I didn't look!"

"Ma'am," the dispatcher again raised her voice. "What is the nearest address?"

"Oh, God, please help! Please!"

"Ma'am, what is your emergency?" the dispatcher asked with growing alarm.

"He's inside!"

"Someone's inside your house? Ma'am? Can you hear me, ma'am? Are you able to get outside? You need to run to an exit, to a neighbor, and tell me your address when you're safe to do so. I'll stay on the line with you, okay?" The dispatcher was silent for several long moments, listening. "I can hear you breathing, are you unable to speak? Are you outside?"

"I am."

"You're outside?" the dispatcher asked.

"Yes."

"Are you safe?" the dispatcher asked.

"See for yourself."

"Excuse me?" the dispatcher asked.

"Look out your window."

Hell Gate

THE AUDIOPHILES

"Mayer." A hand shook my shoulder. "Hey!"

I rolled over and opened my eyes to an audience of four gathered around my bunk. Sergeant Wilson continued shaking me into consciousness. I slapped his hand away and turned back to my other side.

"Fuck off, Wilson," I groaned.

"Git up, Mayer," Wilson continued in his slow, heavy drawl. He kicked my bunk with his boot. "We're takin' the newbie in town for initiation." He spit into an empty soda bottle and added, "'N celebratin' his promotion."

"Seriously, Wilson, fuck off."

"Jus' 'cause ya made sergeant don' mean ya can say 'no' to me. Don' forget who raised ya," he spit into the bottle, "'n fed ya all that leadership know-how. Mayer? Is y'all listenin'?" He ripped my pillow out from under my head, and my face fell onto the greasy, sweat-stained mattress beneath. I shot upright, striking my head off the bunk above me with a heavy thud. There was a light round of chuckles.

"I just spent all night on the range and all morning cleaning weapons. Please, fuck off, Wilson. Please," I begged. My head was beginning to throb with pain and anger.

"Yeah, boo-hoo. Ya didn' git any sleep last night. Nobody did. Whatcha doin' tonight, huh?"

"Sleeping. What do you think I'm trying to do?"

"'Xactly." Wilson smiled, revealing a set of crooked, tobacco-freckled teeth. His bulging lip, like an overwhelmed dam, struggled to manage the pile of dip perpetually stuffed into his gum line. "So, here's what y'all's gonna do up until then: y'all's gonna rub them lil' eyes, y'all's gonna put on some civvies—"

"Oh, fuck you, Wilson," I interrupted.

"No-no-no-no. Listen, y'all's gonna let us buy ya some drinks 'n pay ya for gas, 'n y'all's gonna have a good time." He then looked at the three next to him, Sergeants Ko and Perez, and a third with whom I was unfamiliar. "We all gonna have a good time, right boys?" There was a murmur of agreement. Wilson shook his head in apparent disappointment. "Y'all are killin' me."

"On a Thursday night?" I sighed. "No. I've been through this routine too many times. You pricks tell me it's going to be a good time and we end up crawling back to the barracks at God knows what hour—"

"'N is it ever *not* a good time?" Wilson interjected.

"Yeah, Wilson, yeah," I started.

"'Cause y'all don' want it to be."

"Shut up, Wilson. Just … shut up." I rubbed my head. "You know what time first formation is tomorrow?" He rolled his eyes. "Zero-seven," I stated bluntly.

"Don' y'all worry that sleepy lil' head o' y'all's, Mayer. It gon' be a quick night out. Only a couple o' drinks. Maybe we'll go see some titties, maybe y'all's gonna fall in love, I dunno."

"Yeah, a couple of drinks and the titty bar? I know how quick that always turns out. I could use a calendar to time your idea of a quick night out."

"Look, Mayer," he said, ducking to sit next to me on the bunk. He set the bottle of tobacco-steeped saliva between our feet. "We both know y'all's fightin' a losin' battle here." I shook my head and he squeezed my shoulder. "Y'all's gonna get compensated, y'all's gonna laugh, y'all's gonna cry, y'all's gonna have the time o' y'all's life, 'n then y'all's gonna get some sleep. 'N if ya stay here in the barracks, then what? Y'all's gonna sleep from now until first formation? That's, like, thirteen hours."

I knew any further arguing was just a delay in the inevitable. Sergeant Wilson wasn't a particularly clever man, but he was a brilliant leader. He was the kind of leader who could talk a coward into walking unarmed into a kill zone, or convince a group of sleep-deprived men to pull an all-nighter. He simply wouldn't quit, especially not now, with three other men already rounded up for the night. I might as well have been a child trying to stop a train with a penny.

"Or do I gotta give ya the team buildin' speech?" he asked, reaching under my bunk, removing my civilian shoes, and setting them on my lap with some reassuring pats.

I took a deep breath and rubbed my head. "Why on a Thursday, though?" I groaned.

"'Cause Thursday night's Splash Night," he said, referencing some promotional event of which I evidently should have been aware. He stood up from the bunk. "Now, hurry up. We're waitin' on y'all."

"Do we have to go to the strip club tonight? I really don't have the money to pay for a hard-on I can't use."

"Yeah, Mayer, we gotta. The only tits we gon' see on deployment is gon' be danglin' from under goats. Well, them 'n Sergeant Boone's. That sumpin' y'all's okay with? Ain't sumpin' I'm okay with. That man gotta holster them sum bitches. Ain't there sumpin' in AR 670-1 'bout titties 'n bras?" He made a performative shudder. "Anyway, these Montana titty bars are cheap as hell 'n full-nude. They wasn't like that at my last duty station," Wilson explained.

"They are, Sergeant?" The newbie asked.

"Well, this 'un is," Wilson answered.

"This the guy taking Sergeant Abbott's spot?" I nodded toward the unfamiliar face as I laced my shoes. We had been waiting on the injured Abbott's replacement for weeks, either by transfer or internal promotion. This appeared to be the former and also the latter.

"Tomorrow, 'ficially, but 'til then he's still just a specialist."

"I'm Rich, Sergeant," the newcomer said, offering me his hand to shake.

"Congratulations," I responded, still tying my shoes.

He thought for a moment, then clarified, "No, my name is Rich, Sergeant."

"I'll bet it is," I replied.

"Specialist Smallwood," Wilson corrected.

"Smallwood?" I asked. "That is rich." Smallwood retracted his hand.

"He's y'all's boy, Mayer," Wilson said. "Y'all get to train 'em."

"Yeah, I'll be doing ride-alongs with you in theater, Sergeant," Smallwood stated with enthusiasm.

"Really?" I asked aloud. I turned my attention from my shoes to Smallwood. "That's fucked up." Smallwood's face contorted in a moment of processing. "Well, Tiny Timber, I guess I'm your first-line leader." I looked him up and down. He stood tall and rigid in a t-shirt that struggled to contain his muscular figure. "How'd you score on your last gunner's exam?"

"Expert, Sergeant."

"Expert, huh?" He smiled in affirmation. "You think you're hot shit?"

"Uh, no, Sergeant. I don't."

"No? Then how the fuck are you getting promoted tomorrow?"

A look of perplexity twisted his face. "Um, I guess I am hot shit, then, Sergeant."

"Pretty full of yourself, big guy?"

"Uh ..." Smallwood turned to Wilson for help.

"C'mon, Mayer, y'all fuck with 'im on y'all's own time," Wilson said.

"Did Sergeant Wilson tell you why we're doing this?" I asked Smallwood as I pulled a shirt over my head.

"He said it's team building, Sergeant," Smallwood answered.

"How?" I asked with a stretch and a yawn.

"Um, something about shared experiences?"

I looked at Wilson. "This is my guy?"

"Baby bird's gotta eat. Y'all gotta feed 'im 'fore y'all push 'im outta the nest."

"Okay, let's get the fuck out of here," I told the group, motioning them forward. "Come on, Smallwood, we'll walk and talk."

"All right, Sergeant," Smallwood said.

"So, it's not just about having fun," I started.

Wilson turned. "Oh, we gon' have fun tonight!" he exclaimed while walking backward a few steps.

"Sure," I stated. "But, it's more about the importance of shared experiences. It's about developing trust, Smallwood. I can't trust you if I don't know you. I can't know you without shared experiences. You know what I mean?"

"Um, kind of, Sergeant."

"Huh? What do you mean, 'kind of?' Team cohesion is established through mutual trust. We don't work right as a team unless I can trust you have my back; unless I can trust you'll do your job when the shit is hitting the fan."

"Yeah, I get that, Sergeant," Smallwood said.

"Do you? You're not giving me a lot of confidence."

"Be the mama bird," Wilson reminded me.

"Look, man," I continued. "Yeah, we're going to have a good time tonight. We're also going to start learning each other's character and strengths and weaknesses and shit. That's the real skill of a leader: knowing and coordinating the strengths of the individuals that make up your team."

"And knowin' when to toss the weak bird outta the nest," Wilson added.

"Every soldier can be sculpted," Ko spoke up, correcting Wilson.

"Don't listen to him," I said to Smallwood. "Some guys are great out of uniform but fucking suck when they put it on. They can never be coached because they were never meant to wear it. Keep that in mind when you start doing counselings and eval reports."

"The worst part of getting your stripes," Ko said.

"Nah, it's havin' to be the eyes for the UAs," Wilson said, referencing the urinalyses that required sergeants to be the direct observers.

As we reached the barrack's exit, Perez veered toward a garbage can.

"Hold up," he choked. He braced his hands on the receptacle's rim and hovered over the mess of oily, used cleaning swabs it contained.

"Geez, is my tutoring that bad, Perez?" I asked.

"You all right, man?" Ko asked.

"Yeah," he exhaled. "Just felt like shit all day."

"Well, if it makes ya feel any better, ya look like shit, too," Wilson stated.

"You good to go out?" I asked not out of concern for his well-being, but more out of fear that he would vomit in my truck.

"We just gotta get ya some o' your people's drink, yeah? A little te-kill-ya to set ya right?" Wilson patted Perez on the back and then pulled him away from the bin. "C'mon, amigo, the señoritas are waitin'."

We left the barracks and made for the sidewalk through a strong fall breeze. Streams of dead leaves rattled past us with every gust, falling into place over a bed of dying grass like a dry, crispy quilt.

Across the street, Sergeant Hillman was overseeing a soldier raking a field of its leaves with a mop. We paused in admiration.

"I wish I had that kind of creative aptitude when it comes to smoking joes," Ko said.

Smallwood fixed his gaze on the absurd punishment and snickered.

"What the fuck are you laughing about, *Specialist*?" I asked, reminding him of rank. "You wanna join him?"

"Sorry, sergeant." He fixed his gaze on his feet.

"Sergeant," I echoed. "You see any rank on me right now?"

"No, Sergeant."

"That's because I'm not wearing a uniform. Stop calling me 'sergeant.' Damn, kid. It's like you're new here or something."

"I am new here. Like, to the unit, but also the infantry. I just heard you guys were kinda, like, hardasses, you know? Not that you're a hardass, Ser—, uh, Mayer." To this, the group murmured a collective mix of oohs and chuckles.

"Mayer? So, we're like drinking buddies now?"

"But, Sergeant, you just—"

"I'm just fucking with you, Smallwood." I put a hand on his shoulder. "I wouldn't want to scare away our designated driver."

"Bro," Perez groaned. "How much further? I'm really not feeling good."

"I'm parked by billeting but, Perez, if you throw up in my truck, I promise I will smack the shit out of you, sick or not," I warned.

"Just do a Captain Bochy," Ko advised, referencing a recent bumpy ride in a chinook during which an officer vomited into his own shirt.

"Fuck that," Perez moaned. "That shit was nasty. Ugh, I wanna throw up just thinking about it." He stopped to lean over the grass lining the sidewalk, hands planted above his knees.

"Ya gotta drink 'fore ya puke 'n rally, Lil' Mexico," Wilson teased.

Perez took a breath but only exhaled.

We resumed our pace, shuffling along a leaf-littered sidewalk on light feet. My stride always seemed lighter when rid of my boots. Hell, life itself seemed lighter when I donned my civvies.

We soon traded the crunch of dried leaves for the crunch of gravel as we cut through the parking lot. I unlocked the doors when we reached my truck and the group loaded into the front and back passenger seats, including Smallwood. He shut the backseat door he entered and I reopened it. He gave me a questioning look and I raised my hands in a questioning gesture.

"What are you doing? Get in the driver's seat," I directed him.

"I thought you were joking. I'm not driving," he said.

"Uh, yeah. Yeah, you are."

"I don't feel comfortable driving a truck this big," Smallwood stated.

A chuckle escaped my throat. "You've got an operator's permit, yeah?"

"Yes, Sergeant, but I was told that doesn't work for civilian vehicles."

"No, Smallwood. I mean, how did you get that permit?"

"Um, they printed it out over at the—"

"Stop. If I were to look at your damn operator's permit, you know what I would see?" I did not give him a chance to answer. "A list of big-ass, up-armored vehicles."

"Okay."

"Okay? So, get in the damn driver's seat."

"I ain't driving, and that's not really something you can make do."

"Somebody get behind the wheel. Like, damn, bro," Ko called out.

Wilson turned to me from the front passenger seat and raised his eyebrows. *Praise in public, punish in private,* he would tell me.

"Hey, let's chat outside of the truck for a minute." Smallwood sighed, unbuckled his seatbelt, and exited the truck. "You know what we're doing here, Smallwood?" I asked, once alongside the tailgate.

"Going out for drinks ... for, like, camaraderie?"

"No," I sighed. *He's playing dumb. Even in civvies, he won't put down the sham shield.*

I had to remind myself that I, too, once wore the specialist shield insignia, and that I, too, did my fair share of shamming.

"I mean, as a unit," I continued. "Here. In the mountains. We're training to go to war. We'll be in theater in a little over a month, which means I have just over a month to get to know you before we stage for our first mission. Just over a month. And what you're telling me is that the notion of driving a civilian truck down a stretch of paved highway in a first-world country makes you nervous. What you're telling me is that you're not combat ready."

"What? No—" Smallwood started.

"You tell 'im, buck sergeant," someone teased from inside the truck.

"So, I can't trust you to drive me to town and back in this," I gestured at my truck, "but I can trust you to drive me around a war-torn country on bomb-laden roads in a thirty-thousand pound, top-heavy, rollover-prone, up-armored vehicle?"

"I can drive it—"

"I know you can."

"But I don't want to, Sergeant."

"All right. Why?"

"Well, I thought tonight was about me, and I want to drink."

"Tonight is about us," I corrected. "Let's compromise; work it out like a team, yeah? One of us drives there, the other drives back."

"Can you drive there and I'll drive back?" Smallwood asked.

"Yeah, man." Here died my hopes of sleeping on the road. "Me there, you back. Compromise."

I directed Smallwood to take the middle of the rear bench to allow Perez a more immediate opportunity to vomit outside of the cab. I climbed into the driver's seat, turned over the engine, rolled the windows down for Perez, and made toward the lot's exit.

"Clear right?" I asked Wilson. He sat in the passenger seat next to me, staring out the window, entirely obstructing my view.

"Uh …" Wilson droned.

"Am I clear right or not?" I asked.

"What's with these jokers?" Ko asked. He sat behind Wilson similarly staring out the passenger side.

I was about to ask for clarity when three officers in ragged, filthy uniforms came sprinting past the truck and through the gravel lot. Their panicked gasps were barely audible through gas masks. Had they been lower enlisted soldiers, we would've brushed it off as a punitive exercise. However, the one rank I was able to identify was that of a colonel. And colonels were never subject to being smoked in public, or even in private to my knowledge.

"What the hell was that about?" I asked.

"I dunno," Wilson replied, "but let's get outta here 'fore we git involved. Clear right."

I drove to the nearest vehicle control point and maneuvered around the road barriers to exit the base.

"Ain't nobody in the VCP," Wilson said.

"Not our circus, not our monkeys," Ko said.

"How you holding up back there, Perez?" I asked.

"Ol' boy is passed the fuck out," Wilson chuckled, leaned over the center console.

"Wilson, why in fuck's name would you drag him out here, man? He's going to throw up in my truck."

"Oh, here she is. Ain't even made it to the bar yet 'n Mama Mayer has already flipped the switch to nanny mode. Relax, ma'am. Ain't gonna be no vomit in y'all's truck," Wilson said.

"Just like there wasn't going to be any chew all over my dashboard?"

"Hey, I cleaned that up."

"Hardly," I started.

"Ladies, please, calm down." Ko leaned into the front of the cab. "You'll wake Sleeping Beauty," he said, nodding toward the slumping figure behind me.

"Hey, slow down, Mayer," Wilson said. "Y'all's gonna miss the turn for The Wishing Well."

"They have a full bar at the strip club, right?" I asked.

"Uh, yeah," Wilson answered.

"Then, why do we need to go to The Wishing Well? You told me this was going to be a quick night out. So, I'm just following through on your promise."

"Mama Mayer strikes again," Wilson sighed. "Roll them windows up, it's too noisy."

I did. Wilson then leaned his seat back and joined the other three in a swift descent into slumber. Within minutes, I was the sole conscious being in the cab.

"Fuck me," I muttered.

· ∽ ·

In spite of all these miles, I still could not shake this feeling of unease. It latched on to me out of the gate like a stowaway. The officers running in gas masks. The empty VCP. The lack of traffic. Each of these things on their own were easily explained. It was a Thursday night in rural Montana. Of course there wouldn't be much traffic.

And if there was no traffic out here, there was no traffic in and out of the Fort. So, complacency probably got the better of the gate guard. And officers running sprints in gas masks? Well, every once in a while, the brass did some dumb, tough-guy shit to show everyone under their command that they could embrace the suck as much as anyone else. But the sum of these things added up to the feeling of something apocalyptic, made worse with every glance at Perez in the rearview mirror. Had he been infected with something? Some kind of apocalypse-triggering virus? Had we all? We did just receive another round of pre-deployment shots; unknown vaccinations to which we could offer no opposition. Perhaps I was driving a biological bomb into civilization.

I shook my head. These were the silly thoughts of a self-important man. My mind was as fatigued as my body, and my imagination was thus fully unrestrained. I shifted my attention to my driving.

The hum of the engine and rumble of the tires, the slow, deep, rhythmic breathing of sleep from beside and behind, the steady passing of street paint in headlights … line … after line …

I started to drift toward the shoulder of the road, corrected the truck, and shuffled in my seat to brighten my weary mind. I contemplated waking my passengers and reached for the stereo's power button but retracted. As much as I resented them for using me for my truck, and depriving me of sleep in the process, I felt the temporary tranquility I was granted in their slumber would be the high point of the evening. So, while they slept, I took in the mountainous panorama through which I drove.

Every military installation had some unique quality about it, whether in training, atmosphere, weather, or, in the case of Fort Sula—nestled so snugly in the Hell Gate Valley—its geography. Regardless of the location, however, there was one constant among each: they all had the same parasitic town feeding off the same financially irresponsible soldiers. Fort Sula's was Hell Gate, and its irresponsible soldiers were us. Yes, we knew we were prey, bled dry but ever-eager to feed the leech as it inveigled us with all of an infantryman's necessities: dive bars, casinos, car lots, tattoo parlors, pawn shops, and, most importantly, strip clubs.

This was my life. This was the life of prey. Did I need Hell Gate or did Hell Gate need me? Could my needs be met? Perhaps it was the uniformity. Perhaps it was the hours and hours of cleaning floors and toilets and weapons. Whatever the reason, I was as unfulfilled in uniform as I had been before enlisting. The Army had not—possibly could not—meet my needs. I was still nothing, nobody, and no one. Just another uniformed extra on the set of an unwatched movie.

· ∽ ·

We arrived at Peaks and Valleys in just under an hour, which was no easy feat, given how heavy my eyelids had grown. Peaks and Valleys shared a large parking lot with two other buildings: a hotel that catered to truckers and oil field workers, and a sex shop that catered to truckers and oil field workers. No other structure existed for miles in any direction. My eyes burned with fatigue as I traversed the empty lot to a spot nearest the entrance. Once parked, I looked around the cab, gazing upon my dozing passengers with jealous abhorrence.

"Wake up, assholes," I shouted. "We're here."

One by one, they roused themselves, wiping spittle from their chins and rubbing at dull eyes, save for Perez, who was slouched forward suspended by a locked seatbelt strap.

"Somebody wake up Perez," Ko yawned, "or he'll get all bitchy."

"I don't think he's waking up any time soon," Smallwood said as he shook Perez by the shoulder. "Maybe we should just leave him."

"No, we're not just leaving him. You guys head on in. I'll take care of him."

With Mama Mayer on the scene, Wilson, Ko, and Smallwood were able to depart without objection or even hesitation. As they entered, the rhythmic thumping of a bass-heavy song floated out of the entrance like the cool air of a refrigerator. I was reminded of my headache.

I opened the passenger door, leaned Perez against the seatback, and rubbed my knuckles into his sternum. He moaned and slapped my hand away.

"C'mon, Perez. Get out."

He did not.

A prickle of unease slid up my spine like fingers on guitar strings.

"Fuck it. I guess you get to sleep." I tried to sound uncaring, annoyed, but there was no masking my concern. I reached forward and felt his forehead. There was warmth, yes, but no apocalyptic heat. I was no medic, but if I had to guess (if I was being reasonable), it was likely he had too much sun and too little water. I would let him sleep. "Lucky bastard," I muttered. *When the car alarm goes off, we'll know he's awake.*

I entered the other side of the cab, unbuckled his seatbelt, and carefully laid him across the bench seat in as much the recovery position as space would allow.

"If you can hear me, know that you'll be paying for a professional detail if I catch even the faintest scent of piss, shit, or vomit." I softly shut the door into his head, reopened it, pushed him further in, and then shut the door fully. *Am I locking him in a truck, or sealing him in a tomb?*

With that, I went to join the others inside.

· ☙ ·

There were only a handful of strippers on duty this Thursday night. Not one possessed even a single alluring quality, but, much to my dismay, each was unduly confident in their bareness and physical aggression. Alluring or not, I made every attempt to enjoy both my situation and the services for which I paid. However, my capacity to endure the repelling atmosphere—the loud, brain-shaking, bass-heavy music, the repulsively filthy and worn furnishings, the greasy, obnoxious patrons—was wholly exhausted within the first hour. By the fifth hour, I was nearing a breakdown.

Was this really it? Was this what my life had come to? All night—all fucking night—throwing money at strippers and herding a crowd of drunks. *Be all you can be,* the Army had promised. Was this all I could be?

I once had aspirations—dreams, you could say. Not even that long ago, right before I first put on the uniform. But dreams were dreams because they were not reality. Perhaps I dreamed too big— dreamed of being a part of something too big. Always the bigger, better thing. I dreamed of being heard. More specifically, I dreamed of being sought out to be heard. It seemed so infantile now, these childish dreams. But how vigorously I chased them. So convinced was I that these dreams were achievable, that I started a band, and we practiced and rehearsed and performed with every bit the confidence of future stars. We never left the garage. We never made the right connections, never played for the right crowd on the right night. Simply put, we never became anything. As nobodies we started, as nobodies we ended. I often wondered how many Led Zeppelins and Nirvanas had been left unborn by obscurity, or worse, apathy? All I wanted was to be heard. Was that so large a dream it could not be birthed into reality?

When the band fell apart, I felt small. Never had I felt so small. *Be all you can be.*

Never had a decision been easier. But even after donning the uniform, being a cog in the most powerful machine mankind had ever known, I still felt lacking. I was expendable at a time when I needed to be needed. I suppose that was why I bought the truck, and why I always conceded to these group outings. They needed me. And I needed that.

We sat side-by-side at the tip rail throughout the night, splitting up at times only for private dances; that was except for Smallwood, who had wandered off solo hours ago. Wilson, Ko, and I had all dived into the depths of drunkenness early on, and while Ko and I resurfaced hours ago, Wilson remained ever-drowning in inebriation. When it came to alcohol, Wilson lacked both time management and financial discipline. The latter was especially evident as Ko and I rejoined him at the tip rail after a trip to the truck to check on a still-sleeping Perez. Wilson flung a wad of dollar bills at a stripper who was forcefully providing him a close-up of her c-section scar.

"Let's get out of here," I called out to Wilson over the music once he had been released from the stripper's gripping legs.

"Y'all jus' can' have a good time, can ya?" He slurred. No one's drunken stupor was as vexing as Wilson's. I loathed drunk Wilson. Drunk Wilson's slurred drawl was every bit as unintelligible as the depraved ramblings of a crack-addicted lunatic.

"No, Wilson. We *had* a good time," I explained. "But we've been looking at the same tits for hours and we haven't had anything to eat all night. Can we be done, now, please?"

"Where's Smallwood?" Ko asked.

"Lemme tell ya sumpin' real quick," Wilson motioned for us to sit next to him, as though he were a grandfather gathering his grand-children for an old tale.

"If I let you tell me whatever insane shit is fluttering around in your head right now, will you help us find Smallwood and get the fuck out of here?" I asked.

"Thiz one time, me 'n muh buddies wuz-a huntin', right? 'N we done put down 'tween us 'bout a rack-a cold 'uns 'n 'bout a other rack-a warm 'uns, right?"

"Will this story have a point or are you stalling until Mom here finishes her song?"

"S-shut up, Mayer," Wilson grunted. "So, we wuz-a swervin' a lil' on the way home—"

"As one tends to do when they're pants-on-head drunk," Ko cut in.

"Y'all gon' lemme tell it?" He searched for his mental bookmark. "'N we done hit us one-a them, uh, whatcha call 'ums ... pork-you-pines."

"Why are you telling us this, Wilson? Just tell us where Smallwood is, please," I implored.

"I'm gettin' there, I'm gettin' there." He gave Ko a slow and overly exaggerated wink.

"Oh my God. I will drag you out of here if I have to, Wilson," I threatened.

"So, we done pulled over to check the tires, ya know? 'N that's when I seen the pork-you-pine wuz still mostly good. So, I puts 'em in the coola, 'n when we gets back, I puts 'em in the garage. 'N when I opened the lid, that lil' fella look like he wuz-a chillin' in a hot tub. 'Cept it wuz full o' ice. So, I sits him in a corner 'n I propped his lil' elbows up, 'n I taped a beer to his belly ..." He suppressed a giggle. "'N he look jus' like a lil' people."

I watched him giggle for a moment, attempting to absorb the ill-articulated information I was just provided.

"So, instead of answering my question about Smallwood's whereabouts, you tell me about how you and your toothless colleagues ran over a porcupine and then mutilated its body for your entertainment?"

He burst into laughter. "Yep. 'Til he stunk so awful I throwed 'im away."

I crossed my arms and ground my teeth as I watched him double over in laughter.

"What—" I started.

"But that ain't the point," Wilson informed us.

"Oh, gosh, I was hoping there was more," Ko said.

"Only one of muh buddies got a kick outta it."

"Why? Was the other one sane?" I asked.

"Nah. He wan't there. 'Cause his ass wuz still out in the woods. Wandered off by hisself like an asshole, had to walk home by hisself like an asshole. That the moral of the story: act like a asshole, miss out on the pork-you-pine."

"What an enlightening parable, Wilson," I said. He bowed in his seat and nearly fell forward. "So, your suggestion, as I understand it, is to leave and let our DD walk over fifty miles back to the barracks?"

"That his pork-you-pine," Wilson stated simply. "He been a ass-hole all night."

"There he is," Ko said, pointing toward a doorway in the rear with a glowing sign overhead that read, "Champagne Room."

Smallwood moved toward us with a cool gait. A broad smirk— one emblematic of some great triumph—was smeared across his face, dripping conceit onto his proud, puffed chest.

"Ooh, somebody got their willy wet," Wilson cheered. Small-wood's smirk glowed brighter.

"That true, Peckerwood?" I asked.

"Hell, yeah," he replied, nodding.

I shook my head. "Did you at least use a condom?"

"I can't."

"Why the hell not?"

"Then I don't feel anything," he answered.

"You dumb bastard. Oh, you dumb bastard," Ko tittered.

"What?" Smallwood asked. "She can get an abortion. God knows she's got the cash for it."

"Okay, maybe, but that's only, like, one of your problems. This is a truckstop strip club, my guy," Ko stated.

"So?" Smallwood asked.

"So, I wouldn't touch anything in here with his dick," I said, pointing at Wilson. "And there's a lot of shit I'd touch with that dirty pecker."

"Here, I got sumpin' for ya, Mayer," Wilson said, reaching into his pocket. He then removed an extended middle finger.

I turned back to Smallwood. "What Ko's getting at is that you're getting rodded off the range tomorrow."

"What does that mean?" he asked.

There was a round of mischievous chuckles.

"What does that mean?" Concern had melted his victor's smirk from his face.

"Well, my ignorant, reckless friend," I said, putting an arm around his shoulders. "Tomorrow morning, you'll be pissing fire. And, like any frightened soldier in anguish, you'll go begging the medic for help. And he's going to send you right to the TMC."

"TMC?"

"The clinic," Ko answered.

"Now, the medic has to inform your team leader, me, of your whereabouts," I continued. "And I'm going to inform my first-line leader. So, needless to say, everyone's going to find out about your raw-dogging exploits. And, needless to say, you're going to get the shit smoked out of you when you get back from the TMC."

"That's it?" Relief refueled his smirk.

"Oh, no," I chuckled. "The nurses at the TMC are going to have their fun with you, too. You know when you're leaving the firing range and you gotta have your weapon cleared by running a rod down the bore and into the firing chamber?"

"Yeah …" Some understanding bled into his voice.

"Well, they're going to take a Q-tip and rod you off the range." He stood in silence, unwilling to comprehend my statement.

"They're going to shove a stick up your pee-hole, dude," Ko clarified. "You know, to get a tissue sample from your urethra, stud."

He clutched his crotch. "Well, can't I just piss in a cup?"

I laughed. "Of course you could. But we're all about teaching you lessons. And how are you going to learn if you just pee in a cup?"

He chuckled in nervousness. "That's not really how they do it, is it, guys?"

"Gotta learn somehow, horndog." Ko said with pity.

"You guys are fucking with me, right?" he asked.

"Y'all better believe 'em," Wilson said. "They got plenty experience with it."

"Yeah, this guy," Ko gestured toward me with a thumb, "had herpes so bad he was nicknamed 'Thunderclap.'"

"I don't know how many times I have to tell you assholes," I said. "That was an ingrown hair."

"That wuz the herp, bud," Wilson stated.

"You know what?" I pulled Wilson out of his seat. "Now, you don't get to finish your beer. How about that?" Wilson struggled a moment, reaching for his glass, but went limp once Ko helped in his restraint. We were only halfway into the parking lot when Wilson lost consciousness and had only just reached the truck when he lost control of his bowels. Ko retched.

"Smallwood, help us out here. Open the door," Ko directed through chokes.

"No-no-no, not the cab, for God's sake, no," I begged.

"Where, then?" Ko asked.

"In the bed," I stated.

"Really?"

"Yeah, really. This'll be his missed porcupine or whatever."

"You're cold-blooded, Mayer," Ko said.

"Is this what you want to be smelling for the next hour? Up or down, those windows won't make a difference."

Ko considered this for a moment. "Smallwood, drop the tailgate," he instructed.

Smallwood fumbled with the latch but followed through, then aided Ko and I in loading Wilson like a shit-soaked, rolled up rug on its way to the landfill.

"Help me move some of this gear around so he stays on his side," I said.

"What if he wakes up?" Ko asked.

I lifted Wilson's head by his hair and dropped it onto the truck bed with a light *thud*. "Yeah, no, that won't be a problem. He'll be fine with the tonneau cover. And tomorrow," I raised my voice at the limp body, "you can hose out the back of my truck, you dirty pain in the dick." I turned my attention to Smallwood, ready to toss him the keys to the truck but paused. He appeared to be swaying.

"Let's roll," Ko said.

"Ko, can you check on Perez real quick? I gotta chat with Smallwood." Ko jumped down from the truck bed and went to the cab while I made to sit on the tailgate.

"What's up?" Smallwood asked. He spoke in a tone that suggested he knew damn well what was up.

"You tell me, Smallwood. You look like you're drunk." Anger, nausea, and fatigue were fighting for control of my mind.

"I mean, I've set back a few but I wouldn't say I'm shitfaced."

"Smallwood, you were supposed to be our DD. We agreed on this before leaving post."

"We've been here for *hours*," Smallwood said with a hint of anger of his own, "celebrating *me*. And, what, I wasn't supposed to have any kind of fun?"

"You weren't supposed to have any kind of *alcohol*, you asshole." Smallwood began to clench a fist at this. "You fucked us. What—"

A hand gripped my shoulder. "Hey, dog, how about you just let me drive?" Perez asked. He stood beside the tailgate upright and healthy.

"See?" Smallwood said, still clenching his fist. "You're making a big deal for nothing."

Praise in public, punish in private. Assuredly, there could be no positive conclusion in continuing this discourse with Smallwood. Not in the parking lot of a strip club while intoxicated. It would have to wait for tomorrow; cleaned up, sober, and in uniform.

"Get in the truck," I commanded.

I handed the keys to Perez, slammed the tailgate shut (*sorry, Wilson, Mama's a little upset*), and joined Perez in the front with Ko and Smallwood situated behind us.

"Damn, bro, do you even got enough gas to get to the gas station?" Perez asked once he started the truck.

"Only one way to find out. Best not to sit here idling."

"I feel, like, way better, by the way. Thanks for asking." Perez drove us out of the lot and onto the highway.

"No one was asking, Perez," Ko said from behind.

"Yeah, no shit. I was being, uh ..."

"Facetious?" I asked.

"Yeah. You guys don't give a shit about me. You're all in there, drinking, and looking at titties, and shit. And you left me in the truck."

"Oh, please, Perez," Ko moaned. "We tried to wake you up."

"Not only that, but we constantly checked on you," I added.

"Well, like, twice," Ko said.

"Whatever," Perez said. "You guys owe me."

"For what? Letting you sleep?" I asked. "Well, forgive me."

"No, for being the DD."

There was a moment of silence. Smallwood shifted in his seat.

"Wait, I just realized something," I said, hoping to break the tension. "What did you say your first name was, Smallwood?"

"Rich," he answered.

"Yeah, Richard," I said.

"Rich," he corrected.

"So, your parents named you Dick Smallwood?" Ko and Perez laughed but Smallwood remained ever-stoic.

"You know what?" Smallwood asked. "Fuck you, Mayer."

We were silent once more.

· ❧ ·

I awoke roughly forty-five minutes later as Perez was shutting down the truck's engine.

"Are we already on post?" I grumbled. A terrible nausea was welling in the pit of my stomach and dizziness enveloped my head.

"Not yet," Perez answered.

"Then why are we stopped?"

"'Cause you're out of gas, dummy."

"Oh, yeah. That's right."

I stepped out of the truck and stretched. Ko was asleep, head leaned crookedly against the window. Smallwood was awake, casting side glances at me through his window. On the other side of the truck, Perez was removing the gas cap.

"Premium, Perez," I called out.

"Motherfucker. 'Premium,'" he mimicked. "You're getting a free tank of gas," he explained, removing the nozzle and selecting the standard option.

"Dude …."

"Fucking premium, man. You're running a twenty gallon tank and you think you're getting premium." He looked over his shoulder for a moment and then back at me. "Tell you what: I'll get you premium if you get me a drink. I'm thirsty as fuck, dog."

I looked across the street to the dull glow of a buzzing sign. *The Wishing Well*.

"C'mon, Perez. We've been out all night."

"*You've* been out all night," he corrected me. "Drinking. I haven't even had water since we left the barracks."

"Come on, Perez, don't be like that."

"You want seventy dollars in premium, or fifteen in standard?"

I exhaled a long and heavy groan. "One drink?"

"Just the one."

"Non-alcoholic?"

"Dog … You know I'm good to drive with just one drink."

I paused. "All right, fill 'er up," I said, shaking my head. Given the emptiness of the lot and the late hour, I was sure the building was either closed or closing.

The truck now filled, we made our way to The Wishing Well.

· ↻ ·

"One drink," I reminded Perez as we exited the truck. "The same goes for you, Smallwood. We're not going to be out here all night." He followed but did not respond.

I was desperate to be back at the quiet calmness of the barracks. Like a small snack could awaken a large hunger, the nap on the road from the strip club only reminded my body how depleted it was. My head was aching. My stomach, though full of booze, bile, and queasiness, was hungry. If I was lucky, The Wishing Well had a kitchen.

If I was very lucky, the kitchen was either still open or at least had something left over to settle my stomach.

As we neared the entrance, I could hear the thumping of a strong subwoofer and the ache in my head pulsed, quickly outgrowing my skull. Above us, the building's sign glowed, its buzz playing off my throbbing head, rattling against my eardrums like hail on shingles.

"You good?" Perez asked.

"Yeah, let's just get inside already." I opened the door and waded into the roaring ambience within.

Inside, The Wishing Well was alive; a shocking contrast to the emptiness of the parking lot. We made our way to the bar and took a couple of stools, Perez and I side-by-side, Smallwood at another opening further down the bar top. I scanned the shelves and tap handles. Though a large selection of liquors and beers were available, only one was being advertised: Whet. I did not recognize the name and was not interested in broadening my palate at the moment. I needed a glass of water and a pain killer. *And maybe some bread*, I thought, looking around for a kitchen.

We sat at the bar top unattended for several, several growing minutes before Perez spoke up. "This bitch is old and slow as fuck, bro," he complained.

I looked down the bar at the tired, elderly woman tending the bar. I had mostly kept my gaze down to shield my eyes from the overhead lighting and glowing signs, and thus had not yet observed her work. Presently, she was serving a crowd of four a round of shots. The woman was meticulous in her task and indeed slow—horridly so. When she at last filled the final shot glass, I beckoned her our way with an extended hand. She started toward us and then turned wildly back to the four she had just served. She hit her forehead with the heel of her hand and giggled as recollection shot into her mind like an arrow. She asked one of the patrons for his credit card and proceeded to run their charges through a computer with all the speed and finesse of a moss-covered stone. Her unhurried demeanor seemed to further fuel my migraine.

"Holy fucking shit," I exclaimed.

"For real, bro. Like, don't give her a card. The only machines she's used to are for dialysis," Perez stated. "Hey, I'm going to the latrine real quick. If you get to her before death does, can you hook me up with, like, anything on tap? I really don't give a shit as long as it's not an IPA."

"Yeah, I guess." I waved him off and again studied the tap handles. I then caught the glow of one of the signs from behind the bar top reflecting from a pool of water that must have been the bar's so-called wishing well. For how lively the bar was, the well's water was disturbingly serene. It seemed utterly unaffected even by the music's bass that reverberated through my chest. The tranquility was transfixing. It almost seemed to ease my mind …

"I've been waiting for you all night." The slow voice broke my entrancement. I looked up at the wrinkle-enshrouded gaze of the bartender. "Here," she croaked, sliding a half-full plastic cup toward me across the sticky bar top.

I picked it up and examined it with heavy skepticism. *Did she just hand me someone's half-finished drink?*

"What's this?" I asked.

"It's what you need, honey," she stated like a concerned grandmother addressing a flu-stricken grandchild. "A taste of desire."

I glanced back up at the advertisements decorating the walls. *How do you spell desire?* I read. *W-H-E-T.* I looked back at the pale brew in my hand and then to the bartender once more. The only thing I *needed* was a cold glass of water but the unsettling gaze of the expectant bartender motivated me to humor her. Besides, Perez was driving.

I threw the cup and my head back and downed the brew. As the salty warmth rushed to the back of my throat, I recalled gargling salt-water. My mother would warm a glass of saltwater for me to gargle before every session in the garage. It was supposed to soothe my vocal cords. But this wasn't a garage session. I was on stage—an actual stage!—reaching my fingertips forward, mirroring the outstretched hands of a crowd. *Ow!* A prick. I retracted my hand. No longer was I surrounded by fans, but by cacti, arms forever raised in statuesque rocker's poses, bodies planted firmly in dirt and sand as dry as—

As dry as this cup.

"What's your wish tonight, hon?" The bartender's voice again snapped reality into focus.

"Huh?" I cleared my throat. "Um, how much would a glass of this run me?" If a warm half-cup was so oddly comforting, a cold, full glass would be exceptional.

"Oh, honey," she chuckled. "If this is your first time getting Whet, it's on us. The first one's always on us." Her tone suggested I should have been aware of the fact. "But the next will cost you."

She turned to the tap handles and began pouring a glass of Whet. Again, she dawdled, and again, I was overcome with aggravation. Except this time it was not her lack of speed that antagonized me so; it was my being without that feeling, that … Whet feeling. I needed it. This drink would be the redeeming factor of the night—the highlight of the week, even. But this saggy corpse masquerading as a bartender was nothing more than a hindrance. My hands started to shake.

"Oh, shoot," she muttered. "Too much head." She began tilting the glass in an attempt to clear the thick layer of froth that crowned it. Beer was spilling violently over her bony hands.

"It's fine," I called out. "Just give it to me."

She brought the dripping glass to me and I snatched it from her grip. I raised the foamy lip to my nose and inhaled before drawing in a few quick gulps.

Sawdust. I could smell the sawdust in my father's garage. The bar's crowd and music were immediately muted by a passing car from outside the open garage door. I strummed a guitar. I could feel the steel strings biting into my fingertips. My lips brushed, not foam, but a microphone. Suddenly, I was no longer in my father's garage. I was sitting atop a stool in front of a cheering crowd. I was playing center stage in my high school auditorium. I was living a missed opportunity. No, not quite. I was *reliving* a missed opportunity. No, more than that! This was real, a remembrance of actuality. I was being heard when no one had listened to me. And I was great, I really was. I was getting my big break. Never before had I had an audience. Yet, there they were, within view, within reach. I was being soaked by waves of roars; a rising—no, a receding tide. Roaring cheers were becoming groans of a disgruntled, pained mob. A rising heat. All around me the stage was aflame. The very audience was aflame, eyes still locked on me, taking my image into their dying memories as though I were to blame. The very air was burning, drying out like the glass in my hand. The glass was empty. The obnoxious thumping of a bass-heavy song came flooding back with a deafening force.

"So, what's your wish tonight, hon?" There was contempt in that croak.

Again, that request. She was like an old parrot. Was that dictated by management? Was that how the staff asked for your order in The Wishing Well?

"I need another." A simple answer for a simple question. I held the glass toward her. It was disgustingly light. She did not move. Her wrinkly gaze stayed fixed on me. "Please, ma'am," I added.

She smiled. "Music to my ears. I've got a feeling about you," she said, wagging a finger at me.

"What?" A strong buzz accompanied my throbbing headache.

Was I getting drunk again? Surely not this drunk off a single beer.

She leaned toward me over the beer-speckled bar top. Her pupils grew; like the damned music that thump-thump-thumped, they did not stop growing. Our eyes held. Her pupils dilated, now encompassing … everything.

"What," she pressed, "is your wish." Each syllable was articulated with an unnerving meticulousness. Each word poured over bleeding gums and rode a sour breath that clouded my head. Her nose and cheek twitched as though they were a levee on the verge of collapsing in a storm of rage. I felt ill. But I also felt an uncontrollable urge to speak.

Was there enough time left in what remained of my life to answer a question so vast it contained every possible past, present, and future? What was my wish? Everything. Everything, because nothing was ever enough. I wanted—*needed*—to be a part of something bigger. I *needed* to be looked at exceptionally—to be exceptional. (*Be all you can be.*)

"To be heard," I whispered. Her face grew unfocused through beads of tears.

A slow, raspy chortle crawled out of her throat. "You want an audience."

"Yes," I cried. "Oh, God, yes. To be heard. To be needed. To be a part of something big—something bigger. No, the biggest thing!"

She leaned away from me and the whites returned to her eyes. "Well, why didn't you say so, hon?" She fetched a coin from her pocket and set it in the palm of my quivering hand. I squinted at its brilliant shine and glanced back at her. "Well, what are you looking at me for, honey. You know what to do."

The bartender stepped to the side, leaving the glassy surface of the well's pool unobscured. I flicked the coin into the pool, where it sank to its resting place alongside a handful of other glistening wishes.

"Thank you," I choked.

There was a round of laughter and whoops. I turned around and saw a shoeless, pantsless Perez walking toward me. His face was painted a bright red indignation.

"Let's get the fuck out of here," he growled.

"What the hell happened?" I was swimming in a subdued daze. I was unsure to whom the question was directed.

"That fucking bitch—" He was interrupted by a flash from a nearby phone. He pulled me from the stool by the shoulder. "C'mon, bro, let's get the fuck out of here." He held his middle fingers up to the applauding crowd as we exited the bar.

"What happened in there?" I asked once we entered the parking lot. My fog of insensibility was dissipating into the cool, night air.

"I took this little cunt into the latrine 'cause I was gonna fuck her, you know? And we're in one of the stalls and I got my pants off and shit. And she asks if I got a condom and I'm like, 'Yeah, it's in my pants.' And she goes looking for it and must've felt my wallet and phone and shit 'cause she just turns and books it with my pants. So, I grabbed her by the hair and she starts screaming, 'Rape!' And this fucking asshole turns around from the urinal, mid-stream, bro, dick swinging, pissing all over the floor and my feet and shit and punches me right in the face."

"Dude," I exclaimed.

"So, Teenie Weenie over there," Perez gestured at Smallwood, who was following at a distance, "comes busting in, probably 'cause he heard this bitch screaming. She starts to run out the door with my pants and I'm beating the hell out of this drunk fucker who helped her and yelling at Muscles McGee to stop her. He sees me rolling around on the pissy floor with this dude and then just goes to the urinal to start pissing. That's when the bouncer and some other guy come in and pull me away. And here I am."

I looked at Smallwood, who said nothing, and then back at Perez. "Fuck, man. Well, I've got some PT shorts in my gym bag if you want them."

"Yeah, all right. Thanks, bro."

"So, all that shit went down while I was ordering drinks?" I asked as we walked toward the truck.

"Huh?"

"You were only gone a few minutes."

"Nah, man. We were in there way longer than that," Perez chuckled.

"What? I barely had a drink before you lost your pants, Perez."

"Mayer," he said with humor now totally faded. "You were sitting at the bar just totally fuckin' zoned out, dog."

"Huh ..." I didn't refute this. Perhaps it was the sleep deprivation or ounce after countless ounce of alcohol or both, but I was having a hard time remembering much of anything between entering and leaving the bar.

I dropped the tailgate, checked on Wilson, who, though still unconscious, seemed to be fine. At least, he was alive and breathing. Though he did not smell like it. I quickly removed the physical training shorts, leaned away to take a breath of clean air, then sealed the truck bed once again. I passed the shorts to Perez, who squeezed into them hurriedly.

"Dog, I didn't know the Army made these in kid sizes." He stopped and examined my face. "What's with you? Your eyes are all red and puffy like you been crying and shit."

"You know what? We don't talk about me, I won't talk about you," I offered. "You still good to drive?"

"Yeah, but I don't got my wallet, bro."

"Then don't get pulled over, bro."

"Yeah, but, like, how am I gonna get on post?"

"We'll figure it out when we get there, I guess. Just stop before the turn and I'll swap you out. You can ride with Poopy Pants in the back."

I gestured at Smallwood to enter the truck and we departed.

· ∽ ·

Perez shook me awake. I straightened in my seat and found that we were once again in the gravel parking lot near the billeting office.

"They didn't check our IDs at the V-she—veep … VCP?" I asked.

"There wasn't nobody there," Perez stated.

"Huh. Well, let's grow inside. We have to get up in …" I toggled the backlight on my watch. "Three hours? Oh, son of a bitch."

Perez woke Ko and we all exited the vehicle, gathering around the tailgate.

"Think he'll be mad you guys just threw him in the truck bed?" Perez asked.

"Oh, please," I said. "We *slid* him into the turk bred."

"We tossed him back there like a sack of shit, dude," Ko said. "Also, why are you in PT shorts?" he asked Perez. "You piss your pants?"

"No!" Perez raised his voice. I shushed him. He lowered his voice and continued, "No, dog, somebody else pissed my pants." A round of hushed laughter. "No, bro, for real. This guy was pissing on me in the latrine and then, like, we were on the floor in all the piss—"

"Yo," Ko chuckled. "I told you guys. I told you he was gay."

"Fuck outta here," Perez said, pushing Ko with one hand. "We were fighting, bro."

"Oh, shit, I'm sorry it didn't work out," Ko said, feigning concern.

"Will you two just help me get shithead outta here," I said, dropping the tailgate. I held my breath. We were promptly engulfed by Wilson's fetid reek. Ko gagged, Perez coughed.

"No fucking way am I carrying him into the barracks," Ko said. "We gotta hose him down."

I pulled him so his legs dangled from the tailgate. His pants appeared to be soaked with a combination of urine and liquor-fueled diarrhea. Ko retched.

"Leave 'em," I gagged. I took a few unsteady steps back from the wretched smell wafting from the opening.

"All night?" Perez asked.

"'All night?' It's only a gubble hours to sunrise," I said. "And, yeah, if he gets gold—cold enough befloor—b-before then, he can find his own way back. I'm done babyshitting tonight."

We left Wilson on an open tailgate and made our way for the barracks. The wind had grown in strength since our departure, and the waves of fallen, dead leaves that accompanied it splashed all around us. It added to my drunken vertigo and I found myself stumbling into the grass several times before reaching the entrance to the barracks.

"You guys go ahead and head on in," I said to Ko and Perez. "Somali … *Smallgood* and I need to chat."

"Not interested," Smallwood stated.

I blocked his ingress. "I don't care. I've got somethin' to say and you're gonna listen."

"Geez, now I see why they call you 'Mama Mayer.'"

"You're really pissing me off, Small-guy." I took a deep breath. Wilson had warned me about moments like these. As much as I struggled with him when he was out of uniform, as incoherent and senseless as he was when drunk, Wilson was a sage soldier, and his guidance always surfaced in troubled waters.

Y'all know why we call each other "battle buddies" even when we ain't in combat? he had once asked me. *It's 'cause everybody got a battle they fightin'. Y'all never know what's goin' on up here.* He had tapped his head. *'Member that. 'Cause ya ain't no buddy if y'all forget, just a nobody.*

"Sorry, man," I apologized. "Look, tonight … this morning—tomorrow or however the hell you wanna look at it, you're still Specalist Small. By the end of the day, when you get those stripes punched into your chest, you'll be Chargin', uh, Smar, ahem, Sergeant Wood. And you know what? Not much is gonna change. And that's because it'll be up to you to becomes a bleeder, ugh, leader, to listen to others, hear what they gotta say, and to just be a butter man, y'know? I dunno you. But from what I seen so far, you," I shoved a finger toward him, which he batted away in irritation, "got a bad attitude and an in-indy, hmm, indecisional … in-di-vi-dual-ristic mindshet." I paused, swaying. "*You* only think about *you*."

"Can I go to bed now?"

"Slur, man—sure. But ash yourself this when you glide—lie down: is this who you wanna be? To us, the guys coverin' your ass when we're in the shit? To yourself?"

He said nothing. Then it dawned on me, in all my drunken reasoning, that Smallwood had been transferred to our unit, with deployment imminent, not to replace Sergeant Abbott, but so that the sending party could be rid of him.

When the trash stinks too bad for my bin, I'll just dump it in my neighbor's. Right before collection …

Smallwood pushed past me and entered the barracks. I gave him space and then followed.

· ∽ ·

We found our respective bunks with some minor stumbling about and slipping. The bay floor was wet in several spots, suggesting it had rained in our absence. The ceiling tended to drip and we usually placed the mop buckets under the heaviest leaks to add to the water we used to clean in the mornings. I shed only my shoes and socks and fell onto my bunk with great relief. Much like the bar, the bay was lively tonight. Numerous gurgled snores reverberated about the bunks, as did several dripping leaks. I listened intently. It did sound as if it was raining. Although, we weren't supposed to see rain all week.

Shut up, I told myself in thought. No matter the intensity of my fatigue, my mind always raced when I set head to pillow. Anywhere but bed, and sleep would put me down like an ungloved boxer. *I just need to focus on something,* I thought. I fixed my mind on my hearing once more and listened as the other three joined the rest of the platoon in rest.

Outside, I heard the pitter-patter of an erroneous weather prediction. Inside, the ensuing drip steadied on. *Splish-splosh, splish-splosh.* It was like a metronome, or, rather, the tapping of a conductor's baton. The orchestra began tuning. A fart here, a cough there, a couple of moans and gurgles and creaking bed frames, some shuffling of sheets amidst a series of beer burps and congested snorts. This slowed into a brief period of silence as the dripping droned on. Then, a slight crescendo of gurgling snores filled the musky air and the room began to spin. I set a bare foot on the cold, polished floor to reorient myself, but to no avail.

The spins were setting in and nausea was spreading from the depths of my stomach, leaving me with two options: a preemptive trip to the latrine for a splash of cold water and a quick prayer to the porcelain god; or, I could chase a few minutes of sleep and risk vomiting on my bunk. I spent a moment weighing the options. Getting up now would mean putting on my shoes. Even in my somewhat drunken state, the threats of foot fungus and MRSA persisted in my mind, and the idea of running into the latrine barefoot only fueled my nausea.

I sat up, nearly falling head first off my bunk, and felt around for my shoes, instead finding my boots. I hurriedly slid my sockless feet into the cold footwear. They were still sweaty from yesterday's overnight training. I paused and burped a spot of acid into my throat. Using the bunk above, I pulled myself up and made my way to the latrine door. A few unbalanced steps into the arduous journey brought me to another unseen puddle. My heel slid forward and I threw my arms up, paddling through the air. By some miracle, I was able to recover and pushed the door open to the latrine. I shielded my eyes against the blinding fluorescence and leaned onto the nearest sink, moaning into its drain like a microphone. I ran a heavy stream of cold water over my hands and splashed my face. I rubbed my eyes free of water and raised my face to the mirror to observe my piteous condition. I strained my eyes to regain some facet of clarity, and then I noticed the reflection of a soldier sitting up against the wall behind me. He appeared to be huddled up with some kind of animal.

"Wegner," I rasped, pausing to stifle a retch. "I fucking s-square, ugh, swear, if you brought that dog in here again ..."

As I turned to face him, I became aware of how red the latrine seemed. I shook and blinked more clarity into my vision and was finally able to process my newfound perception. The walls, the floor, and even parts of the ceiling had been doused with gore. Wegner's shredded uniform was saturated with blood. He seemed unable to move save for his darting eyes. He gurgled something incomprehensible and shot his gaze down to the creature on his lap. The thing seemed to have the body of a large fox and a curled, multi-jointed tail that ended in a poised stinger like that of a scorpion. Its bat-like ears sat erect atop an eyeless head, twisting to focus on me. Its face, like a vampire bat, was clamped on Wegner's thigh and it appeared to be draining him like an unweaned pup. The creature braced its paws, shook its head, and pulled itself free from Wegner's leg, tearing away strands of dripping flesh in the process. It oriented its head in my direction, mouth agape, stretching several strands of scarlet saliva along a handful of barbed teeth that curved toward its throat. It seemed to be listening to me. A set of palps unfolded from under the creature's blood-matted chin. They stretched and danced along Wegner's body. It then fixed its maw upon Wegner's other leg, on the inner-thigh, just below his groin. Wegner gurgled a groan.

I stood rigid in disbelief. The icy vines of fear spread across my back, creeping up and down my spine like a thriving ivy. I tried for minutes to break loose from Wegner's shaking eyes before finding success. I unrooted my feet and opened the latrine door. I felt along the wall beside the door frame and flipped the bay lights. Like the latrine, the bay was covered in gore. Puddles of blood were formed all about beneath dripping limbs that hung from the sides of bunks. Bloody shoe prints were tracked to and fro, likely from us four recently returned. A few bodies were strewn about the floor in odd positions. On initial glance, more than a dozen creatures were attached to gurgling soldiers. I walked out into the bay, stepping over splotches and puddles of blood. I trod on slow, light feet, and examined every horrific scene.

"Turn off the lights," Perez called out. Three of the creatures, still feeding, tilted their heads to train their ears on the noise. One of them pried itself like velcro from the flesh of a nearby body and slinked toward him. "Hey!" Perez shouted. He sat up. "Lights! Turn 'em off!"

Shut up! I screamed the words in my mind.

Perez removed his beanie, which had been pulled low over his eyes like a blindfold. Exasperation evaporated from his face, leaving shock and perplexity in its stead. He swung his legs over the side of his bunk to stand and was met with one of the creatures. Before he could react, before any cogs were able to turn in the gears of his mind, the silent stalker shot its tail forward, thrusting its stinger into his chest. He stood with a sharp gasp and the creature dangled from him. He reached for the stinger and his body seized, collapsing to the floor. He writhed a moment, as every muscle in his body bulged and tightened. Then he was utterly still. The creature detached its tail and began running its palps along different areas of his body. It stopped when it reached his inner thigh. The creature fastened its bite and it drank, all the while Perez watched on, grunting with constricted lungs.

I looked for Smallwood and Ko. I couldn't let the same fate befall them. Smallwood was nearest me, and so I moved in silence to his bunk. The expedition was brutally slow-paced. A creature was latched onto the leg of his bunkmate above him. Smallwood's hand began to twitch and his eyes rolled beneath their lids as he entered REM sleep. My heart labored in anticipation. I could feel its rhythm in my skull. Two beasts had torn loose from their meals and were slinking my way, freezing every other step to listen. I halted and still they pressed on. Their ears twitched with each break in their advance, the twitching synced with the pulse in my head.

They could hear my heartbeat.

I stepped quickly to Smallwood's side. With great restraint and adrenaline-drenched hands, I nudged him and eased him free of sleep's embrace. I kept a single palm placed firmly over his mouth. I looked back. The creatures were a mere meter from me. I snatched Smallwood's phone from its charging cord and flung it across the bay. It clattered near the front entrance. The two creatures trotted toward it in zig zags. Smallwood started to mumble something in protest and I gripped his mouth tighter. I turned his head to reveal to him the grisly scene. He looked back up at me with shocked eyes. I placed a finger against my lips, pleading that he remain silent. I pointed at Ko, then the rear entrance. If we could make it outside, the rain would mask our sound and we may be able to reach the truck. Smallwood stood and retrieved a pocket knife from the pants hanging from the side of his bunk, but did not immediately follow me. I turned, saw him considering the exit, and then grabbed his arm. With fading resistance, he followed me to Ko's bunk.

Another creature ripped free from a leg and joined the first two in zig zagging across the floor in search of the phone. They were so silent in their movements. I knew I would have even less time to wake Ko. I motioned for Smallwood to help me pull him from his bunk. I grabbed Ko's face with one hand and wrapped my free arm around his chest. Smallwood took him by the hips and we pulled him from his bunk to a standing position. He fought against our restraint and I tightened my grip against his muffled cries. This brought the creatures to an abrupt stop. They trained their radar ears on us and began slinking our way. Fiery fear flooded my face and sweat beaded. Ko's body jolted as he witnessed the advancing things and his struggle strengthened. I snatched a water bottle from the floor and threw it behind the beasts. The initial two creatures trilled, unmoving, while their newest companion gave chase. Three more beasts freed themselves from their meals. Behind us, Wegner's creature whined through the latrine door like an anxious dog ready to reunite with its owner. This caught the attention of the six stalking creatures and they all trilled a reply. They then rushed in our direction.

Ko broke loose from my grasp as Smallwood dropped Ko's lower body to the floor, turning to flee. I pulled Ko up to his feet and we mirrored Smallwood in flight. Shoulders struck bunks, feet kicked footwear and bottles of water and spit, heels slid through blood. I could hear the remaining feeding beasts detaching themselves and joining the pursuit. Smallwood slipped wildly in a small spill of blood. Ko hurdled him and Smallwood grabbed at Ko's legs, tripping him. Ko struck the floor, the two atop one another in a pile. I turned to lift them. The creatures closed in. As I pulled Smallwood to his feet, he kicked the rising Ko backwards. Half a dozen stingers shot through the air, embedding themselves in Ko's torso. He scrambled to his knees and then fell to his face as his body convulsed.

"No!" My hushed cry was involuntary.

Vampiric heads snapped to face me. Mouths agape under flat noses, crimson drool sliding down blood-matted chins in long ropes, tall, broad ears flexing around eyeless skulls. Behind me, bare feet slapped bare floor as Smallwood continued for the exit. I pursued. He reached the door with one arm and extended another behind to shove me back. I grabbed the striking arm, reached forward, and caught the collar of his shirt. He slid again on wet heels, losing his balance. I took advantage. I wrapped an arm around his thick neck, locking his sweaty head against the side of my face. He thrashed. He was substantially larger and stronger. I had to hold on. If I lost his back, I would lose my life.

Smallwood turned us to face the encircling predators. He thrust backward, slamming me into the door above the crash bar. All the air was forced from my lungs. Static blinded me. I squeezed and flexed my arm under his jaw with all my force. The creatures neared with caution, seemingly thrown off by our violence; measuring; calculating; encircling. Smallwood clawed at my forearm with one hand and fumbled around the pocket of his shorts with the other. He removed the pocket knife and unfolded the blade with quivering fingers. He was losing strength but not fast enough. The creatures continued their slow but steady advance, paw by inching paw. He stabbed behind, first at the door, then at my leg, striking it twice. I clenched my teeth nearly to the breaking point and let out a huff in suppressed agony as the sharp fire pulsed through my body. When the sharpened steel met my leg a third time, I dropped an arm and seized his genitalia in a death grip. A stifled whimper bubbled up in his throat and reflexes brought both his hands to his crotch, leaving the knife sheathed in my flesh. I released his genitals, pulled free the knife, and brought the blade to his throat. He caught my forearm, dug in his nails, and pulled with all his weakened might. My arm—my body—trembled as I strained against his grip. I could hear the blade's edge grazing his day-old stubble.

The poised stingers were within striking distance now. On impulse, I lashed at his head with a bite, clamping my grinding teeth onto his ear. His grip loosened slightly and my strength, fueled by rage and fear, surged. The blade passed along his throat, just above his Adam's apple. Skin began to separate. Still, he fought. I forced the last remnants of strength into my grip. Flesh spread and arteries opened. A single spurt of blood shot outward onto the floor, a splash of sound into a pool of silence. The stingers darted. As he did Ko, I kicked Smallwood forward into the ravenous throng of beasts, simultaneously throwing myself into the crash bar at my back. I fell outside and kicked the door shut.

Some men were never meant to be in uniform. Some were never meant to be at all.

· ∽ ·

I was lying on a dry sidewalk peppered with equally dry leaves. A humvee was abandoned atop a cracked fire hydrant alongside the barracks. A geyser of water was raining down onto the building. The muddy paw prints surrounding the scene suggested it had already been scoped out. It was a miracle considering the situation: the sound of splashing water must have masked my noisy egress.

I stood, folded the knife, and secured it in my pocket. I scanned the area around the barracks (an open field in one direction, a parking lot and more buildings in another) and spotted maybe a couple dozen other soldiers scattered about who somehow survived the night. Some were half-dressed. Others were undressed entirely. Some were in uniforms while others were in civvies. They all stood or sat unmoving and silent. There were hundreds of the vampiric scorpion creatures milling about. I was trapped. We all were trapped. I was overcome with dread. I swiveled my head around in search of anything that would bring hope. The world was spinning. My head spun. My stomach twisted. I felt ill.

Across the street one of the survivors motioned for me to calm my breathing. He pointed to his watch and then at the horizon. I took a deep breath and tried to work some understanding of the gesture. The mountain peaks were beginning to glow, signalling sunrise. Would the monsters retreat from daylight? They were all eyeless, which did imply some nocturnal nature or sunless habitat. But the creatures didn't seem to be withdrawing at all. In fact, they appeared to be waiting for something; organizing, even.

I looked back at the soldier and shrugged. He pointed to his watch again and then gestured as though he was playing a trumpet. The motion brought instant clarity. Wake up. Reveille would soon play over the loudspeakers. And once the recorded bugling polluted the air, our movement would be obscured. Hope washed over me.

As I waited for the automated wake up, I weighed my options. I could run for the truck, though I was unsure I would make it before the song's end, especially given the wounds to my leg. And then what if I became stranded in that large, gravel lot? It'd be like throwing myself into my own grave. I considered trying to get to the firing range and ammo storage but I would not have access to the ammunition. Even if I got a hold of a weapon and some ammunition, I would do nothing more than draw attention to myself with gunfire. I needed a plan—a silent one—and I needed it quite soon.

What do I do? What do I fucking do?

I looked around at the remaining survivors and wondered about their intentions. The open space was ablaze with nonverbal communication. Silent gestures and motions and mouthings of plans or questions or prayers or a little of everything carried from soldier to soldier, near to far like human heliostats.

I imagined the naked survivors had an edge on the rest of us as they needed not worry over the sound of their clothes' friction or the tread on their shoes catching pebbles. I looked down at my own footwear, a pair of unlaced boots. I could remove them and then toss them one at a time as necessary to distract the creatures. I could wait for a gust of wind to move a pile of leaves and take a few quiet steps. It'd be slow but slow was good. I could control my breathing and heart rate with slow. Slow was smooth and smooth was fast, as the saying went.

There was a scurrying through the fields. All the scorpion-esque creatures were forming a line. One of the creatures made an almost musical chitter, which was passed up and down the line before transitioning to a steady click. *Click-click-click.* Like metronomes. Now a clacking noise was passed from one end to the other as the last of the creatures lined up. *Clack-clack-clack.* Rhythmic, like drumsticks on a rim. They were communicating something. A plan. Now the line moved in unison. A plan in action. They were sweeping across the base in zig zagging lanes at a light trot. They were combing their kill zone.

Time's up.

As they made their swift, but diligent, approach, the soldier nearest them stood unflinching. We all spectated his valiance, eager to observe his strategy. The line was nearing him at a steady pace. He raised one leg high as if to step over the creature in whose lane he stood. I held my breath. The steady breeze surged into a strong gust and the soldier, like the surrounding trees, bowed forward, only slightly, but enough to disorient his balance.

He shifted on his planted foot.

Two of the creatures trilled and the sweep was paused. The creature nearest the flamingo-posed soldier slunk forward, its ears twitching in a rhythm synchronized with a severely elevated heart-beat. Its scorpion tail quivered with excitement. The soldier turned a single, despairing glance our way and broke loose into a run, dragging behind him the creature, like a ball and chain. As his muscles seized, his efforts remained unceasing, though increasingly slowed. He collapsed and dragged his body forward with a twisting arm as though every inch of ground for which he fought would bring salvation. When he was at last still, his passenger detached itself and sat atop his contorted mass. It leaned its vampiric head back and made as though to howl. I heard nothing. Its fox-like chest continued to inflate and deflate, mouth open skyward, throat flexing. It must have been screeching in a pitch I could not hear, like a dog whistle.

Save for the rustling of leaves in the shifting wind and the splashing of water behind me, everything was still. Then, in the distance, a small building seemed to be moving our way. I shielded my eyes against the rising sun and focused my vision. The mass neared. It was quite swift for its size, and was upon us in a matter of moments.

A titanic spider was reporting to the unheard shriek in an expeditious scurry. Its legs were thick trunks covered, not in hairs, but in thorns. Like any spider, there were eight legs in total, all pale and translucent with bands of black, as though someone had painted support beams in the style of a zebra and then wrapped them with barbed wire. A stinger hung beneath it much like the tails of the scorpion-esque creatures.

As it drew ever-nearer, I saw that the spider was not unaccompanied. At first, it appeared the spider's body was made of static. As it moved in, I realized that the static was actually a crawling mass on the spider's abdomen. What crawled upon it I could not quite identify until the titan had reached the soldier. Initially, I was under the impression that it was carrying a swarm of its young, as wolf spiders were known to do. That was an unexpectedly erroneous assumption, for, as best my eyes could make out, the wriggling cluster it conveyed was an orgy of dog-sized ticks.

The spider, also eyeless, used its massive palps to investigate the scene. Once it found the fallen soldier, it positioned itself over him and shivered. One of the ticks fell from the spider's abdomen, crashing down into the dead foliage alongside the immobilized soldier. It collected itself and crawled to the paralyzed body. The tick flexed its spike-like jaws and buried its head into the soldier's side. As the tick began dragging the soldier in the direction from which it came, the scorpion-esque creature that had halted the sweep trilled once more and the sweep resumed.

Panic sparked and erupted through the survivors like a firestorm. A handful of the soldiers nearest the line broke into a chaotic flight. The spider jolted and stretched out its legs, feeling the vibrations of the fleeting men's footsteps. With unfathomable speed, the spider chased down the would-be escapees, stinging each and dropping ticks upon them. All the while, the sweep carried on around its eight barbed legs.

Before I could establish a strategy, before I could even mentally grasp the events that were unfolding, a multitude of survivors sprinted toward and past me in the direction of the dining facility, the spider and vampiric creatures in pursuit. Silence had been decimated. Fleeing feet and pursuing paws upon fallen foliage filled the autumn air like monsoon rains. Without further delay, I joined the stampeding soldiers, the spider at my back with less than half a dozen men between us. Leaves, clothes, and limbs were piling up the spider's thorny legs like crocheted socks as they were pierced in the beast's mad pursuit of us.

Scurry. Stop. Feel. Scurry. Sting. Tick. Feel. Scurry. The titanic arachnid moved like a robin hopping about a rain-soaked lawn in search of worms.

Pain shot through my leg with each stride. My injury, combined with my inebriation, slowed my turbulent progress. I stumbled. I strode. I swayed. I side-stepped. The spider's stinger darted past me. Perhaps the unpredictability of my erratic movements spared me this once. One of the soldiers just ahead of me, a chubbier, older man whose towel had long since abandoned him (though, to his disadvantage, not his shower thongs), fell to the ground with a wail that was utter, terrified realization of his imminent death. The spider's stinger spiked him as I hurdled his flailing body. The older man's tick reached the ground just as I reached the entrance to the dining facility, which, to the opposition of shouting within, was being held open by Wilson. I fell past Wilson on failing legs. He tried to pull shut the door but was blocked. The spider's stinger slid through the opening and skewered his forearm before being pinched in the frame. He pulled harder at the door's crash bar and I scrambled onto wavering legs to assist. The spider squealed and there was a subsequent wet *pop* as the door sealed shut. Wilson fell backward with the severed stinger flexing in his arm.

He began convulsing.

· ❧ ·

Though Wilson twisted and writhed on the floor, his eyes never broke from mine. I moved to dislodge the stinger, to comfort him, to do anything to provide even an iota of solace to my friend and mentor. I used Smallwood's knife to saw the stinger loose from the tail and pulled the remnants from Wilson's arm.

I looked around for any available aid. The room was spinning. I was drowning in growing stimuli. A chorus of panicked planning echoed from wall to wall. Shouts and shushes here and there like a choral canon. The metal feet of furniture scraped and squeaked and the bare feet of the shoeless padded as people rushed to build barricades and hide. Percussion echoed from the kitchen, as pots and pans banged, dishes broke, serving utensils and silverware clattered. Moans of anger and dismay grew. Every door and window rattled as that hellish horde—the audience to our symphony of dread—clawed and slammed and scratched and banged, over and over and over again and again, like ceaseless, relentless applause. My head throbbed. My nose retold the story of Wilson's defecation. My stomach begged to empty itself. My leg bled. I was breaking.

All at once, a steady silence began to grow. At first, I thought the shushers were winning the war against the noisy. Then I came to realize even they had quieted themselves. And as the interior grew in silence, so did the exterior. The creatures seemed to be transitioning from aggressive pursuit to unassertive investigation. Rattling glass, creaking metal, bangs and thuds, all subsided to inquisitive scratches and taps, and this development—this hope—forced my eyes from Wilson's once more.

I first observed the enemy, and scanned every obvious entry. Metal doors were bent inwards, but not penetrated. Windows were cracked, but not shattered. Every door and window was still under infernal investigation. Every window still displayed how utterly surrounded we were—we, the remnants of the greatest military force in the history of mankind, who I now studied.

Every surviving pair of eyes in the room was trained on one particular corner. I, too, moved my gaze to that far corner of the dining area, and I, too, saw the thing that demanded so much attention that even frightened hearts were hushed. It was an M4 carbine. It was an M4 carbine loaded with a thirty-round magazine. It was gripped tightly in the hands of a man whose eyes seemed trained on nothing within the room—nothing even outside it—but on something beyond, something imperceptible. Just below those eyes was a mouth agape. And within that mouth was not a silent scream of terror, but something deadly; as deadly to the armed man as it was to his unarmed audience. It was the muzzle of the rifle, pressed firmly into the roof of his mouth.

We froze in uneasy anticipation.

We froze in silent study.

We froze in imminent doom.

One of the underwear-clad men (likely an officer or senior NCO, given his age and paunch) cautiously approached the suicidal soldier, hands raised to show his lack of hostility. The suicidal soldier seemed not to notice. The undressed man gently waved his raised hands, which finally stole the attention of the suicidal soldier's eyes. Those eyes only briefly studied the undressed man before darting down to the rifle. This prompted the ever-approaching, near-naked man to tilt his head down, evidently shifting his own gaze to a very particular point below that drool-dripping, gun-gumming mouth. Like the heads of passengers in a braking vehicle, the rest of his audience dipped their gaze as well. Just below the faded-black, curved magazine (undoubtedly loaded with thirty noise-making, silence-shattering, sound barrier-breaking rounds), was the curved, finger-wrapped trigger of the weapon.

Keep that nose pick off the trigger until you intend to kill! Sergeant Boone's voice echoed in the back of my mind.

The weapon was hot, we all knew this. What I didn't know from this distance and angle was whether it was set to single fire or three-round burst. Was he the kind of soldier who thought a single round would do it, or the kind who didn't like to take risks? Did it matter?

The suicidal soldier's shaking eyes jerked back up to the undressed man, now within arm's reach. More drool drizzled down his chin, followed by a long, hopeless whine. The undressed man shushed him softly like a loving mother to her fussy infant. A harder *thud* against the window nearest the two indicated they were being heard.

It was as though the starting pistol of a race had been fired.

The undressed man shot out a hand to grasp the firearm. The suicidal soldier squeezed the trigger. Three thunderous rounds exploded through the barrel in quick succession as the rifle was pulled from its owner. The first entered the suicidal soldier's mouth and exited his eye. The second passed through his upper teeth and lip and the third joined the first two en route to the high heights of the ceiling, piercing only air.

Chaos erupted on both sides of the windows and doors. Men moved to brace and barricade. Men fled to hide. The undressed man and the sabotaged suicide fought over the rifle.

Snap!

Metal broke from behind me. I turned to see the pointed head of a tick bursting through the door. It flared open its jointed, barbed jaws and ripped the door free from its hinges, revealing an entire world of creatures now rushing inside like daylight into an unsealed tomb. I laid myself atop Wilson like a bride and groom in consummation and rolled, swapping places so he was now on top of me. (*Another shared experience bringing the two of us closer together.*)

Paw after paw pattered past. Screams and prayers were quickly becoming gasps and gurgles. Tables flipped and kitchenware clashed as men fought creatures and fellow men alike. The drool-slick rifle fired another burst of rounds—only one. The man who had squeezed the trigger had evidently succumbed to suicide or paralysis.

A tick shuffled alongside Wilson and me. A pair of palps unfolded from underneath its piercing mandibles. The tick studied us. My heart quickened. Then, a tearing sound, that of clothes and flesh, as the tick lodged its barbed mandibles into Wilson's side. A slight gurgle loosened from his throat; all his disabled lungs could muster. The tick began dragging him toward the door. I wrapped my arms around him and held tight for the ride. We were dragged into the open, past a mob of ticks and scorpion-esque creatures that continued flooding into the building as screams flooded out. The torment was still audible as we were distanced from the dining facility; even over the sounds of reveille.

· ∾ ·

For a long time, I held my eyes shut. My spinning vision and the sights of carnage only further fed my nausea and fear. I was not sure where the tick was dragging us to, but it persisted. On and on we were dragged, pulled through asphalt and concrete, leaves and grass, dirt and gravel. My shirt had long since been pulled up and torn, and my back was raw. Above me, Wilson remained still. Watery shit, perhaps more than had started the morning, was seeping onto me through his pants. The smell was as relentless as the tick.

On, we were dragged. On and on. I opened my eyes.

We were nearing the mountainous periphery of the firing ranges. Wilson and I (and the tick) were in a stream of creatures moving humans and animals further and further into the mountains. Ticks and vampiric scorpions and the spider were slowly moving past us as our tick struggled to maintain pace with my excess weight. With no other option immediately present, I decided to hold on with ever-stiffening arms. Perhaps the rest of the creatures would pass us and I could simply let go.

But the stream continued without end.

I remembered what Sergeant Boone once told me about combat, about what it was like during his first deployment. He fancied himself a type of Hemingway when drunk, especially when he got to ordering liquor instead of beer. And if you got stuck with the man one-on-one, he would pontificate. My God, would he pontificate.

Life marches on like an indefatigable soldier, he had explained. *Then, in the blink of an eye … flashes of hell … like rapid snapshots.* He had paused, either for dramatic effect or in deep, drunken thought before adding, *Then, life, that uncaring fucker, marches onward.*

Minutes. In a matter of minutes, I had lost all of my friends. And here I was, clinging to life as it marched onward. Not even a pause to consider that entire worlds had been destroyed.

Life was indeed an uncaring fucker.

Eventually, we passed a fenced off trailhead and entered the mouth of a limestone tunnel. There were strings of lights secured to rows upon rows of support beams. Each bright bulb brought pain to my eyes and I clenched them shut again. On, we were dragged, now through loose soil and rocks. Dust danced about the passage and I fought the impulse to sneeze. The tunnel seemed to stretch miles in length. We were nearing … we neared …

Every foot brought closer the unsettling sound of misery. Lamentations echoed and re-echoed. I opened my eyes once more, and once more I saw that we were being dragged like food carried back to an ant colony. I leaned my head back. Still, there were creatures. Some carried, some dragged. Most had fully intact prey, others did not. Some brought only pieces of prey. Some prey and pieces of prey were bare, but most were clothed; or, rather, gift-wrapped in camouflage.

The lamentations grew louder, nearer.

The tunnel fed into a large cavern, whereupon we finally came to a halt. Howls, screams, squawks, and bleats reverberated about the cavern like an overcrowded amphitheater. Man and animal and every other living thing able to utter anguish had been collected here. Suffering was all around. It was deafening. Moreover, it was masking; the kind of raucousness that could conceal my movements.

I wriggled out from under Wilson and stood. The stream of eyeless creatures continued its course into the cavern. I continued to sway. (*How could I still be drunk?*) There was space by the tunnel's mouth. If I could reach it, I could regroup and plan my escape. More of the things were arriving. There were so, so many. More and more marched in every moment. (*Life marches on* ...) The limestone chamber was beyond full. How could I step over and around so many moving monsters in such a drunken, injured state?

I held and released a deep breath. With each incoming creature, my stepping areas diminished. If I was to do the impossible, I would have to do it now.

I carefully removed my boots and held one in each hand, ready to throw one or both as a distraction if needed. With cautious tempo, I lifted and set my feet over, between, and around barbed tails and pulsating stingers and shuffling paws and twitching ears. I straddled. I swayed. I lost and regained balance. Every wary step a mere inch from doom. One more. Another. Just one more. A long stride this time and—

I fell forward. I reflexively shot an arm out to catch myself, boot still in hand, and made contact with—oh, God, I touched—

The limestone wall.

My heart, tired of my exploits, rattled my ribs like a prisoner demanding freedom. I slowly, shakily, quietly let loose the long-expired air my weary lungs had been holding for so many steps. I rested my head against the rocky wall and caught my breath.

I examined the cavern when I at last felt the strength and courage to turn from the wall. I was surrounded, utterly surrounded. I was completely confined in this cavern with creatures in all directions. And the sound—that hellish sound. A symphony of moaning, groaning, sobbing, and screaming men and animals. Multitudes of animals and soldiers lying in piles scattered about the cavern's floor. All paralyzed, all of them. All unable to do anything other than moan and wail in pain. Vines, too. Everywhere vines. There were vines attached to every living thing, save for the eyeless.

From where I had just ventured, Wilson was being dragged once again. His eyes were trained on me as he was pulled toward a dead, withered deer. Another tick, one free of body and limb, dragged the deer carcass to a pile of dead animals, on which hundreds of melon-sized maggots fed; pulsating, throbbing, undulating. Wilson's tick moved him to where the deer had been, tore loose from him, and left him. The vines crawled onto him, under his clothing, under his skin. If he moaned or whimpered or screamed, I could not distinguish it from any other vine entangled being. The vines continued to swarm him. As they inched their way across and into his flesh, they turned blood-red. I watched through drunken vertigo as Wilson's lifeforce traveled through them like veins. Away it went—his blood—away from him, along the walls, up the ceiling, and toward the center of the cavern, feeding into the monstrous maestro of this madness.

At the heart of the chamber hung the heart of the nightmare: a gargantuan humanoid suspended above a writhing mass of tortured souls by a web of veins. Its loose, decayed skin barely clung to the skeletal form within. The monstrosity, like all the others, was eyeless. Though, while it had no eyes to emit emotion, I could nevertheless discern it was enjoying—no, *savoring* the sounds of sorrow surrounding it.

I was witness to an infernal resurrection, deep in the core of this inescapable cavern. Except, this was no cavern. This was a theater:

the colossal creature a conductor; the captives a cursed chorus; the cacophony of crazed cries concert concessions. It was too much to comprehend. It was simply too much.

Nausea flooded my head once more. I wobbled on my feet and fell to my knees. I hurled. I sobbed. I retched. I repeated. When I at last lifted my head, I gazed upon my audience.

To Be Heard

THE EMPATH

I have awoken again in the realm of pain. It is endless, this pain. There is no solace. There is no comfort. There is only suffering … and me—only me. I suffer in solitude, but not for long.

The banishing lights have faded in the other realm. I step through once more, emerging, as always, in the dark chamber with the hanging skins. My nails scrape the wooden surface of the chamber's door as I search for its orb-like release. The release squeaks, as it always does no matter how slowly it is turned; as does the door creak, as it always does when pushed open, even unhurriedly.

The room into which the door opens is as dark as the chamber of hanging skins, though at least thrice the size. I shuffle into that darkness with deliberate slowness, but the occupant has evidently already noticed me, as its breath is quickening. Likely, it had not yet fallen asleep. I have to reach it, perhaps calm it even, before it alerts its keepers, who bring with them the banishing light—always that hellacious blaze, conjured in an instant by merely touching the wall.

The occupant shifts in fear. I try to speak—to croon, really— but, much like the door, my voice can only creak. This serves only to frighten the occupant.

I continue my approach. The small soul begins to whisper; a welcomed act. Though not directed to me, the magnetism of its speech— of its fear—draws me nearer. It suffers. Oh, how my companion-to-be anguishes. I can share its pain. More importantly, it can share mine. We can indulge in each other's pain in the other realm. I reach out to feel its distress; it is almost tangible. Its whimpers and whispers grow louder. I catch words in brief: "Please," and "God."

I am now at the side of the sleeper's resting place, gazing down upon it. How small it is. Its eyes are clenched shut. I am stricken with envy. If I had eyelids with which to blind myself, I could keep from observing the torment wrought upon me in the other realm; so much reprieve from so simple an act.

A long rope of drool slides past my teeth, falling onto the occupant in its bedding. I cannot help this. I have not the lips to refrain from drooling, much like I lack the skin to keep from bleeding upon the floor. Although, lips may not offer much benefit, as the shape and size of my teeth would not allow for such flesh to function properly.

I am uncertain it can understand my creaking voice, but I thank it nonetheless: for its presence; for the companionship it will soon provide; for praying, most of all. "I'd have never found you otherwise," I try to speak. Something about these words—these prayers—allows them to be heard in the other realm—allows me to find their speaker. Perhaps it is the nature of the prayers that allows them to be heard: that they are directed to another realm; that they are so liberally seasoned with fear.

Another rope of drool falls from my jaw. The sleeper shrieks. The footsteps of the keepers approach. I reach out to grab my companion but it is too late. The other door bursts open and the banishing light returns.

· ∾ ·

I have awoken again in the realm of pain, alone. I was close, so close to obtaining it: empathy. I will try again, when next the banishing lights fade. I will share my pain. There is so much of it, this pain, that there is no other way, for it is more than any one thing can endure. Or, is there another way?

Prayers in the distance. No, something else; something more alluring. There is desperation, desire, and … anguish. Oh, yes, there is anguish. It beckons, guiding me toward another passageway into the realm of companions-to-be: a flooded stone tunnel, littered with small, metal discs. Just beyond the passageway, just on the other side of that wet veil, is the source of that beckoning anguish. There stands the anguished soul before the stone tunnel, solitary in its suffering, casting a metal disc into the tunnel's water in some sort of ritual. It craves companionship. Here am I, its succor.

The anguished will have me in solitude's stead, and I will have empathy; each of us fulfilling the other's desire.

Please, God, forgive me

THE UNHOLY

A faint but no less comforting aroma beckoned me into consciousness. Dishes clinked and the mixer whirred. Mother was making the first Christmas breakfast! I picked encrusted tears from my eyes, grabbed a shirt from the clean pile, and opened the door. The whole hallway smelled like Christmas breakfast. Christmas breakfast was my favorite of any holiday meal. I liked it even more than Thanksgiving, because there was only one Thanksgiving meal. There were two Christmas breakfasts: one on Christmas Eve and one on Christmas Day.

I was about to run downstairs but remembered my blessing on my desk. I folded it, made sure it was tucked in nice and snug in the envelope, and licked the glue to seal it. I always hated that part. My brother told me they used earwax in envelope glue. That was what made it so sticky and yucky.

I ran downstairs, jumping to skip the bottom two steps. I wasn't supposed to run or jump in the house, but it was Christmas breakfast! Besides, God forgave (Mother said so), and if there was a day for forgiving, it would be Christmas Eve. Just listen to that culinary melody! French toast was being patted on the griddle, eggs were being tapped against the countertop, bacon sizzled throughout savory air like radio static. That kind of music spoke to me—hurried me to the kitchen. But, I couldn't, not yet. Even though my mouth salivated and my stomach ached, I passed the kitchen and went instead to the living room. Father called this "delayed gratification." If Jesus could spend forty days fasting in the desert, I could finish my chores before breakfast—even Christmas breakfast.

There were not yet any presents to be found; that would be tempting, and temptation was a tool of Satan. No, Jesus wouldn't bless us with gifts until tonight, but everything else was set up for Him just the way He liked. The tree was covered in strings and lights and balls (I got to put the star on top). There were big socks on the wall. Mother's porcelain Bible toys sat in their little manger in the corner. And everybody's letters wishing Jesus a happy birthday and thanking Him and the Lord for their blessings and making a Christmas prayer were stacked in the blessings bowl next to the cookie plate. I was on my way to place my blessing in the bowl when Father called to me.

"Did you shower?" Father asked.

"Huh-uh."

"Well, get on over to the sink, stinky, and wash those grubby little grabbers of yours. And don't say 'huh-uh' to me. Honor thy father."

"Yes, Father." I obeyed Father's command and helped Mother set the table. Then we sat down to pray.

"Our heavenly Father, we are so thankful for the meal with which You have blessed us and pray that You will continue to bless us. And, please, Lord, look after our son as You have looked after us. I pray that he finds Your forgiveness ..."

Dad was praying for my brother. He was at a special faith camp for the winter because Mother caught him doing something awfully sinful in the bathroom. Father was so angry. Mother cried all night. I was scared for a long time. I had never seen Father's wrath like that before. Scarier still was that I did not know what sin my brother had committed. I still did not know. I tried to figure it out, so that I could avoid committing it myself, so that I could fix it. I looked all over the bathroom for any sign of his sin but all I could find was Mother's lotion left out and some trash on the floor. We weren't supposed to leave things out, especially not trash, but that didn't seem like a super serious sin. I put the lotion away and picked up the trash—an easy fix. It was just a little bit of toilet paper and a small cardboard picture of the man from the underwear bags. I told Mother I cleaned it up, but still she cried. I asked what happened. Mother said he strayed from the path of the Lord. If that was an answer, it did not feel like one. Whatever had happened, it must have been exceptionally sinful, for he had the prayer lock on his door for three whole days. That was the longest either of us ever had the prayer lock.

"... in Your name we pray ..."

"Amen," we all finished.

Then, we had Christmas breakfast. And it was wonderful! Oh, the cheese was stringy, the bread warm, the milk cold, and the bacon was a little less than crispy, just the way I liked it. This Christmas breakfast was nearly perfect—nearly, but not quite. Only Jesus was perfect.

Once every crumb had been eaten from my plate, I helped Mother clear the table. This would not normally have been an issue, except that the milk was still mostly full. It was heavy when it was mostly full, and my brother, who was bigger and stronger, would usually put the heavy things away. But, he was at camp, so I had to be the big and strong one today. I stood on my toes, grabbed a hold of the table, and reached up with the cap to screw it back on top. I was being a big boy but I wasn't a tall boy. I started pulling the tablecloth while I was steadying myself and the milk jug was inadvertently being pulled to the edge of the table. It was going to fall over! I pushed the jug back, but in my hurry, I knocked it over on the table. This was an accident! All the world and God above could have seen that. Accident or not, though, milk was spilling all over Mother's tablecloth. My heart started beating so hard my hands were shaking. So when I tried to pick it back up, I knocked it onto the floor—onto Mother's dining room rug. That was an accident, too, though no less punishable.

Please, God, forgive me. I could feel my heartbeat in my fingers and toes and all throughout my body. No, it was worse than that. I could feel Father's presence—his wrath—right behind me.

"Wasting milk?" His voice was low, as it typically was when he was coerced into wrath by one of us.

"Oh, no," Mother sighed, turning to see the growing mess beneath the table. "I needed that for baking."

"N-no, Father, it was—"

"Pick it up." Still, the deep tone of wrath. I could not move—not quickly—for I was weighed down by fear, anxious anchors in body and mind. Father hurried me with a push to the floor. "Now!" he commanded.

I handed Mother the milk jug from the floor and she handed me the hand-drying towel in return. She sloshed the remaining milk in the jug, feeling it out.

"No, it's not going to be enough ..." Mother stated, more aloud to herself than to either Father or me.

"What did Jesus say in the Gospels?" Father asked me.

"'Let nothing be wasted,'" I answered.

"Pray while you're down there on your knees, child. Pray." He set his foot atop my back. "Pray," he commanded. "That the Lord may forgive you for the waste you have created."

I prayed. I cried. I wanted to pee.

"I'm sorry, Father," I cried.

"Not to me, child, to the *heavenly* Father."

"I'm sorry, Lord."

"'Gather up the fragments that remain, that nothing be lost,'" Father spoke, quoting the Lord. "And when you've finished here, you will walk to the store to replace what you've taken from your mother."

How blessed am I, I pondered, for I merely had to make amends for the sin I had committed rather than be punished outright.

When I had sopped as much of the milk out of the rug as the towel would allow, I went to the entryway to don my clothing for a winter trek to the grocery store. I didn't like my snow boots. They were too big. They used to be my brother's before he went away. Father said I'd grow into them, but I hadn't, yet. They still flopped and I still got blisters. Mother helped me with my scarf (she always wrapped it nice and snug) and then gave me five dollars.

"Be sure it's whole milk. It should have a red label."

"Okay, Mother. Do you want to come with me?" I hoped she would so that I wouldn't have to walk.

"Sorry, sweetie, you know that isn't your father's command." She spoke quietly. "Be safe, okay?"

"Okay."

· ⁀ ·

"That was a pretty atypical punishment for me back then," I explain. "My father didn't really let us out on our own. I think probably because we would have said something that would have attracted the wrong kind of attention to our house, even in a town as rural and religious as Hell Gate." The therapist remains quiet, listening. "I don't know why that day was different. Maybe because it was Christmas Eve and he figured there wouldn't be much of anyone to talk to apart from a store clerk. Maybe he didn't really have a choice because my mom was busy in the kitchen and he had a scheduled call with my brother's camp director for the holiday. Or maybe something else compelled him to send me out ..."

· ⁀ ·

I stepped out of the warmth of our home and into the cold embrace of a late morning's winter day. The snow was already blindingly bright in its whiteness but some flashing thing still managed to call the attention of my eyes. I could see that glint from half a block's distance. It was like I was supposed to find it—fated to. So, I went to it, scooped it out of its cold resting place, and blew away the snow from my palm. It was a coin—a rather unique coin; so much so that even in my child's mind I could reflect on its profoundness.

"Neat," I reflected.

I cannot today recall the details of that coin but I know that on one side was inscribed my birthdate—not just the year, but the whole date. I looked about the surrounding properties for a place that may provide some insight, and to my good fortune I spotted a nearby building marked "Coin-Op." Perfect! (Nearly perfect.) A coin store, not miles away but immediately accessible. Indeed a fortuitous morning to maintain my uplifted spirits. I crunched and shuffled through the snow toward the building, all the while imagining the fortunes that awaited. I would approach the counter and slap the coin down before the clerk, who would undoubtedly gasp at its sight.

"Where did you find this?" he would ask.

I would have a clever response prepared; something along the lines of "finders keepers."

The clerk would stammer in excitement. He would beg to purchase it for a million dollars. I would, of course, talk him out of two million.

Oh, what a morning!

But when I approached the door, I encountered only misfortune. The door was locked. Worse yet, there did not appear to be any showcases with ancient coins and such. Only laundry machines. Perhaps I was at the wrong entrance? How frustratingly misleading.

Then, much like the coin in the snow, something else caught my attention: a glowing sign, just across the street. The one semblance of life on the entire block: "The Wishing Well." I knew I wasn't allowed to deviate from Father's commands. The store and back was the path and to stray from that path would have been nothing short of an act of defiance. If God forgave, though, surely my father could forgive, especially with upwards of two million dollars on the line. More than that drove me to enter the bar, however. I was overwhelmed with a feeling I could not comprehend in my child's mind; something entrancing. Maybe I weighed my options, maybe I was pulled in without thought, guided by God's hand, so to speak. In any case, to the bar I went, and through its door I entered.

The Wishing Well was empty, save for the bartender, who was sitting atop one of the stools, ankles crossed, left hand clutching the right in his lap. He brightened with impossible magnitude upon seeing me. He patted his lap, gesturing that I come sit upon it. He straightened his red sweater and checkered tie, as though to give me his very best, neatest, least threatening appearance.

He did so vainly. I was both frightened and repelled.

"Hello there, young man," he called out with a little wave. His lips struggled to keep his smile as he spoke. Everything about him seemed to struggle. He was like some type of ill-crafted robot whose springs were on the verge of bursting out. His arm shot up seemingly uncontrollably, a single finger pointing accusingly at me. "You look like a boy in need of a hot chocolate," he exclaimed. He used his loose arm to pull his stiff, accusing arm back into his lap. "Hold the schnapps, right?" A forced, mechanical chuckle was spit from the smile of his overtaxed mouth.

"I'm not supposed to talk to strangers," I muttered.

"Well, aren't you a cautious little scamp …" He was grinding his teeth, which were all too visible within that monstrous smile of his. "Tell you what, son," he said, waving me over. He moved around the bar top with strangely stiff legs, like one of those wind-up dolls. "I've got some paper behind the bar. You know, for orders and stuff." He rummaged underneath the cash register and retrieved a notepad. He tried to set it on the bar top but that tricky arm of his seemed unwilling to comply. He pulled the notepad free with his more controlled arm, set it down, and gently slid it in my direction. "How about you write it out instead?" He reached back under the register and brought out a pen. His ungovernable appendage snatched the pen from his other's grasp and slammed it into the pad of paper, where it stood erect like a freshly planted flagpole. "It's not talkin' if it's writin', right? Why, we'd just be penpals."

To obedient me, a child of disciplined upbringing in which dissent was utterly proscribed, the bartender's reasoning was inarguably factual.

Still with some caution, I took short steps toward the bartender. The seating area was full of rows of benches all facing the bar top, just like pews at a church. I walked an aisle between them like how the Catholics walk to the priest to receive communion. When I reached a barstool, the bartender helped me up but he did not immediately go back behind the counter. He lingered. He kept his hands on my shoulders and kind of ... rubbed them ... almost exactly like the pastor; a (nearly) perfect imitation.

He did eventually return to the other side of the counter, to take the notepad and pen. He wrote around the piercing he had made on the first few pages and passed the notepad to me.

What brings you in today? The words were smeared from left-handed writing.

I found a coin, I wrote in reply.

The bartender's right arm jerked as he read that. He quickly shoved it into his pocket, then scribbled with equal haste and passed the pad back to me.

Cool. What kind of coin? A very special coin for a very special boy, no doubt.

I went to set the coin down on the bar top but reconsidered and instead held it up for him to see.

He continued to write. *That is indeed a special coin, little buddy. You know what that coin can buy you here?*

What? I asked in writing.

Anything you want.

I looked around. There were barstools and benches, of course. Those were the big things. There were posters and signs on the walls. I studied one of the posters, which read, "Feeling dry? Try getting WHEt! Drink responsibly." I wondered how anyone could drink irresponsibly. Through your nose? Until you got a tummy ache? With your tongue like a dog? "WHEt," whatever that was, was everywhere. Three capital letters and a lowercase "t"—more a crucifix than a letter, though. But even that did not keep my attention. There was nothing in view that was of interest to a boy my age. Nothing, that was, until I locked eyes on the fixture that was the bar's namesake: a wishing well. It was situated on the floor behind the bar's counter like a stone kiddie pool. I speak literally in saying my eyes were locked, as they could not pull away from the sight of this thing. So unnatural was this structure, so unnerving, that my compulsion to gaze upon it could not be considered a curiosity but a sickness of the mind, like a morbid fascination that felt less voluntary and more like a physical force holding my head in place, spreading my eyelids with invisible fingers. I was an unwilling spectator of the abyssal water within. It was frighteningly dark, that water; contradictingly a consuming blackness but also mirror-like, as though the well held not a liquid but a reflective shadow. Frightening, yes, but I could not look away. It was as though my sanity was in question and thus my mind forbade I look away, that I may grant it a further opportunity for study in the hopes

213

it could make the incomprehensible comprehensible.

The bartender's arm flung out from his pocket and its open-palmed hand struck him in the forehead. The act broke my trance and I blinked and shook my head to bring back awareness as he wrote again on the wounded pad of paper.

Not like that, dear boy. Let's start with a drink and we'll flesh it out.

The bartender swiftly snatched a mug from a cabinet, like he was plucking a golf ball from a gator's mouth. It shattered in his grip. Shards of bloody glass showered onto the floor. An embarrassed chuckle escaped his ever-smiling mouth, though the rest of his face gave no indication of happiness. He carefully retrieved a new mug with his uninjured, controllable hand and set it before me. He pulled a can from a shelf and set it next to the mug. While he warmed up the milk, I spun the can in examination. It was labeled "WHEt Cocoa Mix." And in smaller print, "If it's not WHEt, you're probably dry." I had never heard of it.

· ❧ ·

"Never before and never since had I been drugged. I honestly don't know if I was ever actually drugged that day. I just don't remember anything else. I don't remember how it tasted. I certainly don't remember drinking any of it. I don't know if the guy ... touched me or something. The only thing I can recall—mostly from dreams—are his eyes. It was like the ink from that pen had bled into them. They were like black holes feeding on my very soul ..."

· ❧ ·

I returned home without the coin, but with a gallon of whole milk, which I promptly put in the fridge. Whether I was given the gallon by the bartender or purchased it from the store, I did not know. Mother was grateful either way. Father was in the living room. I went to him and passed off my blessing, just then noticing it was unsealed. The bartender must have opened it. Or, perhaps I opened it for him, I wasn't sure. Open or closed, Father did not seem to care. He appeared distracted, likely due to his earlier phone call with the director of the faith camp.

Father added my blessing to the blessings bowl and went to his chair. All four envelopes stuck out of the bowl of crinkle cut paper like feathers, my open one the sole ruffled feather of the bunch. Father plucked first my brother's to read. He always read the first blessing, for he was Father, the husband, and the husband was the head of the wife and so on.

"Well, I suppose we should see what our oldest has to say first and foremost." Father opened the envelope and unfolded the letter within. He glanced over it for a moment, murmuring. "He's sorry. So sorry. He wants to come home. He's righted the ship. Making amends … back on the path …" He looked up at me. "Son, I want you to read Leviticus tonight; seventeen through twenty-six, but especially eighteen."

"Yes, Father."

He made me read Leviticus frequently since my brother committed his sin. I knew most of the passages quite well already (particularly chapters seventeen through twenty-six), and I really wanted to object, but questioning Father's commands was sinful.

He turned over the letter. "Ah, here we are. 'Lord Christ, happy birthday. I am so grateful for Your sacrifice, that humanity was granted a second chance. This year, I pray that I may be granted a second chance; a return home; forgiveness. I know in Your supreme benevolence I may be afforded this blessing.'" Father crumpled the letter and tossed it aside. "Perhaps," he muttered. He then handed the blessings bowl to Mother.

Mother pulled my envelope from the thin shreds of paper and removed the letter from the envelope with the kind of gentleness that came so naturally to a mother's hand. As she unfolded the letter with similar tenderness, I noticed it was written in pen, rather than pencil. Ink was forbidden in the bedrooms and it would have been reasoned that I had written this letter at the desk within my room, but Mother brought no attention to this matter. She only gave a light chuckle at first look. She then showed the letter to Father.

"What is he, dyslexic?" Father asked, more amused than bemused. I didn't know what he meant.

"'Dear Jesus,'" Mother read. "I hope You're enjoying Your birthday in heaven. Thank You for my family and for Christmas breakfast. It's my favorite. I like it better than Christmas dinner, which is why this year for Christmas, I wish ...'"

"We don't wish," Father reminded me. "We pray. To wish is to covet. You know this, child. Things don't simply happen by magic. It is either by our own doing or by the Lord's intervention that we achieve or fail or attain or lose."

"Yes, Father," I replied.

Mother continued. "'... I *want* to invite,'" she paused, "*Santa* for tomorrow's Christmas breakfast.'" She started to turn the page over.

"No, I didn't invite Santa," I told Mother, remembering now the revision I had made while at the bar. I knew Santa didn't exist. Father told me so when I asked. He was always honest. To lie was to stray from God's path. There was someone else who was real, though. I knew because I asked Father about him. "I invited Satan."

Father jumped out of his chair and stood over me. I shrank to the floor. He poised the back of his hand above me and Mother stopped him.

"Please, sweetie." It was the closest I had ever seen Mother to questioning Father's authority. "Listen." She continued reading aloud. "'I know he was once an angel. So, he used to be good. If there's still good in him, I'd like to invite him to Christmas breakfast to prove it. Maybe if I can show the good in him, there won't be any evil in the world anymore, and then I can play outside, or go to school—real school—and I can have my brother back and he can join me.'"

Father continued to stand over me. "The Deceiver has visited this house once already and tainted your brother's mind. Now you wish for his return? You would welcome him, the Father of Lies, into our home?"

Father snatched the prayer lock from the key rack on the wall.

Not on Christmas Eve, I thought. My stomach dropped. I thought I'd puke right there on the carpet. But, oh, if I did, how I'd burden Father further with rage, and Mother with cleaning.

"Father, please," I cried. I swallowed hard to keep anxiety from emptying my gut. "Forgive me."

"The Lord forgives, child, not I." He grabbed me by the arm and pulled me to my feet.

"Ow, it hurts!" I bawled.

"Quiet, child. God hates cowardice."

He dragged me up the stairs and shoved me into my room, slamming the door behind me. I got to my feet and ran to the doorknob but it was too late. The prayer lock had already clicked. I rattled the door but it would not open, not with the prayer lock fastened.

"No! Father, I'm sorry!"

I remembered how my brother shook, pounded, and scratched at his door. I remembered seeing his shadow under the door as he whimpered and begged for me to help him, for Father to forgive him, for Mother to slip him food. No one approached the door for three days. His pleas went unanswered but not unheard. I could still hear them.

I pressed my ear to the door. Father was walking back down-stairs. I wiped my eyes and nose, then shuffled to my bed on my knees and prayed. I prayed all day. I prayed for forgiveness. I prayed all evening. I prayed that Father would release me. I prayed that my hunger pangs would be subdued. I drank a bottle of water I kept hidden in my box spring, peed in it once empty, and then prayed that I would be forgiven for hiding the bottle from Father in the first place. I prayed until I felt God was no longer listening, and then I climbed into bed, eager to fall asleep and awaken to an unlocked door on Christmas morning.

· ∽ ·

"I still can't fall asleep with the bedroom door shut." I eye the closed door behind the therapist. I understand the need for a closed door during these sessions, but it will never be anything other than dis-comforting. I also understand the need for therapists to position themselves between the client and the door. While it feels confining to me, as though they are blocking my escape, it is more for the therapist's safety, especially in this setting with so many violent clients, that we the clients are not the ones blocking the therapist's escape.

· ∽ ·

I tossed and turned on my bed in childish anger. I knew I was just in my reasoning, though that line of thinking implied I was not honoring my father. Still, my intent was not malicious. Father just didn't understand. If only he would allow me to explain. I knew Satan was the Deceiver and the Father of Lies. I knew Satan well from the Bible. I secretly really liked Satan's story. He used to be an angel. All bad

218

people used to be good, which meant they could be good again. Even Father said there was good in everyone. So, there had to be good in Satan. Like Darth Vader from the Star Wars books my brother snuck in. He wasn't always evil. But even when he was evil, there was still good in him. That was how he saved the universe at the end. He was ultimately a hero, not just Luke. But someone had to show Darth Vader how to be good, and that was Luke, which was kind of like me. I was going to be Luke Skywalker bringing the good out of Darth Vader.

What a feat that would be. Father always told me that for every true, good deed, God would pay me back tenfold. And if I were to make Satan good again, could you imagine all the blessings I would get from God?

I tossed and turned even harder. How could I ever get to sleep on Christmas Eve? All I could think about were the blessings I was going to get. I would surely be forgiven the next morning. I'd run downstairs and there would be boxes upon boxes piled up under the tree. More boxes than any other Christmas. Tenfold … If I actually got Satan to be good … Maybe Father would throw away the prayer lock. Maybe he already had. I couldn't take it! I was going to have to check, now—right now!

I got out from under the covers but just before I was going to jump out of bed, I heard the tinkle of a little bell. Was it coming from outside? I put all my focus into my ears. The sound was faint but it was clear this little bell was ringing from somewhere inside the house; maybe even my room. A little louder now. It was definitely in my room. Was it a kitty, one with a little bell on its collar? Did God bless me with a kitty for Christmas? Now another bell. Did I get two kitties for Christmas? Even more tinkling. Three—four kitties?

I laid myself down onto my pillow. I wasn't sure if I was allowed to lay eyes on God, or even hear Him for that matter. So, if He entered the room, I'd cover my head with my pillow. But I did not see God. What I saw in His stead was a group of little pointed hats bouncing around my bed like fishing bobbers. There was the pitter-patter of little feet. Some whispering that was just too quiet to make out.

All at once, several little ropes were thrown across the bed from one side to the other. Just as fast they were thrown, they became taut. I struggled against them but every movement was met with a further tightening of the ropes. There were giggles and titters. My lamp clicked on.

I looked toward the nightstand and saw a little person. Father said I was supposed to call them little people because "midget" was a sinful word, but this wasn't quite a little person. This was *nearly* a little person. It was wearing a green jacket and a green hat. Well, mostly green. They were stained and tattered, barely clinging to its gaunt, not-quite-humanoid form; simply hanging from its equally stained and tattered skin, like a partially shedding reptile. No, not a little person. This was an elf, it had to be; or someone's attempt to portray one. Not just someone either, no. A demon. Indeed a demon in inadequate disguise. A sliver of a smile spread from cheek to sickly gray cheek, like a spreading incision from a scalpel. A predatory smile. The thing studied me for a moment with eyes too wide for such a small face, then left the lamp and went back to holding one of the ropes.

"The fear within you, like blood, runs. It beckons him, your judgement comes," one of the little people tittered.

"Wh-who comes? Mo—" I started to shout for Mother and Father but a wet, ragged little hand clamped my mouth shut. The taste of salty copper just breached my lips.

The room darkened and the demonic elves chattered like insects. A shadow was growing on the wall. More than growing, it was pulling itself out of the wall and into the room. It grew and grew, gaining mass and depth and shape until it was no longer a shadow but a man—more than a man. Of course, a child's eye skews the perception of size, but I cannot understate the enormity of this creature and how it filled the room. As my child's eye witnessed, this was a big, big man, with a big, big belly, and a big, big bag on his back. And only one such man came to a child's mind.

"Santa?" I whispered through ragged little fingers.

The little people giggled. I didn't think it was funny. He looked just like Santa (nearly perfect). Except, he wasn't jolly. Jolly Santa would greet me with a cheerful laugh, loud and happy, like "ho-ho-ho!" not the heavy wheeze I was hearing now. For a long time, this Santa just stood there, watching and wheezing. Like Jolly Santa, this one had a substantial paunch that moved as it wheezed, but it wasn't a jolly paunch. It was too distended, too pendulous to be jolly.

I was about to attempt another call for Mother and Father when the Santa-creature started walking closer. It was wearing a hood, so I couldn't see its face too well, but it didn't look like it had a beard. It lumbered closer, nearing both me and the light, becoming more and more visible with every unrushed shuffle. The robe was similar to Jolly Santa's only in color, as it was stained red. Like the elves, the behemoth was tattered, clothes and body alike, and it had a foul odor so sour it burned the back of my tongue. I could see its face a little better now. Its mouth was open, unnaturally unhinged, like a python prepared to partake of some particularly portly prey. Its jaw was hanging loose, as though too lazy to stay attached to its head. Similarly, the Santa-creature's pale, fat, loose tongue draped lazily over its chin, dripping long strands of drool as it pulsated like a maggot.

The Santa-creature neared and wheezed and stank a noxious reek of evils unknown. Was this what death smelled like? Every wheeze brought forth a miasma of old cheese and festering fish that had been sitting in the sun.

"Santa, I'm scared," I whined.

The Santa-creature sniffed and inhaled a deep wheeze.

"Not yet, you're not scared. You're much unprepared." The raspy voice was coming from the Santa-creature, but not from its mouth. "I will have to wait while you marinate."

I didn't understand what it was talking about. I just kept staring in dread and disbelief, like a blinded deer waiting for impact.

"To give you reasoning, there is no seasoning, not quite, my dear, like fright and fear."

I looked again around the room, at all the demons dressed like elves.

"Satan?" I asked.

"Satan and Santa are so much a lie. They are not as real as you and I."

"W-what are you?"

"I am many things but what I am most is what terror brings: the Unholy Ghost."

"Am I in trouble?"

"I feed on fright and tonight, little one, I'll feast on you until daylight's begun."

The Unholy Ghost unshouldered its sack and held it at the foot of the bed. It was going to put me inside and take me away! My mind raced with the dreadful possibilities. There could be anything in the sack. It could be taking me anywhere. This wasn't real. This was a bad dream. I really had to pee. If I didn't wake up soon, I was going to pee the bed. Mother would be so angry with me. She may even have Father leave the prayer lock on the door. I'd miss Christmas. Christmas breakfast, Christmas dinner, God's blessings, I'd miss all of it.

"Wake up," I sobbed.

Two of the nightmarish elves latched onto my ankles. Their calloused palms and broken claws scratched into me. A tingle ran from my toes to my neck and I started peeing. Warmth spread across my hips.

"I'm sorry, Mother!" I wailed.

The Unholy Ghost sniffed and wheezed. Its face hovered over mine. Its eyes were bright and motionless, like those of a dead fish. It didn't blink. I didn't think it could. It didn't have the eyelids to do so. I saw myself in the reflection of those vacant discs; watched as drool draped around my throat and shoulders like a sludgy shawl. Its lazy, pulsating tongue crawled over my cheek like a slow, slimy slug. I held my breath. Another whiff of that miasma would empty my stomach of its bile.

"Mmmmy, that's fine," it croaked. "Time to dine on thine dread." He pointed at the elves. "To the foot of the bed."

Two of the elves dropped the lower ropes, grabbed my ankles, and jerked my legs over the edge of the bed. The Unholy Ghost re-adjusted its sack and opened it at my feet. I peered over my heaving chest, past my pee-soaked pajamas, and into the maw of the Santa-sack, seeing now it wasn't a sack at all. It had teeth; rows of crook-ed daggers jutting out in every direction from a wet tunnel of pulsing gums. A tongue, like a sentient, hungry tendril, slithered out to lap at my legs, coiling and clinging and wetly embracing. The sack swal-lowed a squelchy gurgle, the peristalsis rippling through what must have been an umbilical cord conjoining the end of the sack's throat and the Unholy Ghost's distended belly. I screamed.

Footsteps pounded down the hallway.

"You keep quiet in there, boy, or I'm coming in with the wrath of God," Father boomed from the other side of the door.

"Father, help!" I howled.

The prayer lock clattered against the door and hit the floor with a *clunk*. The door burst open.

"I warned—" Father halted at the door, absorbing the scene, and then flicked on the overhead light. He gasped dreadfully, as though just breaking the surface of a pool with empty lungs. Mother piled into the doorframe beside him and froze. She seemed as unable to make an utterance as she was to make a move. The creatures also halted and the Unholy Ghost wheezed in ecstasy. From my parents wafted the fetor of fear.

The Unholy Ghost gestured toward my parents and the elves dropped my binding ropes and charged Father. Father kicked at one and made to grab me. He was tripped and collapsed to the floor. An elf grabbed at one of his ankles and he kicked wildly with both legs. The Unholy Ghost threw its belly-sack onto the floor toward the kicks. Father's feet were caught in the teeth and the sack worked its way up his calves like a python swallowing its prey. Father screamed.

· ∽ ·

"That was the first time I had ever seen him frightened. Or injured, or helpless, or anything other than the unquestioned top of the hierarchy." I shift in my seat. I have never revealed so much of that night before. Every other therapist, every psychologist and psychiatrist and counselor and any other inquiring individual has only ever heard that I fell asleep, had a nightmare, and awoke the next morning to the aftermath of the night.

"I remember one time I asked my father about his fears. I had just learned about phobias when my mom explained my fear of spiders to me. I was just a curious kid, you know? So, I asked my father about what frightened him. And, of course, this angered him. He accused me of probing him for weaknesses and punished me." I pause, allowing the therapist a moment to speak—hoping for a response, for some insight or validation or something. But I hope in vain. Likely, it is obvious that I am delaying retelling what happened next.

"I, uh, jumped off the bed and pulled at his arms." I clear my throat. "My father's arms."

· ∾ ·

"Get the gun out of the nightstand!" Father bellowed at whomever would obey him. "Hurry!" he yowled.

One of the elves latched onto Mother's leg and bit into her thigh. She batted at it while I tore it loose from her. She took me by the arm and we sprinted down the stairs. She pulled the keys from the hook rack with such force the drywall screws were nearly stripped from the wall. We bolted shoeless into the icy driveway and toward Father's snow-swathed truck, which was blocked in by some kind of sleigh.

The sleigh had been pulled by an entire team of what appeared to be harnessed dogs. They snarled and barked and fought against their harnesses to reach us. They were partly covered in flesh and fur, partly bare with exposed muscle and tendon, but entirely drenched in a thick, viscous blood, as was the snowy ground around them; glistening crimson in the moonlight. They snarled and growled nearer, tugging behind them the sleigh—their anchor. Their fleshy harnesses dripped blood with each strained pull. No, it was clearer now that they weren't attached to the sleigh by mere harnesses but by their own intestines, which wrapped around their midsections like steaming cummerbunds.

Mother frantically pulled at the door handle before realizing she hadn't yet unlocked it. She squeezed wildly at the key fob and the truck beeped again and again. She pulled once more at the door handle and the door ripped free from its icy frame. She then dropped to the ground. One of the dogs, its intestinal lead stretching from the mainline, had snatched my mother by her leg. The rest of the dogs

225

were straining against their own organic tethers, further rupturing their bellies to pile onto her. I climbed into the cab, slammed the door shut, and watched Mother's demise through a rapidly fogging window. I was spared from much more than a single shriek, as her throat was the starting point for one of the hellish hounds.

I remained in the truck for hours. I prayed. I prayed I would awaken. I prayed for warmth. I prayed for my brother.

I asked Father once when he would return—my brother. He told me he could come home when God forgave him and freed him of Satan's influence. I asked why Satan had interest in my brother. He told me that Satan and his own have no interest in those destined for heaven or hell. That Satan worked solely on those in between—the ones with feet on both paths leading to heaven and hell. I prayed, now, to know what path I walked. I prayed to find an end. But, this time, I didn't feel God was listening. For the first time, I didn't feel there was one to hear me.

· ∾ ·

"My brother never came back, of course." I pause and wait for welling tears to recede. *"From the camp, I mean. He just ... ran right out onto the highway. I don't know if he knew, you know? About our parents. Like, would he have done that if he knew? Or did he do it because he knew?"* The tears escape. *"I never got to say goodbye."*

· ∾ ·

I was either deep in prayer, shock, hypothermia, or sleep when a tap at the window snapped me conscious. A very large, very dark shape was barely visible through the fully fogged window of the driver's door. It was the Unholy Ghost, impossibly larger; engorged, undoubtedly, on Mother and Father. Its Santa-sack was draped over one shoulder by its umbilical cord, which continued its pulsing peristalsis, apparently still in the midst of digestion. The Unholy Ghost was opening the door. I knew it meant to finish feeding, but I was too cold and too overwhelmed by hopelessness to impede it.

The door opened. I waited. I anticipated. But only cold air entered. The creature did not take me. It merely spoke.

"You've seen me once, you will see me twice, for I'm what hunts the naughty and nice." The Unholy Ghost leaned in and inhaled a couple of wheezy sniffs. It made what I assumed was a scowl. Probably, I had exhausted my fear—had now smelled as bad to it as it had to me. "You've made my list, so I insist you do not resist what's due. You will be found, we will persist, my hounds and I will find you."

The Unholy Ghost, lumbering now with greater, overfed effort, boarded its sleigh and dissipated into the shadows.

· ∾ ·

"And that is how you remember the events of that December?" the therapist asks, breathing heavily. She is an impressively hefty woman. The room is otherwise mostly silent, save for the ticking of the clock on the wall. We are nearing the end of the session.

"To the best of my recollection." I inhale deeply, consider one line of thought, then speak another. "I think they rhyme. Uh, demons. For some reason. I don't know why, but I think that's just what they do. The elf things did it. The Santa thing did it ..."

"These things, were they seen by others? Aunts or uncles, friends or brothers?"

"No, just me ... and my parents, of course."

"These ... sights and sounds that only you could understand, did they ever give you instructions or commands?"

I shiver. "Like what?"

"Like hurting yourself or another? Perhaps like your father or mother?"

"Are you implying that I killed them?"

"Sometimes in the shadow of trauma and when drowning in depression, we see or hear things we don't want to. I never said you killed your momma, please do not get that impression. I just need to know the real you."

The room feels colder. My heart is growing anxious. "Please don't speak like that—in rhyme. It's very triggering."

"I am not speaking in rhyme." She shifts her backpack and checks her watch. "Now, before we're out of time, I'd like to clarify a discrepancy at hand." She repositions in her seat and the couch creaks, sounding more like the pangs of hunger than the groans of weary springs. "The statement that you were never given a command."

"How do you mean?" The room seems to be darkening. Likely a stormfront outside is obscuring the sun's light, I reason—I hope—I pray.

"On that cold Christmas Eve, you were told, I believe, as you sat in that truck, to keep your mouth shut." She stands up from the couch, a massive figure, and unshoulders her backpack. "Now you're out of luck!" Her voice bellows and deepens and her jaw falls loose and her maggot tongue slides past her chin. "And I warned and swore on that ice and gore that on you I would feed if my word you'd not heed!"

There is nowhere to go but into the maw. The therapists always keep themselves between the door and the victim.

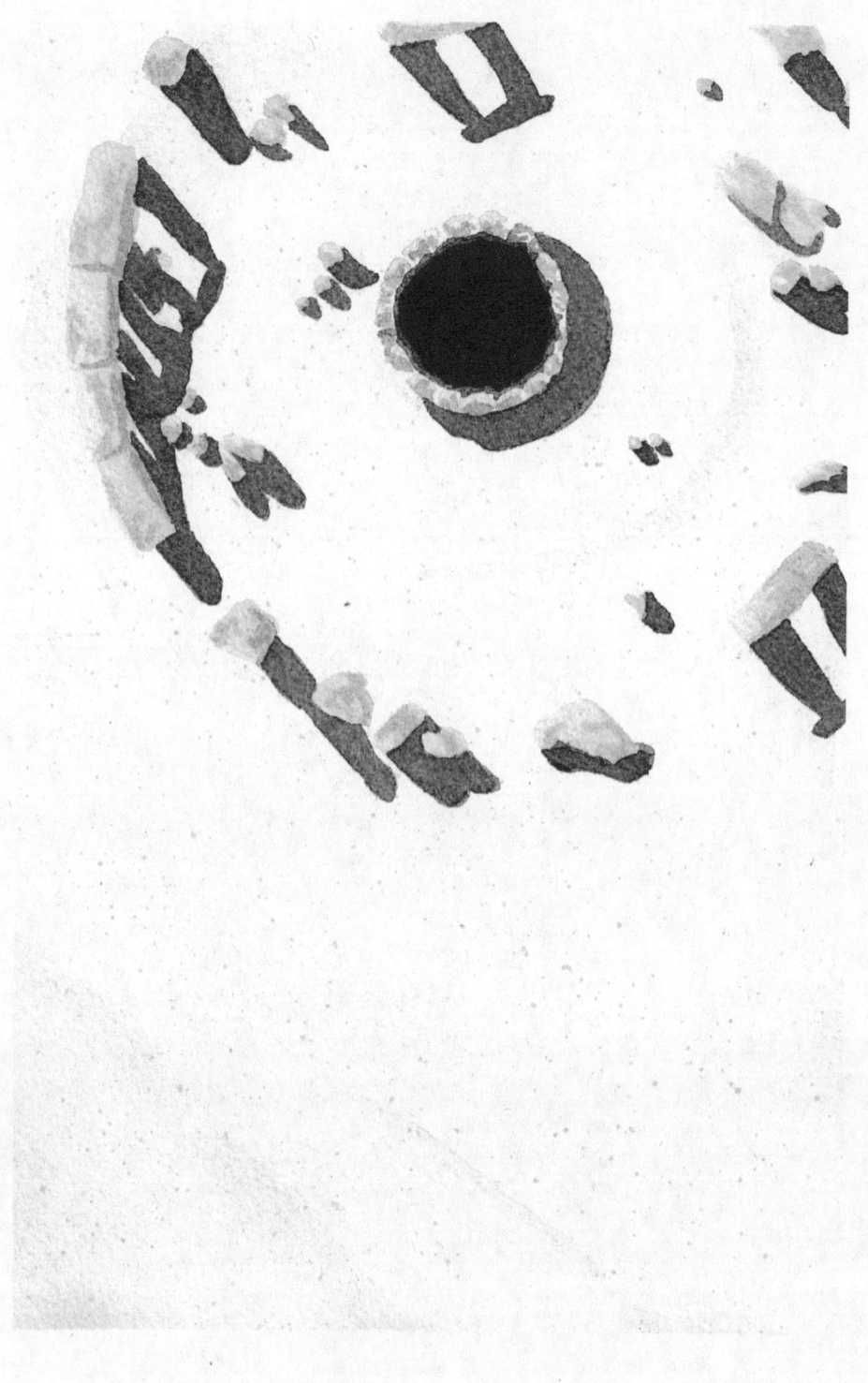

Deep, deep in the depths of this unfrozen water

THE BLIND

I trudged across a blanketed winter ground under a sunny winter sky. My car had long since been abandoned alongside an icy winter road. I had waited—all through a cold winter night, I had waited. Even after the engine stopped burning gas and the cold winter air riding gusts of unrelenting winter winds seeped steadily into the cabin, I had continued to wait. In my active mind, I had told myself I was waiting for rescue. My subconscious, however, had been deluged with passive thoughts … Those ever-present thoughts … Swarms of whispering gnats …

But even they had been stymied by the cold. The cold. To say that I was merely cold would be the type of understatement a child would make. Yet that was the regression it had wrought upon me. The deadly chill that had crept its way deep into my flesh suppressed even my cognition, and, as it was, "cold" was the sole descriptor—my last active thought—my subdued reasoning had granted me.

My body pressed on, seeming to move on old orders dictated by a once warm and functioning brain. The numb piston of my leg pulled its equally numb foot up high out of its icy grave and shoved it back down into the cold, white burial dirt mere inches ahead. Where was it going, my body? What destination had my now defunct brain once had in mind? Now the other leg was pistoning. Where are you going, legs? Someplace warm, perhaps?

The sun was bright overhead, the sea of snow beneath it even brighter. I closed my eyes. The backsides of my eyelids were as blindingly bright as the hovering sun and its grounded mirror. There was no reprieve from the whiteness.

My body pressed on. Every action was autonomic. My lungs expanded, filling with cold air, freezing the hairs in my nostrils together. My lungs contracted, expelling my waning warmth, expending my dwindling moisture, moistening the frozen hairs of my upper lip. My tongue reached out in search of that frozen condensation, scraping chapped lips. My face was a frozen mask of flesh, my hands frozen gloves within frozen gloves, and my persistent, persevering, pistoning feet were cold marble swathed in ice wraps that were once soggy shoes.

Still, my body pressed on, fueled by the furnace within my coat. As cold as my extremities were, my torso felt warm—hot, actually. I had been sweating at one point, possibly even now. It was difficult to tell if this was a cold sweat or a hot sweat seeping through my coat. I should probably remove it. The gloves, too. I wouldn't want my clothes getting wet with sweat. I wouldn't want to overheat, and it was already starting to feel uncomfortably warm.

I made to unglove one hand with the other, but my fingers would not work, the oppositional little bastards. So, I bit the end of one of its fingers and pulled the glove from my hand. I tried to flex my fingers but was unsure of my success. The blinding white in my eyes was obscuring most of my vision. I moved my hand to the side of my face to use my peripheral vision and while I could not see my fingers curl, I could almost see their color: white, like everything else. Or perhaps gray?

My body pressed on. I could not be distracted. I needed to get this coat off. I pawed at the likely places the coat's zipper would be, but was unable to feel the zipper's tab. Even my peripheral vision—now a fuzzy halo—offered no assistance.

My body faltered. One of my lifeless feet had struck some sort of

stone stumbling block. I could not quite identify it through the whiteness that blinded my eyes, though I likely would have been unable
to process the sight of the thing anyway. My mind could no longer
process the complex, just as my body could no longer advance.

I stood frozen and statuesque for some time. Perhaps moments.
Perhaps lifetimes. Then, the stumbling block rushed nearer my white-
washed eyes as my body collapsed to its knees. Would it lay itself—
my body—onto the soft, pillowy clouds it had been traversing for
so many countless miles? No. It would apparently lean forward and
collapse onto the stone stumbling block.

From what my mind could gather over the several minutes that
followed, there were multiple such blocks, all situated in a ring. Within the center of this apparent well or fountain was a pool of water—
obviously frozen, as was everything else my body had encountered
since leaving the frozen car. A shame. My body would have quite
enjoyed a drink of water. My mind would have quite enjoyed making
a wish. For rescue? No, there was no rescue. As magical as wishes
were, they still required some modicum of likelihood. No, my mind
would have liked to have figured out who I really was before expir-
ing. There had to have been some probability of that, at least.

Who was Cole? What was Cole? Cole was cold. Ol' cold Cole.

What was this shining so bright in the corner of my eye? Not the
blindness. A coin, perhaps? An unfulfilled, uncast wish? I reached for
it, an exceedingly arduous task, as my elbow—that frozen hinge—
would allow no bending. I think I set my hand upon it, whatever it
was. I could neither see nor feel the object. It was likely a coin; my
mind would have reasoned so, if it had the capacity to do so. As it
stood, I was not sure what force, be it internal or external, motivated
my body to interact with that object. My body just had … a feeling.
Was that what one would call a "gut feeling?"

My stiffening shoulder urged my arm forward, pushing the

glinting object toward the edge of the stone, toward the frozen pool. Perhaps I could wish upon the coin. Perhaps I could drop it upon the pool's frozen surface. Perhaps, if there was an afterlife, I could be posthumously granted a wish—once the pool had melted, of course. These were the things my functioning mind would have pondered. But the only cogs that turned within me were in my shoulder. Further, the coin was pushed. The sound of frozen friction filled my ears, but I did not hear this. It mattered not to my dying mind. Further, my arm extended. My muscles were tight and stiff, but I did not feel this, for this, too, mattered not to my dying mind. My eyelids shut, though everything remained white. I would fall asleep before the coin fell into the well.

Plop.

My body was shutting down, ready to sleep. My mind had been following suit but something deep within—an infinitesimal ember— was desperately sending signals to my body, as if it knew something the body did not. With great reluctance, my lower half pushed my upper half over the lip of the stone structure, just as the shoulder had done with the coin. My nose was wet. As slow and shallow as my breathing had become, my nose had remained wet for nearly the entirety of this trek. This, however, was a different kind of wetness. My eyes opened—only partially. The coin shimmered far away; deep, deep in the depths of this unfrozen water. My head tilted. My lips outstretched, meeting the water's surface. Neither warm nor cold. I drank.

The sound of dry, frozen crunching. The sound of worry. The sensation of being bound. The sensation of being dragged. My mind processed none of it.

· ∽ ·

"Cole!" Someone shook me gently by the shoulder. "Is it Cole?"

"Yeah, that's what the ID says."

"Hey, Cole, buddy? Can you wake up? Kinda need you to stay awake. Stay with us, Cole."

"I told you we should've put him in a warm bath."

"I'm telling you, that would probably kill him. Or fuck up his skin or something. Slow and steady. When you're cold, you rewarm slow and steady. When you're hot, you cool fast, with the ice blanket thing or whatever."

"Well, what the hell is a pile of blankets going to do when he isn't even generating heat?"

"Shut up, his eyes are open again."

The room was white. Everything was white. I blinked, but it made no difference.

"Hey, Cole?"

"I ... I'm blind," I wondered aloud, softly.

"What did he say?" asked a scruffy voice.

"He said he's blind," answered a nearer, more pleasant voice.

"Huh. Ask him if he was always blind," the scruffy voice directed the pleasant one.

"Holy shit, Andy. What am I, some kind of interpreter for the blind? I'm sure he can hear you just fine. It's his eyes that aren't working." The pleasant voice softened as it was directed back to me. "Cole? You think you could drink something warm? We've got tea and cocoa. Take your pick, buddy."

"I ... I ..." I coughed weakly. "I can't see."

"You think it's snow blindness or does hypothermia mess with your vision?" asked the scruffy voice, apparently Andy.

"I don't think it's really important right now," answered the pleasant voice. "Cole, buddy. Let's get something warm in you, all right? Try some of this cocoa. I made it, not my brother. So, rest as-

235

sured it's actually drinkable."

"I, uh, I can't move my hands," I said.

"Ah, yeah ..." Andy sucked air through his teeth. "I don't think you've got hands anymore, my guy."

"Andy!" the pleasant voice hissed. "Would you get the fuck out of here?"

"Oh, excuse me for being forthright—"

"Blunt."

"I'd want to know if my hands were fucked up. But I'll see myself out and leave you to your feminine touch."

"What-what's wrong w-with m-my hands?" I asked. Shivers, which had long been absent, had briefly returned.

"Uh, well, Cole." The pleasant voice cleared his throat. "Ahem. You got some wicked frostbite, buddy."

Silence.

"I don't usually say this, but I think my brother's right. Well, probably ... definitely half-right. One of your hands is a goner for sure."

I tried to feel my hands but my weakened brain could only become aware of the stinging pain that was rapidly growing in my arms and legs.

"It hurts," I said.

"C'mon, let's try that drink, Cole." He leaned my head forward. "My name is Ricky, by the way."

A warm—but not hot—liquid met my lips. I drank. The warmth was not gentle on my throat. The shock of pain jolted me into a coughing fit.

"Sorry!" Ricky said, taking back the cocoa. "Oh, my God, I'm so sorry."

"It's okay," I said between weakening coughs.

"Oh, you poor thing." Ricky placed a warm palm against my

cheek. There it lingered, fingers brushing my sideburns. The gesture, the feeling, and the warmth … It was worryingly comforting. I
turned my cheek away.

"Sorry," Ricky said quietly, quickly. He stood from the bed.
"Um, do you need anything?"

I did not answer. It was such a complex question and my mind
was in a state of recovery that could not manage such questions.

"Ricky," Andy called from down the hall.

"Yeah?" Ricky answered.

"Need a gameplan, brother. Let's make it happen."

"Please," Ricky spoke, presumably to me. "Please holler at us if
you need anything at all, okay?"

I did not respond. I was drowning in fatigue, bobbing in and out
of its waters; one moment barely awake, the next barely drowsing.

· ❧ ·

Down the hall, the brothers were softly arguing with each other.

"Ricky, the guy needs actual medical help. Like, a hospital or
something. More than just blankets and hot chocolate."

"Then go, Andy. But I'm not leaving him here to die blind and
alone."

"I'm not going to try to beat out a storm by myself. Have you
seen the wind? It's only getting colder and snowier."

"Okay, yeah, but can they even get a helicopter out in this?"

"Not if we keep waiting."

· ❧ ·

A weight compressed the side of the mattress.

"Cole?" It was Ricky.

"Mmm ..."

"Hey, buddy, if you can hear me, we're headed out. I really, really hate to leave you like this. But we gotta get you some help. Please, just ..." He cleared his throat. "Just hang in there, okay?"

The weight lifted from the mattress.

· ᴄᴏ ·

The cabin was silent. Had the brothers left, or had I dreamt it? I listened for them. Outside, an unfaltering winter wind was steadily growing in strength. Similarly, the passive thoughts were emerging, a growing cloud of whispering gnats.

Alone.   *Sleep.*

          Die.

               Clown.

          Go to sleep (just do it).   *Loser.*

Alone again (alone).

                    Nobody here (because you're nobody).

          Let go (if you're lucky you won't wake up).

Fuck you.

               The pain (go outside) will go away.

          Go away.

Who are you (nobody)?

                    Nobody.

     Loser.   *Alone.*

               You're a nobody.   *Don't wake up.*

     Don't ...

My body, consumed by exhaustion, depleted of energy, could spare nothing more to keep my mind or even the passive thoughts operating. Everything shut down.

· ∽ ·

The sound of rustling around a kitchen—of pots and pans and dishes and drawers clanging, clinking, and clashing—drifted down the hall and nudged me awake. How long those sounds had been nudging me, I could not know. I knew only that I had fallen asleep in pain and was now awake in substantially more pain. Needles of pain, burning pain, throbbing pain, cramping pain; there wasn't a single part of my body that wasn't reporting pain.

Though engulfed in affliction, I was regaining my faculties, a slow strengthening of command over all but my dominant right hand and, to my greatest dismay, my eyes. Had they been lost to frostbite, my eyes? Could eyes freeze in the living? What else of me had the ravenous winter cold so greedily devoured? I curled the fingers of my left hand, their tips feeling only stinging needles. My right hand obeyed none of the signals my brain was sending. My toes? Did they curl on command? I could not tell. They communicated, yes, but only in shouts of pain. Lost or not, my nose still seemed operational—at least, whatever part of it managed the olfactory senses—for it spoke to my brain the story of the cabin's construction. Old wood (pine, perhaps) was all around. Something else, though. Some kind of decay? Something dead? Perhaps I had lost my nose. My ears, however ... Those were in working order. Yes, they heard well. Dead or alive, they heard. Crackling ... popping ... An active fireplace. The bedroom door had been left open, likely to receive the heat from the living area in which the fireplace was undoubtedly situated.

From down the hall, the kitchen sounds continued. The brothers must have returned, unable to beat the storm. Or maybe they had not yet left, were now unable to do so because of the storm. Or, hopefully,

239

one had gone, one had stayed behind, and that one was now making me something warm to eat and drink.

"Hell—" A dry cough cut in. The kitchen sounds abruptly halted. Save for the whistling winter wind in which the cabin was enveloped, there was now only silence—studious silence.

In an instant, the hallway erupted with the thunderous patter of a heavy, four-legged clamber. Claws scratched wooden floorboards in search of traction. Then, the sound of friction and a sudden collapse into something solid, as whatever had been attempting a sprint in my direction had seemingly slid wildly into one of the hallway walls. More clambering, as the seemingly four-legged thing returned to its feet.

Once more, silence.

The unwavering winter wind whistled without end.

By machine gun beating, my heart saturated every ounce of my frostbitten flesh with icy adrenaline. My breathing quickened and I was becoming more and more overwhelmed with the need to cough. I looked in the presumed direction of the door. I saw only whiteness. I looked in all other directions but the room and everything within was equally white. I clenched shut my eyes. The world remained just as white. The itch in my throat reached its breaking point and an involuntary cough broke free.

Once more, a clawing patter.

I braced myself—eyes, teeth, hand, anus, and anything else that could, clenched. The weight of a hundred—two hundred, or more— pounds of scrambling flesh slammed into the bed frame. Again, the four-legged thing collapsed, and again it rose, paused, listened.

Death.

Die.

You're gonna die. Ha!

Bear.   *You're dead.*

Torn apart.

Fucking dead (die).

Blind (you're blind).

You can't (see) see.

You can't (see) anything. You just can't.

Blind ...

Something was in the cabin. A bear? Had a bear broken in? Wandered into the kitchen in search of food—a last minute binge before a late hibernation? Or was it rabid? Fuck, it was rabid. It had to be. Oh, fuck. I was going to get rabies. I was going to die blind, crippled, and rabid.

Not like this, I prayed to anyone or anything listening to my pleading thoughts. Sure, I have had ideations in recent weeks, but ... *Not like this.*

Movement. Pausing. Sniffing. Little *clicks* softly emanated from here to there and back as it stalked about the room, undeniably the sound of claws tapping wood. *Click.* Pause. Sniff. There were animal attributes, and the smell—dear Lord, the smell—was certainly that of an animal that had recently rolled in something dead to mask its scent, but there was something off about this thing. *Click.* Pause. Sniff. It moved in a halting, uncertain manner ...

My God, it's blind, I thought. An affliction to mirror my own. This creature had no edge over me. I needed only remain silent and still beneath this pile of scent-smothering blankets. And not for long. Help was on the way. The brothers were absent, so help was assuredly racing this way.

The bed shook as the animal stepped into it. The mattress sank as the animal stepped onto it. My body leaned as the animal stepped toward it. My heart—that tired little thing—beat an aching warning

241

like an organic klaxon. *Fight or flight! Fight or flight!* it warned. Now the pillow was sinking under the weight of the thing.

Perhaps I was wrong. Perhaps the thing wasn't blind. Perhaps my punishment for such an erroneous assessment would be a slow mauling of my face—the only part of me exposed. I tried to sink into the mattress, to will myself through its springs so that I could take refuge within. But I could only do now what I had done outside in the snow: freeze.

The animal again halted and sniffed. Its hot, foul breath bathed my face. Another erroneous assessment. It hadn't rolled in a decaying animal, it had been eating one. Death was on its breath. I held my own. I braced and waited. It took in another breath and then moved, but not to eat, bite, or even taste me. It was turning to move toward the foot of the bed. One step. A second step. A third. I could feel the weight shift from the mattress to the floor.

That's right, go back to the kitchen. No food here. Nope. All in the kitchen.

A weight pressed down onto my shin. I stifled a pained grunt. The animal paused. Its back half then joined its front half on the floor. I could hear it shift about. Another pause. I listened. There was nothing to hear. I felt. There was nothing to—

An exploratory appendage was moving across the blankets. These were not the inquisitive pattings and pawings of an animal but the gliding investigation of something more percipient.

Fight-or-flight! Fight-or-flight! my panicked heart implored.

The weight of the blankets began to ease from my lower body. Cool air spilled across my legs. The exploring appendage took hold of the damaged flesh wrapped about my shin. My cold-burned skin shot pain up my spine and out my mouth in an uncontainable "h-agh!" As though the sound were an authorization of sorts, the appendage tightened its grip and yanked. I was hauled from the mattress into a mess of frostbitten flesh and blankets, which had become like embers, so fierce was the pain that burned me.

"Help! H—" Another coughing fit erupted from my pained throat.

Again I was yanked. My skin screamed in agony as my naked body was being dragged from blankets onto the rough, wooden floor. Though the thing had me in hand—an unnervingly humanoid hand—it continued to move in its halting, uncertain way. A set of clicking and scraping told me its claws were searching for something within the room. I tried to look for its apparent destination, as that was likely my deathbed, but I saw only whiteness. I tried to kick at it with my free leg. Only once did I try this, as I missed and the pain that ensued from my damaged foot falling onto the floor was as blinding as whatever had afflicted my eyes.

Again I was yanked. Yank. Pause. Feel. Again and again and again. Then, a different kind of *click*. Something metallic. A door had been opened.

I was yanked once more, this time with more confidence. My side struck a doorframe and I attempted to anchor my arm onto it but the gripping, yanking thing was too strong. With a single pull, I was stripped from the doorframe and dragged through a pile of boots and under a row of coats, scarves, and all manner of clothing. I had been dragged into a closet.

I swept my arms, as though molding a snow angel. My right hand felt nothing, gripped nothing, could do nothing. My left was too slow, its grip too weak. In, I was dragged. In and in, further and further. My God, how deep was this closet? My arms continued their flailing search for anything of potential aid. Boots and shoes were feeling more like ... knots of muscle and sinew? The floor, the walls, everything on which I was being dragged, everything my limbs encountered, felt warm and moist. What now brushed my torso and face was not hanging garments but loose flaps of skin, dangling ligaments like fleshy vines. Decay was all around, on everything, in everything. This was a dimension of decay, of death, of decomposition and necrosis.

The walls were abuzz with whispers. Every word was a reassurance of my impending demise. Here, assertions. I was nothing, came from nothing, returning to nothing. There, postulations. I was immoral, lecherous, hellbound ... I was being dragged into hell.

My left hand had at last secured something. Or, rather, something had stuck to my trolling hand; something wet and fleshy. Gristle, or something tumorous. But, what would I do with it? It was too soft to bludgeon anything, too light to be thrown with any intention of harm.

Deeper. Ever deeper into the depths of the closet. The creature was now fully confident in its movement. It halted not, faltered not. Then it did. All at once, a great collapse. My leg was jerked, but only slightly, as, for the first time since being pulled out of bed, the creature's grip loosened. The thing must have slipped, or fallen into a cavity of sorts, or tripped. How it happened mattered not. I was loose, but not free. I backed away in a frenzied squirm. Squelching burst in rapid fury at my heels as the creature slapped at the decayed floor like a hand drummer, either in search of me or in search of purchase by which it could right itself again. I continued to distance myself.

The creature was up on all fours now, squelching in my direction. I paused and cocked my arm to the extent its cramped muscles would allow. With all my weakened might, I hurled the tumorous knot away from me, away from the closet entrance, beyond the creature. The creature halted. There it remained in contemplation, as I remained in propitious waiting. It sniffed, inhaling deeply. It tried again. With death all about, I was sure it was unable to smell me. Another moment of contemplation, then the thing turned to investigate the thrown mass.

I rolled onto my stomach and pursued a careful but steady crawl in what I was mostly certain was the direction of the closet's entrance. The rotting flesh of the floor dampened the noise of my retreat but also dampened my skin with what I presumed to be blood, its warmth burning my damaged skin like acid. Whatever coated the floor—whatever seeped from it—was slick, and my slithering flight was becoming increasingly hopeless in my crippled state. Without vision, I could not tell if I was making progress. I may very well have been moving as a child moves up a descending escalator.

From behind, the sounds of hastened squelching informed me the four-legged creature was back on the hunt; frenzied patting like someone in desperate search of fallen glasses, hither and thither, nearer and nearer. I could afford to crawl no more. I braced my right forearm and left palm and pushed myself up onto numb feet. I attempted a jog but, unable to properly feel for traction, my foot slipped back and I fell into the fleshy floor with a *splat*. The hunting creature began its own rush. I stood once more and strode forward on stiff legs, as though running on stilts. The floor underfoot was hardening, transitioning from flesh to wood. Pain erupted with each strike of my impaired feet.

I fell forward once more, this time tripped as my foot had encountered the pile of boots within the closet. Within less than a handful of rapid heartbeats, a chaotic crash of creature and clothing came beside me. I remained still. The creature scrambled upright and began its familiar ritual of listening and sniffing. Could I blend in with footwear?

Loud static emanated from the bedroom. The creature started. "... wishing you well. Stay warm everybody." The creature burst through the closet opening, knocking the door into the wall with a *bang*. What must have been an alarm clock radio continued. "Stay indoors. And stay tuned." Then, a soundbite. "Thirty-three-point-three

... The Disorder."

Destructive chaos now emanated from the bedroom. It sounded as though the creature was attacking not just the radio, but the entire nightstand. This was my opportunity. To do what? I did not know, but this was it. I stood from the pile of boots and shoes and torn down clothing and set forth from the closet with arms outstretched like some kind of naked, classic movie monster. Beside the bed, the destruction continued.

I let my left hand guide me, as my right was still as blind as my eyes. I stepped carefully, both to ensure silence as well as to lessen the pain of setting weight onto my injuries. I wanted to hurry. The nightstand would offer me only so much time to leave the room. I begged my hand for a positive update but it reported only the same feeling of a rough-hewn log barrier. I continued to step. *Wall ... wall ... wall,* my hand described. To my back, now, the destruction was dying down, becoming more an investigation of the remnants of the furniture.

C'mon, c'mon, my mind pleaded. There. At last. This must have been the doorframe, or the opened door itself. My left hand functioned only well enough to faintly describe the sensation of touch.

I sidestepped and entered the opening in the wall, what must have been the hallway. I set my first step onto this new path to safety and freedom, and the floorboard—that treacherous timber—creaked in declaration. *He's here! Hurry, he's getting away!*

At once, the creature became silent; my heart—ever the contrarian—did the opposite. It was as though hope was an egg in a race that had shattered at the finish line. It wasn't fair. I had done everything right and would still suffer some otherworldly torment.

Fight-or-flight, fight-or-flight, my heart screamed. I was too frightened to defy natural instinct. My mind was retreating into the primitive brain and it eagerly gave control to the body. My legs continued their movement. I'm sure if my feet had not been so damaged, had the muscles of my legs not been so cramped, they would have set a pace to match my heart. As it was, they did not. They moved in the same careful stride my thinking brain had commanded only moments earlier.

From behind, the creature gave no impression it was doing anything other than waiting. I could feel it, though. It was that indescribable, inexplicable, extrasensory perception: the feeling of being watched, of being stalked. Yes, that was it. I could feel its stalking presence, creeping behind me, reaching for me. Was that a breath of hot air against the nape of my neck, or the pins and needles of sensation returning to my frostbitten flesh? My legs continued their soft march. My pulse grew thicker and heavier, rushing fear and adrenaline throughout my trembling body. A soft *click* from behind. My leg froze mid-step. My breathing halted, choking on the swollen piston that was my heart. A hundred images flashed through my mind as I visualized the soft sound my ears had picked up: jagged teeth meeting as a drooling muzzle snapped shut; two clawed fingers tapping each other on an outstretched arm; wood expanding or contracting with temperature change (*please, God, let it be that*).

My legs progressed. It was not a precise progression. I found myself leaning into either wall of the hallway multiple times. This time, however, my shoulder bumped something protruding from the wall; a picture or knick-knack, perhaps. I paused, braced in anticipation of its fall, but nothing happened. I scanned it with my left hand. It was something hanging from twine, either a picture or a small sign. As my fingers still lacked dexterity, I hooked the twine with my thumb and carefully lifted whatever it held away from the wall. I carried it a few paces further down the hall until a change in the air told me I had at last entered the living area.

The fireplace, though unattended, continued to crackle with

great vibrancy. I could feel its warmth even from here, radiating to my right. To my left, I could only guess there was the kitchen, or some other open space. As I had with the tumorous distraction, I would throw the object I pulled from the wall and make my way in the opposing direction, toward the primitive safety of fire. I stepped two paces to my right, enough to leave the opening of the hallway, I hoped. Then, I cast the twine-bound object just ahead to my left. It struck something—multiple somethings. Seemingly every damned thing in the cabin began to clatter to the floor. The sound was utterly jarring.

From beside me—right beside me—the creature jolted. It had indeed been stalking me, likely within inches of me. A brief patter of claws against the floor; a brief patter and nothing more. The creature would not be fooled twice.

I waited. I hoped. But the creature did not move.

A pop from the fireplace. A steady whistle from the wind. A stubborn silence from both predator and prey.

A muffled *crack* from outside, somewhere overhead. From the roof came the soft thud of what must have been the crash of a cumbersome clump of snow. This must have interested the creature at least enough to consider it, as the thing paced leisurely forward; not leftward, but neither in my direction.

My lungs released a long overdue sigh of relief, which seemed to remind my throat of its need to cough. I suppressed it. No itch would outmatch my resolve. I was a survivor. I survived three decades of being me. I survived a winter car crash. I survived winter itself. I would survive this.

No (no you can't).

Ha.

Weak.

Coward (clown).   Die.

No, I mentally swatted at the swarming gnats. *No more.* But it wasn't as easy as "no." They were always there. Always whispering. Sometimes a couple of nagging reminders. Sometimes a swarm. For now, though, it seemed the swarm had withdrawn; standing by, but not gone—never gone.

The creature's clicking claws came to a halt several paces ahead of me. With arms outstretched like insectoid antennae, I made my way painstakingly rightward, in the direction of the fire's warmth. The living area was either carpeted or covered in a large rug. In either case, my footsteps were muted. I sidestepped a recliner, circumnavigated a coffee table, and steadily approached the heat.

The stinging caress of ambient warmth was overpowering. My cheeks burned, and tears began to well uncontrollably. I would need to distance myself from the fire or risk further injury to my skin. However, I first needed to arm myself. If this was a wood-burning fireplace, there were likely tools beside it to manage the fire; and not just any tools, but heavy, iron ones. Could I swing something so sturdy and heavy? Perhaps not now. But every moment I continued to survive was another moment of recovery, another bolstering of my strength. Who knew what I could and could not swing in another handful of minutes … or hours … or days.

How long? How long would it take for rescue? How long would I have to survive this?

My hand painfully scanned the hot stone or brick or whatever comprised the mantel and jambs. Nothing to the immediate left. Nothing to the immediate right. I would need to venture a little farther in either direction but which? Too far to the left, and I risked bumping into the creature. Right it was, then.

I felt along the log wall, my hand kept low in search of the small stand in which fireplace tools were usually kept. I was losing hope with each cautious step that distanced me from the fire. Then, my hand encountered the wooden framework of a storage rack. It was tall, likely a rack for pool cues. No iron rod, but it would suffice.

I reached for a cue. Carefully, inch by painful inch, my cramped bicep loosened, guiding frostbitten fingertips slowly into the rack, slowly, that I would mitigate any bumping or knocking or any other inadvertent contact that would rattle or dislodge one of the sticks. Fingers met cue. I gripped the shaft to the extent my fingers would allow and made to lift it but found my weakened shoulder was unable to manage its weight with arm outstretched. I stepped closer. Still with considerable struggle, I managed to lift the stick from the grooves in which it leaned. If my body perceived such heft from a mere pool cue, I was rather glad I had not discovered an iron fire poker in its stead.

As I turned to bring the stick toward me, something glanced off the framework—something attached to the stick. It must have been a rake—a bridge cue or whatever they were called—and I bumped it. I bumped the fucking thing. Just barely, though, just barely. Imperceptibly so. How could anything have heard? The creature wasn't moving. Perhaps it wouldn't. Perhaps it didn't hear. Or, if it did, perhaps it considered this another trick.

The creature exploded into a gallop. Each stride produced a sound of ripping carpet or rug. I tried to tighten my grip, to ready the stick to swing at the thing, but my muscles were too slow and the creature too quick. The beast tackled me with a freight train-like momentum, slamming my body into the storage rack. I clutched the stick to my chest but its end was still caught in the framework of the rack. The beast dropped to the ground, pulling me with it. My arm locked around the stick and the rack toppled over, spilling its contents onto us before topping the pile. Three or four of the sticks struck my face like the rattan canes of corporal punishment. They couldn't possibly be pool cues …

The creature writhed beneath me, wriggling violently to free itself from the pile. I held the stick tight to my abdomen with my right forearm and moved my left hand down the shaft in quick investigation. At its midsection was mounted something cylindrical. It was a scope. I was in possession of a scoped rifle.

A clawed, humanoid hand gripped my throat. The creature had mostly crawled out from beneath the gun rack and was attempting to jerk my body out as well. I ran my left hand with its partially working fingers to the underside of the firearm, toward where I would imagine the trigger guard would be. A jolt as my body was violently pulled. Now only my legs were beneath the rack. My fingers found the thin, round guard and I forced my thumb—my most functioning digit—into the ring. Another jolt. I was no longer pinned to the floor. I tried to raise the muzzle toward the creature, but lacking both sight and the use of my right hand, this proved to be impossible.

I was choking. The creature's grip was unfaltering. Again I was jerked. I was being dragged toward the hall, toward the bedroom, toward the closet. I flailed my legs in the hopes of catching any of the furnishings in the room. My feet—no hooks were they—offered only pain, not salvation.

I tried again to lift the rifle's muzzle. I was moments from losing consciousness. Another jerk, this one into an immediate halt, as the creature ran my head into a recliner or sofa. It climbed the furniture, pulling me up by the throat, bringing my face to its shoulder. I gnashed my teeth and bit with all my might. Death spilled onto my tongue. I was thrown over the furniture and onto the bare, wood floor, whereupon I retched. I tried to catch my breath but the pungent taste of decay in my mouth commanded my body to vomit.

The creature pounced upon me. Its foul breath splashed over my face. It was going to bite me. An injury to mirror its own. I wedged my right forearm beneath the rifle's barrel and shoved it upward. The steel of the barrel struck the creature's face with a *clack* as the metal met bared teeth. The beast pushed back, leaning into me with what felt like hundreds of pounds of knotted muscle. Its barrel-like chest pinned the rifle against my own. Its strength surged. Its breath grew hotter against my face as its mouth grew nearer. I could sense it. A mouth of deadly design. I could almost feel it. Slimy lips were peeling back from overlapping, carnivorous dentition. Less a mouth, more a bear trap; made not for the mere act of consumption, but to lethally shred its prey—me.

I flexed my thumb. Where the muzzle rested was of no importance. I flexed and squeezed and pressed, but the trigger would not give. Either the weapon had a safety engaged or it was unloaded.

Teeth pierced the scalp on either side of my skull as the creature clamped shut its jaws onto my face. I screamed into its throat. It repositioned itself, straddling my body with its four limbs set wide to my sides. It began dragging me into the hall. I fumbled at anything—everything—on the rifle. I grabbed hold of the bolt handle and twisted, but it did not budge. I pulled and pushed but it did nothing. The creature continued its crawl. I lifted and the bolt moved. Hope soared. I pushed the handle out and something clattered to the floor. At this sound, the creature paused. The rifle had been loaded. Was that its only round?

The creature carried on.

I set the bolt back in place. Safety. There had to be a safety. Fingers fumbled once more. Where was it? Would I even feel it? *Thud.* The creature's arm and my shoulder struck a doorframe. We were entering the bedroom. Where in fuck's name was it?

Click.

Faint but undeniable. That must have been the safety. *Or a dry fire,* a tiny voice whispered in the back of my mind.

I was being dragged over a pile of boots. We were in the closet.

I jammed my thumb into the trigger guard. Before I had given my right arm any strength to push against the rifle, to raise the muzzle, it discharged.

A thunderous explosion instantly muted the world, silencing everything but a strong ringing noise. The creature recoiled, dropping my head to the floor. Blood was filling my mouth and nostrils. I was choking again, and rolled onto my side. The creature writhed in silence. I tried to secure the rifle once more but found only the capacity to cough. The creature clambered further into the closet, retreating into the unknown depths within.

I tried again for the rifle, tried to do anything other than cough and gag, but I was losing strength. Fatigue was weighing on my eyes like unbearable weights. Like a closet-lurking monster, sleep took me.

· ❧ ·

The sound of heavy footsteps on wood flooring. The sound of worry. The sound of tinnitus. The sensation of gentle rocking. The sensation of being dragged. My mind processed all of it.

"Cole?" A worried voice. "Oh, my God. He shot himself. Cole, can you hear me?"

The world was bright in one eye, then bright in the other. Someone was shining a flashlight in my eyes.

"Gnah—" My lips seemed unwilling to meet. "I can see," I remarked slowly. The world was blurry but distinguishable. I had been dragged out from the closet into a semicircle of four men: the brothers and two first responders.

"Looks like a self-inflicted gunshot wound," one of the first responders noted to the other. "An aborted attempt."

"I can see," I repeated, more to myself than anyone in the room.

"You can see?" The responder repeated this in much the same

way a distracted parent would when entertaining a hyper-verbal child.

"I 'as 'lind."

"What's that, sir?" the responder asked.

"He was blind," Ricky announced.

"Oh. You're lucky," the responder spoke up, as though I had also been deaf.

"Lucky ..." I echoed.

"Yeah. You just caught a glimpse of blindness. For some people, it's a lifetime."

"Cole, I'm so sorry," Ricky said. "We couldn't beat the storm. We got into Hell Gate and they called for Life Flight out of Kalispell, but they had to wait for the storm to die down."

"How long?" I asked. I was being situated onto some type of board with restraints.

"No time at all," one of the responders spoke. "We'll have you at St. Sebastian's before you know it."

"No ..." That was not what I had meant. I wanted to know how long I had been left in the cabin, but lacked the physical capacity to ask this.

"Sorry, buddy," the responder stated passively as he continued securing me to the transportation device. "That's the nearest hospital, that's the one we're taking you to."

Ricky knelt and held my left hand. Another lingering touch. "I'll come check in on you," he said.

I felt his hand—the warmth and sincerity of it. I let out a shaking sigh and squeezed both his hand and a steady stream of salty solace from my eyes. "I 'ould like that."

AFTERWORD

If you are reading this, it is likely that you have read all the preceding pages, and for that I thank you. Your time matters, and I am so grateful that you spared it for a debut collection of short stories from an unknown like me.

I would like to further share with you a bit of the journey behind these stories. First, though, some final appreciation to three great gals from my support group: Carissa Switzer, with your professional knowledge of death; Erin Kirkpatrick, with your professional knowledge of life; Julia Jacobs, with your professional knowledge of mental health. For generously offering your time in reading, reviewing, and improving these works prior to their release, I am forever thankful.

Most of the stories in this collection have existed in some form since 2012. Needless to say, this publication feels long overdue. For most of my life, mine were the only eyes laid upon any of my written work, and I long feared that would remain the case into my final days. I was haunted by these things—my unfinished, unpublished, but not quite dead stories. They were a looming presence, following me like a demon attached and inescapable. You know the feeling. If you've ever been assigned a make-or-break, pass-or-fail project at the start of an academic semester, you have felt that feeling—its weight and dread—grow with each nearing day of its deadline. That feeling has stuck with me for a lifetime.

This collection began, I believe, in my earliest youth. I struggled with nightmares and sleep paralysis throughout much of the 90s and

00s. I was terrified to go to bed at night. I wasn't fearful of the night itself, or of the dark for that matter, but of falling asleep. The sleep paralysis episodes had been occurring with such terrible frequency, they became a nightly expectation. It drove me to research sleep and how to prevent it, where and how I could in a time in my life and of the world with limited resources. I checked the dictionary, I scanned books in the school library, I searched the Internet, when that became available to me. None of it was of any use, of course. I quickly learned that sleep is an unavoidable necessity. I did find some advice on managing dreams, however. Tips that included not eating peanut butter or drinking apple juice before bedtime, as that was likely to increase brain activity and, thus, the likelihood of dreams. I didn't know if I was doing any of those things, but added them to my list of actions, inactions, and rituals. I would have done or avoided anything to mitigate those dreadful experiences.

Nothing worked.

At its height, I was tormented day and night. Be it through sleep deprivation or depression or a combination of the two, I was seeing shadows in my peripheral vision in my waking hours, and demonic shadows at night during sleep paralysis. These experiences were so vivid and seemingly real that I can still recall them with great clarity. While I do not write of the following experiences as specifically factual, they were greatly inspirational in my writing of the stories of this collection, and thus demand some notation here.

As it happened, by my recollection, I half awoke into paralysis one night with the top sheet of my bedsheets covering my face. I was almost entirely unable to see my surroundings, save for the faint glow through my bedsheet of the streetlight outside my bedroom window. In spite of this, I became increasingly aware of a presence in my room. Someone (something) was moving about my room, shuffling across the carpet. I could hear this. I could feel them (it) bump into my bed. I tried desperately to regain my motor skills so that I could uncover my face and identify the presence. Of course, I could not move. As usual, even my breathing was uncontrollably limited to the slow, deep rhythm of REM sleep, which further burdened me with the feeling of suffocation. I tried to control my lungs, to blow the sheet from my face. I could almost feel it working. Then, the glow of the streetlight was gone. The bedsheet was dark. Just on the other side of that thin, threaded veil, no further from my face than the length of an eyelash, no louder than a cat's purr ... a voice. "Thanks for breathin' kid. Never woulda found ya in the dark otherwise." My heart panicked. My throat and feet, of all things, throbbed with adrenaline-thick blood. My face was warm. (Was I sharing body heat with the presence?) The pain in my chest forced me fully awake. At last I had control of my body. I could fight. I could flee. But I froze. I remained under the covers, and curled into a ball. And I cried.

It was typically the severity of the pain in my chest that would bring me back fully into consciousness. There was not much else that seemed to break that paralysis.

On another night, I awoke to the familiar sense of dread to which I had become well-acquainted but never acclimated. Everything was heavy: my body, the bedsheets, the air. This time, I was able to look about. My eyes were well-adjusted to darkness from half a night's sleep, so I was able to scan the room well enough. I observed the shadows of the room, its structure, and its furnishings. There was the familiar, and then, at my feet, the unfamiliar. A head. More specifically, a forehead. My feet jutted like goalposts beneath the covers and between them, rising just over the bed's horizon like a black sunrise was a humanoid head. I say head, but it was more a shadow in the shape of a head; a tangible shadow, one with depth and solidity, and two eyes opened unnervingly wide so as to show the entirety of their whites. Then, movement. Slow, slow movement. Not of the shadow, the head moved not. It was the bedsheets. The comforter was being rolled up over my feet. That being the breaking point for my heart, I was pulled far enough into consciousness by pain that I regained control over my body, or maybe just my as yet unmoving lungs. I gasped, either by fear or suffocation. At that instant, my right calf was grasped and I was pulled toward the assailant. Likely because I was dreaming, I was able to kick myself free and flee to my brother's room to spend the remainder of the night.

When I returned to my bedroom the following morning, I found the comforter rolled up from the foot of the bed, and the top sheet was untucked from beneath the mattress. Believe it or not (coincidence or not), I have forever since had a "bruise" on that calf. It has often been asked about, worried about, pointed out. I'm sure it's nothing more than a group of veins sitting a little too close to the surface, based both on its appearance and warmth to the touch. Someday, I'll have it looked at. But not anytime soon. Reasoning tends to dull the shine of storytelling.

Dear reader, you have given me so much of your time. I still must ask one more thing of you: your honest review. Please consider reviewing this collection wherever you typically rate and review online. Each rating increases the likelihood this collection may find another reader, and as my readership grows, so too will my bibliography; for it is you, the reader, who makes this possible.

ABOUT

The Author

Christopher Ruiz is a fiction writer specializing in horror. Born in the City of Angels and raised in the shadows of the Rocky Mountains, he now writes of the demonic, supernatural, and psychological in the Midwest. A veteran of both combat and crisis response, his stories draw inspiration  from both the real and the unreal, from years of sleep paralysis and nightmares, revealing the darker corners of the human experience.

The Illustrator

Amy Myers is an artist and an award-winning graphic designer based in Central Illinois. She first rose to prominance when her pencil drawing of a mermaid appeared on the family refridgerator at the tender age of two. Now specializing in book cover design, her work is recognized for its ability to convey mood and atmosphere through various mediums.

ABOUT

The Author

Christopher Bork is a fiction writer specializing in terror. Born in ... of America ... raised in the shadows of the Rocky Mountains, he now writes of the delirious, supernatural, and psychological. In the Midwest, a veteran of Evil, youth and critics expose the ... for ... draw inspiration from both the rational and ... from years of sleep paralysis and nightmares, recalling the darker corners of the human ...

The Illustrator

Amy Myers is an artist and an award-winning graphic design embraced the Campus ... work. She married to ... her pencil drawings ... a recent ... experience in ... her residence at the ... stage of ... Now specializing in ... work, every detail of her work is recognized for its ability to convey mood and atmosphere through various medium.

www.ingramcontent.com/pod-product-compliance
Lightning Source LLC
Chambersburg PA
CBHW010737130726
47899CB00015B/3315